THE CASE OF THE CANINE AC-COMPLICE by John Lutz

Meet Milo Morgan and his partner, Sam Spayed—a mixed breed with the nose of a bloodhound ...

DOG ACT by Herbert Resnicow

When you need to sniff out a suspect, call a dog ...

A ONE-MAN DOG by William Bankier

Nothing comes between a man and his dog—not even death ...

A DOG'S LIFE by Ray Davidson

When you're looking for a lost dog, you can find some very surprising things ...

... and many more "tails" of mystery and suspense!

CANINE CRIMES

CANINE CRIMES

A Jove Book / published by arrangement with
Dell Magazines, a division of Bantam Doubleday Dell Direct, Inc.

PRINTING HISTORY
Jove edition / December 1993

ISBN: 0-515-11250-X

A JOVE BOOK®
Jove Books are published by The Berkley Publishing Group,
200 Madison Avenue, New York, New York 10016.
JOVE and the "J" design are trademarks belonging to
Jove Publications, Inc.

PRINTED IN THE UNITED STATES OF AMERICA

10 9 8 7 6 5 4 3 2 1

CANINE CRIMES

MARGERY ALLINGHAM • JOHN LUTZ • REX STOUT
and other "masters"
Edited by Cynthia Manson

JOVE BOOKS, NEW YORK

Table of Contents

Editor's Note

The dog has been used by writers as a dramatic and comic instrument in novels, stories, and films over the years. In this unique collection of mystery short stories, drawn from *Alfred Hitchcock's Mystery Magazine* and *Ellery Queen's Mystery Magazine*, the dog has a significant role in plot and thematic overtones. The mystery writers herein present the dog in a variety of guises: as detective, suspect, clue, and hero.

For example, in many of the stories our canine character's behavior is the primary clue to solving a murder. The detective's reliance on either the dog's animal instincts, such as smell, or its sense of protectiveness and loyalty to its master consistently lead to the resolution of the crime. Classic examples occur in stories by Rex Stout, Thomas Walsh, Donald Olson, and M. M. LaCour. A supreme example is Jean Potts's masterful "The Withered Heart," where not only is the dog's role key to the capture of a killer but the dog is also symbolic of the murderer's moral conscience.

On a lighter note, Ed Hoch's detective Nick Velvet is hired to find a missing dog; the clue lies in the dog's bark. If you find this puzzling, read on! We hope you enjoy this collection of entertaining and often poignant canine crime stories featuring man's best friend.

CANINE CRIMES

The Theft of
<< the Barking Dog >>

by

Edward D. Hoch

NICK VELVET HAD come to England to steal a dog.

"It's no Hound of the Baskervilles," the woman in blue had told him. "If he didn't have those guards around his place I'd go after it myself. It's just a big Old English sheepdog named Rodney, the friendliest creature in the world."

"This Manuel Curzon is your former husband?" Nick asked, making notes as he spoke with Evita Curzon. She was a dark, Latin type with a slow, seductive smile.

"That's correct. Rodney should really be my dog, but Manuel won't give him up. He's being very unreasonable about the whole thing."

"My fee would be twenty-five thousand dollars plus travel expenses. Is Rodney worth that much to you?"

"That much and more."

Nick's original plan had involved a dog substitution—replacing Rodney with an identical pooch while he made his escape with the original. Using photographs of the sheepdog that Evita had supplied, he was about to purchase a passable substitute to accompany him to England when he learned about that country's rigid pet-quarantine laws. If he wanted to complete his assignment in a reasonable length of time, he would have to obtain a dog in England.

So Nick flew to London alone after kissing Gloria

goodbye at the airport and promising to bring her back a gift. His first stop after checking into his Mayfair hotel and renting a car was a big kennel on the outskirts of the city. He asked about large Old English sheepdogs, but the only ones available were either too small or had the wrong coloring.

"He has to be grey and white, like the one in this picture," Nick told the young man in charge.

"Funny, there was someone here a few days ago asking for the same thing. In fact, he had a photo that could have been the same dog. He didn't care about the coloring, though, as long as the size was right. I'm supposed to call him if one turns up."

Nick found this extremely interesting, and possibly more than a coincidence. "Do you have the man's name handy?"

"I put his card in my drawer here. It should be near the top. Yes, here it is—Percy Apjohn. Lives in Wembley."

"Thank you," Nick said with a smile. "I'll contact him. If we're on the same mission we should pool our resources."

He tried phoning Apjohn's number, on the pretense of having a dog available, but there was no answer. Because Wembley was on the way to Manuel Curzon's home near Oxhey, he decided to swing by there first. Apjohn lived in a small detached house across from a neighborhood pub. When no one answered his ring, Nick crossed the street and ordered a pint from the bartender.

"I'm looking for Percy Apjohn," he said quietly. "Seen him around?"

"Not in a couple of days. That's odd for him. Usually stops in every night for his pint."

Nick finished the beer and recrossed the street. The little house seemed far too quiet, and he noticed something he'd missed earlier. There were two newspapers on the front stoop, half hidden by a flowering plant. He walked around to the rear of the house and used a credit card to force the bolt on the back door.

As soon as he stepped into the kitchen he caught the

odor. It wasn't pleasant and he knew what it meant. The man's body lay halfway into the living room, in a pool of dried blood. He'd been dead for some time. The cause of death seemed to be a gaping wound in his throat. Nick hoped it had been caused by a weapon of some sort and not by a large, vicious dog. He glanced quickly around the room and noticed a business card on the table, from someplace called Essex Storage Facilities. He stuck it in his pocket, for no special reason.

He went out the way he'd come and cut across the back yards so no one from the pub would see him leaving. Finding a man's body wasn't the best way to start off an assignment, and he could only hope the two things were just coincidental. In any event, he would visit no more kennels for a time. The road to Oxhey lay just ahead.

Manuel Curzon was well known in this suburb of Greater London. He owned several acres of land along London Road and seemed to be well-off, though the people to whom Nick spoke were vague as to the source of his income. Pausing in his rental car along the side of the road, Nick affixed a large circular insignia to each of the two doors. They read: Oxhey Animal Control Unit. From a distance he thought they looked quite convincing.

Nick parked in the driveway of the Curzon home and walked up the stone path to the front door. His approach immediately set off the deep-throated barking of a large dog that was most likely to be Rodney. The door was not opened in response to his arrival. Instead, a broad-shouldered young man in a chauffeur's uniform appeared suddenly behind him. "Can I help you, sir?"

"I'm looking for Manuel Curzon. We've had a complaint about a barking dog." His words seemed to enrage Rodney even more, and the barking from within grew noticeably louder.

"Mr. Curzon doesn't receive visitors."

"I'll have to issue an official warning about the dog," Nick told him. "What's your name?"

"Gilligan, sir."

Nick's British accent was none too good, but he tried to

act bureaucratic as he filled out an impressive-looking form and handed it to the man. "Well, Gilligan, here's a warning for your employer. If there are any more complaints I may be forced to confiscate—"

"What's this?" A young woman in jeans and a man's shirt had come around the corner of the house. "What's the trouble, Gilligan?"

"He's from animal control, miss. There's been a complaint about Rodney's barking."

"I'll handle this."

Gilligan hesitated only a moment and then retreated. Nick faced the young woman and saw at once the familiar features and coloring of Evita Curzon, the women who'd hired him. This could only be her daughter, and she quickly confirmed the fact. "I'm Mr. Curzon's daughter, Catherine. Can I be of help?"

Nick waved the form at her. "Complaint of a barking dog."

"It couldn't be Rodney. He never disturbs anyone."

"Could I see your father?"

"He's— He's quite ill. He suffered a stroke last month."

"I'm sorry to hear that, miss."

"He still can't speak, though the doctor thinks he'll improve somewhat." She hesitated and then decided. "You can see the dog if you'd like, though. I'm sure you'll agree that Rodney is a lovable animal."

She opened the front door and led him inside. The large sheepdog came bounding to her at once, his red tongue about the only thing visible through the coat of long white and dark-grey hair. She dropped to her knees and hugged him, then said, "Look, Rodney! Here's a nice man from the town to see you, Mr.—?"

"Velvet," Nick supplied, taking in the expensive furnishings.

"Mr. Velvet likes big dogs, but he likes them best when they're a little bit quiet."

Rodney's answering bark did indeed seem to be a bit subdued. Nick patted him to show approval. "You behave yourself like a good dog," he cautioned, "and I won't have to give your mistress another warning."

As he straightened up, a framed photograph on the piano caught his eye. It was in among several family pictures and showed five men grouped around a red sports car. He'd never have noticed it except that the second man from the left was clearly Percy Apjohn, whose body he'd found and abandoned earlier that day. "Who are these handsome fellows?" he asked casually.

"Friends of my father's. That's him in the center." She eyed Nick a bit dubiously.

Nick studied the dark, pockmarked face. Even the smile Curzon allowed for the photograph with his friends seemed hasty and forced. Nick could understand why Evita Curzon might have found life difficult with such a man. He turned back to Catherine and said, "One of these men looks familiar. It's Percy Apjohn, isn't it?"

"That's right. He's been a dear through all of this, driving over frequently to visit my father."

"Do the others live around here?"

"Two of them do. The other, Matthew Kane, is out of the country somewhere. I don't even know if he's heard about Daddy's stroke."

"It almost looks as if they're a team of some sort, the way they're posed."

She chuckled at that. "Hardly! Except for a little hunting, Daddy has never been a sportsman. The five of them used to get together to chat and play cards on Saturday nights. A few years ago they started to drift apart."

"Well, you will keep Rodney under control, won't you?"

"Certainly. Thank you for being so understanding, Mr. Velvet."

He went back to his car, aware that Gilligan's eyes were on him all the time. Still, if the chauffeur was the only guard to be overcome, it wasn't such a difficult job. Rodney could be in his hands by the next morning. He took a room at an inn for the night.

Evita Curzon had planned to arrive in London that evening and Nick phoned her hotel after dinner to inform her that Rodney would be delivered the following day. "I scouted out the place today and met your daughter."

"Catherine? How is she?"

"Better than your husband, apparently. Are you aware that he suffered a stroke last month?"

"I heard that, yes."

"But not from your daughter."

"It's not important who told me. Deliver the dog and you'll get your money."

"Do you know a friend of your husband's named Percy Apjohn?"

"I know him. I don't admire him."

"Why is that?"

"Look, Mr. Velvet, I hired you to do a job. You specialize in stealing items of little or no value and I'm paying you to get back my dog. It's all that need concern you."

"Of course. I do have one important question, though. Is Gilligan the only guard at the house?"

"Yes, but don't underestimate him. He says he killed a man once."

Or maybe twice, Nick thought, remembering Apjohn's body. "I'll be careful."

He hung up just as a knock sounded on the door. Thinking it might be the innkeeper, he opened the door without hesitation. A tall man with a vaguely familiar face hit him on the chest with the flat of his hand. "Inside, mister!"

A second man crowded in behind the first and Nick saw that he had little choice. The door was closed and he was alone with them. "Is this a robbery?" he asked, dropping all pretense of an English accent.

"Not yet it isn't," the second man snarled. "And we're here to see it doesn't become one, Mr. Nick Velvet! Catherine Curzon phoned me. She said some animal control person called Velvet was at the house, acting a bit strange. Showed an interest in our picture, among other things."

"I don't know what you're talking about," Nick insisted, but he knew only too well. They were two of the group standing with Manuel Curzon in the photograph on the piano.

The tall one took a folded newspaper from his pocket. "Try to tell me this isn't you."

It was a full page ripped from a London tabloid dated nearly four years earlier. The story dealt with one of Britain's periodic great train robberies, in which a gang of thieves had held up a train in the north country and escaped with a fortune in banknotes. Nick's picture, somewhat fuzzy but still recognizable, was part of a sidebar article on great thieves. In fairness, the story admitted that he'd never been known to steal anything of value.

"That's me, all right," Nick agreed with a smile. "No doubt about it. But you have the advantage on me. Who are you?"

"Phil Banyon," the tall one said. "And this is Roger Green. What are you doing here?"

"I'm on holiday. What about you?"

"We both live in Oxhey. We're friends of Manuel Curzon and we're worried you've been snooping around there."

"Oh, hardly snooping around!"

"What would you call it, with that fake sign on the side of your car?" Green asked. "Oxhey doesn't even have an animal control unit."

"Then they might be willing to let me establish one."

Neither man smiled. Banyon's right fist shot out before Nick realized what was happening. It caught him on the tip of the jaw and sent him reeling backward onto the bed. He started to get up and the other one hit him.

Nick met Evita Curzon in London's Green Park the following morning as scheduled. She walked up to him, trim and proper in a tailored blue suit, and removed her sunglasses. "Where's Rodney?" she asked.

"I don't have him yet."

"Don't have him? Why not? What happened to your face?"

"A couple of gentlemen visited my room last evening.

We had a bit of a tussle and I'm afraid they won. I was dozing when they left and by the time I woke up it was too late to go after your dog."

"Who were these men?"

"A couple of your old friends—Banyon and Green."

"They were my husband's friends, not mine. What did they say to you?"

"They accused me of snooping around. Then they just started punching me."

"Yes, that sounds like them."

"Perhaps you should tell me what this is all about."

"I only hired you to steal my dog, Mr. Velvet. You needn't concern yourself with anything else."

"You didn't tell me about your daughter."

"Catherine's not involved in this."

Nick stared up at the trees. "Tell me one thing, Mrs. Curzon—how did you learn about me?"

"How—?"

"You sought me out and hired me. How did you hear about me here in England? Was it through a tabloid newspaper article? They showed me the article before they started punching me. One of those great train robbery things you Brits are so fond of."

She was silent for a moment. Finally she said, "You're right about the tabloid. That's where I first saw your name."

"Your husband and the others were especially interested in that article about the train robbery—interested enough to keep it for nearly four years. Could they be the ones who robbed the train? All five of them?"

"I don't know," she replied. "Certainly the thought has crossed my mind. The press agreed that the bandits would have to keep their loot hidden for years, until after the statute of limitations ran out. I saw no evidence of anything around the house."

"If your husband was the guardian of this money, his stroke might have made the others nervous." Nick had suddenly remembered something.

"I've no interest in train robberies," she insisted. "I only want to get my dog back."

"All right," he agreed.

"Tonight?"

"Tonight."

But first Nick Velvet had another stop to make. He'd remembered the business card for Essex Storage Facility which he'd found on the table at Percy Apjohn's house. It might mean nothing, but if there was hidden loot a storage facility was certainly a likely hiding place. It was located closer in to London, not far from Apjohn's place in Wembley. When Nick reached the address, he found a long low building with a line of overhead doors, capable of storing motor vehicles if necessary. The painted sign on a side wall read: Essex Storage Facility–Key, Combination, and Voiceprint Locks Available.

Nick found the manager, a robust young man named Jennings. "I am making inquiries regarding the estate of Manuel Curzon," Nick said in his most officious banker's voice.

Jennings seemed surprised. "Has he died?"

"He's clinging to life since his stroke, but the family feels the need to make certain preparations for the inevitable."

"I see."

"We understand he maintains storage space with you."

"That's right. Comes down about every six months to check it over."

"How much can you tell me about what's kept in his space?"

"Nothing. Against the regulations, you see."

"You mean I'd have to have a key?"

"No, no—Curzon rents our top-of-the-line option. He has a voiceprint lock."

"Just what is that?"

"Sort of a computer thing, as I understand it. The client's voiceprint is kept in the memory and compared to a voiceprint of anyone trying to gain access. If they don't

match, the door remains locked. We're one of the first facilities in the country to offer it."

"The speaker has to say a certain word or phrase?"

"That's the idea. There's a slight leeway for natural var-
iations, but the voice has to be pretty much the same.
Someone imitating the voice wouldn't know the secret
phrase, of course."

"Well, that's part of the problem, you see. Curzon's
stroke has robbed him of the ability to speak. It's doubtful
that he'll ever recover."

"With the voice lock we insist on a second speaker for
just that reason. In the event one person dies or is incapac-
itated, the second person can open the lock."

"Who was Curzon's second person?"

"I have no idea. We only record the name of the primary leaseholder."

Nick sneaked a ten-pound note from his pocket and held
it casually between his fingers. "It's important that we find
this person."

"No chance, governor. I just don't know."

"What number is his unit?"

"The records will tell me that," he replied, his eyes on
the banknote. "Come into the office."

He flipped through the pages of a loose-leaf record
book. "Here it is—number sixty-five, around on the other
side."

"Does it say what he stored?"

Jennings replied with some reluctance. "A Land Rover."

"That's all?"

"That's all he listed."

Nick nodded and handed over the ten-pound note.
"Thank you, Mr. Jennings."

That night, after dark, Nick parked his car some distance from the Curzon estate. He carried a number of
items with him, some clipped to a gadget belt around his
waist. He was dressed all in black and even his flashlight
had a black rubber casing. Crossing the yard toward the
house, Nick was careful to avoid the obvious alarm sys-

tems. There was no sign of Gilligan patrolling the grounds, and he wanted to keep it that way.

It had been obvious on his earlier visit that Rodney spent the nights indoors. This was no animal to be relegated to a doghouse. Nick found some open ground-floor windows and taped small tubes of chemical scent to the sills. Wherever Rodney was, he would soon be getting whiffs of a female dog in heat.

Nick retreated to the road where he'd left the car. He was barely back to it when he heard the big sheepdog begin to bark. He stuck the animal control signs back on the sides of the vehicle and slipped on a tweed jacket that made him appear more businesslike. After ten minutes Rodney was still barking. He started the car and drove up to the house.

Before the car had come to a full stop, Gilligan was out the front door, a powerful Webley air pistol held at the ready. He was wearing a dressing down, but it didn't seem to interfere with his aim as he leveled the weapon at the car. "Put that down!" Nick commanded in the most authoritative voice he could muster. "You're interfering with the Oxhey Animal Control Unit!"

"Get off this property!"

"Not until I take that hound with me! He's disturbing the peace and quiet of the entire township."

Gilligan kept the pistol steady. Nick knew that British-made air pistols could be deadly, and he had no desire to test this one's velocity. At that instant, Catherine Curzon appeared in the doorway behind the chauffeur and snapped, "Put that weapon down, Gilligan! What's the meaning of this!"

"The dog—" Nick began, getting out of the car.

"I don't know what's wrong with Rodney," she said, truly distressed. "He's never behaved like this before."

Before they knew it, Rodney himself was on the scene, trailing a broken rope with which he'd been tied. Nick bent down and grabbed the rope, reining him in as he tried to escape out the front door. "I've got him," he announced. "I'll have to take him with me, I'm afraid. You can apply for his release tomorrow morning at the animal control center." By that time the dog would be in London with Evita Curzon and Nick would be counting his fee.

"Mr. Curzon would never let this happen," Gilligan said, anxious to use the weapon he still held.

Catherine walked up to him and placed her hand over the gun. "There'll be none of that. I don't know what your game is, Mr. Velvet, but I can see from your bruised face that you're a hard man to convince. I'll be on the phone to the animal control center first thing in the morning, and you'll be out of a job!"

Nick opened the rear door of his car. He'd left some of the chemical there to induce the dog in, and it offered no resistance. Then Nick got behind the wheel, handed Catherine Curzon an official-looking receipt for the dog, and drove away. Rodney gave a final bark from the back seat and then settled down in frustration.

The following morning, on a cool but sunny spring day, Nick Velvet took Rodney for a romp in Green Park. It was truly a magnificent sheepdog, attracting admiring glances from virtually everyone they passed. He'd expected his client to be there waiting and was mildly surprised when she was nowhere in sight. A smaller dog's approach brought a woof from Rodney, who was ready to give chase until Nick tugged on the leash.

Fifteen minutes later, he began to suspect she wasn't coming. Something had happened. Something Nick didn't know about. He pondered what to do next, saddled with a big friendly dog who liked to bark.

"Mr. Velvet?"

Nick turned and saw a middle-aged man with a round face and thinning hair standing behind him. It was the fifth man from the photo at Curzon's house, the missing Matthew Kane. "Yes?" Nick replied, not showing any recognition.

"Evita couldn't make it. She sent me for the dog."

As if in understanding, Rodney gave a low but distinct

growl. "Do you have the money?" Nick asked, tightening his hold on the leash.

"You're to see her for the rest of it. She just sent me for the dog."

"No deal."

The man's eyes hardened. "I have a gun in my pocket, Mr. Velvet. I won't hesitate to use it."

"Take me to her. Take me to Evita Curzon. As soon as I get the money, you get the dog."

"All right. No funny business."

"Which way are we going?"

"She's leasing a flat on St. James Street. It's only a block away."

Nick fully expected that the flat would yield Evita Curzon's dead body, and he'd be fighting for his life in a matter of minutes. Instead she opened the door when they arrived, smiling and seemingly quite healthy. "I should have known you wouldn't give up the dog without the balance of your money, Mr. Velvet. I was making travel arrangements."

"I was expecting you, not one of your ex-husband's friends."

"Oh? You know each other?"

"I saw his photograph at your old house. Matthew Kane, I expect, back from a long absence."

Kane and Evita exchanged glances. "I told you before that none of this concerned you," she told Nick. "You've delivered the dog and here's your money."

He accepted the envelope and did a quick count of the money. "Thank you," he said with a smile. "It's been a pleasure doing business with you, Mrs. Curzon. With both of you, in fact."

Rodney gave a final bark of farewell as he went out the door.

Nick Velvet should have headed for the airport and forgotten the whole thing. Percy Apjohn was dead, but that meant nothing to him. He hadn't even known the man, and the whole crowd of them might be train robbers for all he knew. It was odd he hadn't seen anything in the papers about Apjohn, but maybe the body hadn't yet been found.

That was one thing he could do before he caught his plane. He'd drive up to Wembley, and if the body was still undiscovered he'd phone the police. Then he'd catch the next plane to New York. He stopped at a store and picked up some Waterford crystal for Gloria, then headed to Apjohn's house. It looked the same as it had two days earlier.

There was a man mowing the grass at the house down the street and Nick asked him, "Has Percy Apjohn been around lately? I have some business with him."

"He was there yesterday," the man replied. "I was talking to him. Did you try the bell?"

"Yesterday?" Nick wondered if his mouth was hanging open. "Are you sure?"

"Of course I'm sure! You think I'm feeble-minded or something? I say yesterday, I mean yesterday."

Nick went up to the door and rang the bell, half fearing that the corpse he'd seen would answer it. But no one came. He glanced back at the neighbor, waited until he pushed the mower around the side of the house, and then circled to the rear of Apjohn's house. He forced the bolt with the credit card as he'd done on his earlier visit.

This time it was different. This time there was no body in the living room doorway.

All traces of dried blood had been removed, and if there was any odor in the air it was the sweet smell of a strong disinfectant.

Nick thought about Percy Apjohn dead and Percy Apjohn back to life. He thought about Rodney and he thought about the photograph of those five men. Then he went back to his car and drove to Curzon's home in Oxhey.

For once he was greeted by someone other than Gilligan. Catherine Curzon herself answered the door and stepped aside to let him enter. "There is no Oxhey Animal Control Unit," she told him angrily. "Suppose you explain yourself!"

"I will, in due course."

"Where's Rodney?"

"First let me see your father."

"What? Are you crazy? My father's a sick man!"

"It's very important that I see him. I don't have to speak to him. I just have to see him. I can stand in the doorway of his room."

But she was firm in blocking his path. "You'd better tell me what this is all about."

"It's about the great train robbery of four years ago. I believe your father and his four friends were involved in it. Your mother knew it, and I think you must have had your suspicions, too."

"Those men in the photograph are no longer close friends of my father."

"There's a good reason for that. The loot from the train robbery is hidden away and everyone is lying low until the statute of limitations makes prosecution impossible. The conspirators seem to have split into three groups—Banyon and Green are still together, your mother seems to have taken up with Matthew Kane, and Percy Apjohn may or may not have been murdered."

"What?"

"I've seen the photograph and I've seen the people—all except your father, that is. I have only your word that he's still alive."

She bit her lip uncertainly and then turned toward the stairway. "Follow me, Mr. Velvet. Please try to be quiet."

She led him to an enclosed sun porch at the rear of the second floor. There, seated in a wheelchair with a blanket over his legs, was the fifth man in the photograph, Manuel Curzon. His head lifted as they entered and he tried to speak, but only jumbled fragments of sound came out.

"Are you satisfied now?" she asked Nick.

"I'm sorry. I had to be sure."

She led the way back downstairs. "Sure of what?"

"Did you know your father rents space at the Essex Storage Facility?"

"I never heard of it."

"He has a space the size of a small garage where he keeps a Land Rover."

"He used to have one years ago. I thought he sold it."

"The lock is controlled by a voiceprint."

"What's that?"

"A graphic representation of your father's voice, with the frequencies analyzed by a sound spectrograph. His voice, speaking some code word or phrase, was used to unlock the storage compartment."

"But he can't speak!"

"That's why his stroke threw the other four conspirators into a panic. He'd used someone else's voice as a backup, in case he died or was disabled, but none of them knew who it was."

"If what you say is true, he must have told someone."

"He did. He told your mother."

Nick knew they'd be there ahead of him, and common sense kept telling him he was only looking for trouble by returning to the Essex Storage Facility. Still, he needed an ending when he told the story to Gloria back home.

This time he didn't stop at the office but swung his car around to the back of the building, to storage space number 65. Another car was already there, and he spotted Evita Curzon and Matthew Kane at once. They had the big sheepdog with them and Rodney gave a bark of recognition as Nick came forward.

"What are you doing here?" Evita Curzon asked. "You have your money."

"I had to see if this thing will really work," Nick said with a smile. "I never saw the barking of a dog open a voiceprint lock before."

Kane reached under his jacket and brought out a snub-nosed revolver. "I warned you earlier that I had a gun, Velvet. You should have stayed in London."

"Let's hurry," Evita urged. "Banyon and Green might show up any minute."

"I have to correct an earlier misstatement," Nick told the round-faced man. "I called you Matthew Kane, but of course you're really Percy Apjohn. You murdered the real Matthew Kane at your house in Wembley two days ago."

"You seem to know a great deal."

"I jumped to the wrong conclusion when I entered your house and found his body. But today I learned you were very much alive and at home yesterday. The body was gone, so you must have removed it and cleaned up. You must have killed him. It had to be Kane because everyone else in the photograph is accounted for—even Manuel Curzon, whom I saw for the first time today."

"How is he?" Evita asked.

"As advertised. He can't speak. That's why you needed Rodney, the back up voice." A bark from Rodney, right on cue. "I should have known you two were in this together because what led me to Apjohn's house in the first place was a kennel owner who said I was the second person try- ing to buy an Old English sheepdog. Mr. Apjohn, he said, didn't care about the dog's coloring so long as the size was right. If the dog wasn't important for its looks, why was it important? I had no idea until I learned of this voiceprint business. It seemed likely that two sheepdogs of the same size might have the same tonal quality to their barks. But you couldn't find a suitable duplicate so I was hired to steal the original. If you both knew of Rodney's importance, I guessed you were working together, except that made it Evita and Apjohn, not Evita and Kane."

"Keep him covered," Evita told Apjohn. She took Rod- ney from the car and led him to the microphone mounted on the lock of the storage door.

Nick kept on talking. He always figured it was better to talk when a gun was pointed at him. "Matthew Kane heard about Curzon's stroke and came back from overseas. He wanted to make sure of his share of the loot. He con- fronted you at your house and you killed him, probably with a gardening tool. I don't know what you did with the body."

Apjohn chuckled. "You'll find out soon enough."

With a bit of urging from Evita, Rodney barked twice into the microphone. There was a distant click as the mechanism unlocked. Evita opened the wide overhead door to reveal a dark-green Land Rover in fairly good condition. She dropped to the ground and pulled herself under the vehicle, starting to tear away pieces of tape from the undercarriage. "It's still here," she told Apjohn.

"Good!"

Bundles of plastic-wrapped currency began to litter the floor of the storage garage. "You're cutting the others out of this?" Nick asked.

"Damn right we are!" Apjohn hefted the gun. "But you're in for the same share as Kane. His body's wrapped in oilskin in the trunk of my car. You're both going in there, in place of the money. They'll find your bodies one of these years."

"A car's coming!" Evita warned.

Percy Apjohn cursed and swung around. Nick couldn't wait for a second chance. He was on the man in an instant, grabbing the gun and wrestling it away as they both toppled to the ground. Nick landed on top and the fight ended just as the car pulled up. It was Gilligan, the Curzon chauffeur.

"I was expecting Banyon and Green," Nick said, holding onto Apjohn.

"They've been delayed," Gilligan said. "They're cooperating with the authorities."

"What's the meaning of this?" Evita Curzon asked. "Are you still my former husband's chauffeur?"

"Scotland Yard Special Branch," Gilligan told her. "We've been waiting four years for this day. We couldn't prove a thing until we found the money. Don't try to run, I'm not alone."

Nick saw the other cars converging on them then, and knew that his return home would be delayed by a few days. No one was likely to prosecute him for stealing a dog, though. He walked over and gave Rodney a friendly hug.

<< The Chocolate Dog >>
by
Margery Allingham

THERE IS A time-honored theory that the mysterious, the uncanny, the miraculous, or even the plain honest-to-goodness peculiar are all properly appreciated only in a half light.

Mr. Albert Campion, sitting on a lump of rock in the blaze of a pure white dawn, reflected on this belief and rejected it. He rubbed his eyes cautiously with his bathing towel—yet the man, the girl, and the dog did not disappear but remained in earnest consultation just below him on the dazzling sand.

They had not seen him, and since it is natural to prefer not to intrude oneself upon any sort of visual phenomenon, he remained perfectly still, his lean body melting into the pinkish crag behind him.

In all directions there was loneliness. There was not a sail or a ripple on the glassy water, not a parasol or a beach pajama on the sand, and in the near distance the planes and pinnacles of the discreet esplanade were as deserted as an empty plate.

The man and the dog sat facing one another, and the girl looked down at them. They were all creatures of that slight fantasy which is the most fantastic of all—the not *quite* right.

The girl was perhaps the most nearly normal, although sheer female beauty of the idealistic kind is still unusual

19

enough to be surprising; and as she stood with her weight on one hip and the dawn light turning her hair to white fire, she was quite sufficiently miraculous to take any ordinary man's breath away.

The man and the dog were more definitely unlikely. They were both so astonishingly formal. The man sat on a flat stone in much the same attitude and costume in which he might have presided at a board meeting. He was a smooth elderly person, meticulously shaved and clad in pearl-gray suiting and spats. A ring glistened on his little finger and an eyeglass dangled from his neck.

The dog sat on the sand and he sat as anyone else might sit, with his legs stretched out in front of him, his solid four-inch tail, supporting much of his weight like the flap at the back of a photograph frame, being his only curtsey to dog construction. He was smooth-haired and chocolate-colored, with the lines and contours of a miniature carthorse, and he sat and surveyed the sea behind his friend with the thoughtful, contemplative air of one who rests.

Far up over the cliffs behind Mr. Campion a cock crowed and the girl straightened herself.

"It's getting late," she said unreasonably.

"Yes," said the man regretfully. "How do you feel about it, Theobald?"

The dog turned his head slowly, as though loath to take his eyes from the shining water. He sighed, an exaggerated gesture, and got up with dignity. He stretched himself carefully, each leg separately as dogs do, and then, before Mr. Campion's startled eyes, went through a further process of limbering up which dogs as a rule do not.

He raised his left paw and let it dangle alarmingly, as though the bone were actually broken, repeated the exercise with his right, dragged his left back leg behind him limply, and afterward did the same thing with his right back leg. He hung his head until his nose was buried in the sand, rolled over on his side with his eyes turned up, and finally, having satisfied himself that every single part of him was in reliable working order, set off at a portly stroll scarcely faster than his companions, who walked after him quietly.

They passed out of sight at length, not with any haste nor yet with the dilatory luxury of those who stroll. They went purposefully, all three of them, as if such a promenade was part of their career.

Mr. Campion watched them go and afterward went back to his hotel feeling a little light-headed and uncomfortable. The tall houses of the watering place still had the blank eyes of sleepers and he felt like a trespasser in a dormitory.

He slept most of the day, as people who get up very early in the morning because they cannot sleep, sometimes do; and when he descended into the lounge of his hotel about cocktail time, the light over the sea was the familiar blue and gold, the esplanade was dotted with parasols, and the sands were alive with children of all ages and their colored toys.

The magical quality of the dawn had entirely disappeared and the world was once more a solid material place of ice-cream vendors, evening papers, and white-coated waiters carrying drinks on trays.

He remembered the vision of the morning with self-tolerant amusement and decided that the girl could not have been so beautiful, the old man so formal, nor the dog so—well, so businesslike.

This was his first real introduction to his hotel, at which he had arrived very late on the evening before; and as he sat in a corner tasting his sherry a misgiving nudged him. The wine was good and the room was charming but he began to regret the well-meaning friend who had recommended the place as the ideal retreat for three days of complete rest.

The annoying thing was, of course, that the hotel was *exactly* as the friend had described it—exclusive, quiet, and thoroughly English, with good food and superlative service; but Mr. Campion had forgotten the natural corollary of these attributes, which is, of course, the next best thing to the silence of the tomb.

Everybody was there, all the dear old familiar faces; the Colonel and his lady drinking in whispers in a corner; the elderly lady and her companion knitting with muted needles; the pleasant plump Mama with the two pretty twin daughters who looked away regretfully when the Colonel's young son glowered at them.

The Anglo-Indian widow was also there, languishing alone over an iced drink and a magazine; the two bachelors who did not know each other but who sat close together for protection; the hearty young woman and her girl friend who lowered their happy healthy voices the moment they laid aside their golf clubs in the hall and came to join the father of one of them dozing under a palm—these and several others, all exclusive, English, and perfectly quiet.

Mr. Campion was not a jolly person himself, but a long association with all sorts of people in the course of his profession, which was criminal investigation, had cured him of his native self-consciousness; and the presence of so many people who clearly all liked—or at least considered each other so much that they were prepared to become virtually dumb lest they offended or discommoded anyone else—got on his nerves.

It seemed to him that among people who had this one great quality of self-sacrificial politeness in common there must be other less Spartan grounds of compatibility; yet he knew, as the others did, that one unguarded remark addressed to a stranger must produce the swift change of color, the guilty glance round, and the frigid commonplace which would add another layer to the ice.

It was actually while he was wondering if a great national disaster would break the barriers, or a natural phenomenon such as pink snow shatter this stultifying delicacy, that the chocolate dog came limping in. He was in a most pathetic condition. His left forepaw hung helplessly and he dragged himself across the parquet on three faltering legs. In the center of the room he collapsed with a thud and turned up his eyes.

Immediately there was a general rustle and a scraping of chairs. Then the silence became absolute. The dog looked round him mutely, made a gallant attempt to sit up and beg, collapsed again, and howled very softly once.

"Poor chap, he's hurt." It was one of the golfing young women. But before her solid brogues could carry her across the floor, the Colonel had thrown down his paper, the elderly lady had cast aside her knitting, and the two bachelors had risen to their feet. The Anglo-Indian widow was the nearest and she got there first.

Five minutes later Mr. Campion himself joined the anxious throng. The dog was a little better. A committee of experts had examined his foot. The Colonel gave it on his word that no bone was broken. The father of the golfing girl, who had a pack of hounds, suspected rheumatism. The Anglo-Indian widow was inclined to agree with him. The plump Mama had persuaded the invalid to take a lump of sugar and the elder of the bachelors was holding the basin for her.

"A nice chap," said the Colonel's son to one of the pretty twins. "What is he?"

"Spaniel and labrador, first cross," submitted the young bachelor.

"Terrier somewhere there," said the Colonel.

"Hound, I should say, sir," ventured the elderly lady, "with those ears."

"What's his name?" asked the prettier twin.

They tried them all and the dog was helpful. At "Jack" he looked blank, at "Jim" bewildered. "Rover" seemed to amuse him. "Smith" left him cold. But as "Henry" he barked.

"That's the name of a friend of his," said the Colonel. "Seen a dog do that before."

" 'Rumpelstiltskin'? " suggested the elderly lady's companion and everybody thought what a nice woman she was.

Mr. Campion forgot his superiority complex and cheated.

"Theobald?" he suggested.

The dog sat up and stared at him in astonished contempt. Never in all Mr. Campion's career had he met such a glance of withering disgust. A nark! The words were not uttered but they went home and Mr. Campion blushed.

"He doesn't like that, does he?" said the Colonel, laughing. "What is your name, boy? 'Rex'?"

The abashed Mr. Campion turned away from the crowd and came face to face with the girl of the morning. She really was beautiful, he was surprised to see, as beautiful as she had first appeared. She was looking at him reproachfully, a puzzled expression in her eyes.

"I'm sorry," he murmured.

"So you ought to be," she whispered and pushed through the crowd.

It took him all evening to get hold of her alone. The little hotel was like a parrot house. Since everybody now knew each other, it was only late arrivals who were not talking.

The Colonel, the elderly lady, her companion, and the elder bachelor played bridge in an alcove. The plump Mama and the Colonel's wife chatted happily about their children. The widow listened to the father of the golfing girls and those young women joined the twins, the spare bachelor, the Colonel's son, and a group of other young people.

Mr. Campion found the beautiful girl in the hall waiting for the elevator.

"You're not going up already?" he protested. "It's livening up now. Won't you join us all?"

She shook her head. "It's not in the contract."

Mr. Campion felt a little helpless.

"I'm so sorry about the name," he began, "but you see I saw you on the sands this morning with Theobald and your . . . ?"

"Father," she supplied.

"With your father," he repeated. "I still don't understand, you know."

The beautiful girl laughed.

"Don't you? I thought you were a detective."

"So I am," he said desperately, for the elevator was descending. "That's one of the reasons for my disgusting curiosity. Look here, will you promise to give me an explanation tomorrow?"

"Tomorrow we shall be gone," she said and, stepping back into the elevator, was whirled up out of his sight . . .

But the following morning, when he was lying awake wrestling with a distinct sense of frustration and regret, he was roused by a discreet tapping rather low down on his door.

Theobald was in the corridor, fit and hearty as ever, with no trace of paw trouble. He cocked an eye at Campion, gave his tail a perfunctory wag, and dropped a small white card at his feet before he galloped off to the staircase.

Mr. Campion took up the pasteboard and found it to be a professional card neatly engraved.

Theobald and Co., it ran. *Introductions arranged. Hotel service a specialty.*

On the back, in a round clear handwriting, a single line had been penciled.

Primbeach next week.

<< The Withered Heart >>

by

Jean Potts

AT THE SOUND of the car turning into the driveway, Voss was instantly, thoroughly, awake. Not even a split second of fuzziness. His mind clicked at once into precise, unhurried action, just as it had last night. He sat up on the edge of his bed—Myrtle's, of course, was empty—and reached for his watch. It was only a quarter to eight. Already? he thought, as the car stopped in the driveway. He had not expected anyone quite so soon. Not that it mattered; he was ready any time.

He waited for the next sound, which would be someone knocking on the screen door of the veranda. The bedroom seemed to wait too, breathlessly quiet, except for the whir of the electric fan, tirelessly churning up the sluggish air. The heat—the relentless South American heat—shoved in past the flimsy slats of the window blinds. Even now, in the early morning, there was no escape from its pounding glare. He ought to be used to it; he had been here long enough. More than ten years stagnating in this unspeakable climate, in this forsaken backwater where nothing ever happened except the heat . . .

There. Someone was knocking. In his pajama pants and scuffs, Voss shuffled out to the veranda. Frank Dallas—good old Frank—was waiting at the screen door, peering in through the swarming purple bougainvillea. He looked fresh and hearty. His white linen suit had not yet had time

26

to wilt; his thinning hair still showed the marks of a damp comb.

"Rise and shine, you lazy bum! Top of the morning to you!"

Was there perhaps a hollow ring in Frank's voice? Voss could detect none. Nor any trace of trouble in Frank's open, beaming face. Relax, he told himself; it's too soon— he's come for some other reason.

"Hi. What's the idea, rousing the citizenry at this hour . . ." Yawning, Voss unlocked the screen door. "What the hell hour is it, anyway?"

"Quarter of eight. Time you were up. Look, Voss—" Frank lowered his voice to a conspiratorial whisper— "Myrtle's gone, isn't she?"

"Sure." He said it automatically, without hesitation. "She's gone up to her sister's for a couple of days. Left early, before six this morning."

"Yeah. She told me she was planning to. That's why I figured it was safe to stop by. I've got this letter that Enid wanted me to give you. She was all upset yesterday, poor kid, resigning the way she did. Well, it kind of threw me too. Anyway, this letter, I promised to see that you got it . . ."

Poor old frank had never gotten over being nervous about his role as go-between. He was as jittery—and, Voss supposed, as secretly thrilled—today as he had been six months ago, when Voss and Enid started their clandestine affair. Happily married himself, Frank had the romantic, inquisitive disposition of a maiden aunt. Besides, as American consul, he was Enid's boss. Very natural, very convenient for him to get into the act. Fun for everybody. Great fun at first. Lately—well, it was over-simplification to say that Enid was too serious, too impetuous, too intense. Those were the very qualities in her that made this affair different from the others, that made Enid herself such an irresistible magnet to Voss. Only he couldn't respond to them any more. He did not want to be a philanderer; he wanted to be a true, star-crossed lover—and he had lost the power. It was as if Myrtle had withered his heart.

This envelope in his hand, addressed in Enid's headlong writing—her farewell note, or so she must have thought when she wrote it—even this could not penetrate his benumbed and crippled soul. To be losing, through his own inertia, a love like Enid's, and to feel nothing more than a kind of guilty weariness . . .

He had felt something more last night, all right. Sudden and vivid as lightning, Myrtle's face flashed into his mind. Alive with malice, as it had been last night—the vulgar, coarse, knowing face of his wife. "So your girl friend's leaving," she had said. "I hear she's resigned. My, my, I never thought you'd let this one get away . . ."

Gloating over her own handiwork—because it *was* her doing; the deadly years of being married to Myrtle had very nearly destroyed in him the capacity for feeling anything. Very nearly. But not quite; last night proved that. Hate was left. And if he could hate, he could also love. So Enid need not be lost, after all.

It was going to take time for the numbness to wear off. Voss was still stunned by the impact of release—which, considering everything, was really very fortunate. This morning, if ever in his life, he needed a mind uncluttered by emotion—a mind as cool and accurate as a machine.

"You're all right, aren't you, old man?" Frank was asking anxiously.

"I'll be all right." He paused, conscious of his own pathos as he placed Enid's letter, tenderly, on the wicker table. "It's just that—well, I guess you know how I feel about Enid."

"I know. It's rugged."

Frank was brimming with sympathy. It would be unkind—more than that, it would be indiscreet—to deny him the chance to spill over. "Have a cup of coffee with me," said Voss. "We'll have to make it ourselves. Myrtle always gives the maid time off when she's going to be away. I'd rather eat at the club than up here alone. The maid's a lousy cook, anyway, but we're lucky to get anybody to come this far out." Their house was set off by it-self, on the outermost fringe of the American colony. What a break that had turned out to be, last night!

Voss felt a spasm of nervous excitement, rather like stage fright, as he led the way to the kitchen. Here was where it had happened, right here by the sink ... Another break—the tiles had been a cinch to clean. But might there be some telltale sign?

There was none. Not the smallest. He breathed easy again.

Back on the veranda, with the coffee tray between them, Frank launched into earnest, incoherent speech. The way he looked at it, it was just one of those things. Not that it was any of his business. But look at it one way, and it was the best thing all around—for Enid to pull out, that is. She was really too young for Voss, so she'd get over it. And there was this much about it, a man just couldn't walk out on a wife like Myrtle, not if he had any conscience.

"No," agreed Voss with a wan smile. "I couldn't walk out on Myrtle." But not on account of his conscience, he added to himself. He thought about last night, probing for some tiny qualm, some flicker of remorse. There was none. This extraordinary lack of any kind of feeling ...

"Myrtle's a good egg, too, you know." Frank took out his handkerchief and mopped his moist red brow. "I've always liked Myrtle."

Oh, sure! Myrtle was more fun than a barrel of monkeys. Everybody said so. The life of every party. Suddenly the memory of the endless chain of parties, monotonous, almost identical, pressed down on Voss like a physical weight. He used to sit and drink steadily, with every nerve stretched rigid in protest against Myrtle's raucous voice, against the flushed, blowzy looseness of her face. For some reason—maybe because it was her lushness and vivacity that had attracted him in the beginning—her antics had a kind of excruciating fascination for Voss. Your wife, he used to tell himself; look at her, listen to her—she's all yours.

"What I say is," Frank floundered on, "when two peo-

ple have made a go of it like you and Myrtle for this many
years, why, they can't just throw it away at the drop of a
hat. Myrtle doesn't know, does she?"

Unprepared for this particular question, Voss hesitated.
But it took him only a moment to see the danger in assur-
ing Frank—as he would like to have done—that of course
Myrtle did not know. Only a romantic innocent like Frank
could imagine that the affair had been a secret; in all likelihood Myrtle herself had unloaded to everybody she
knew. Much better to play it safe, just in case the question
should arise later. "She probably suspects," he said slowly.
"But I don't think she has any idea that it's serious. You
know how it is in a place like this—flirtations going on all
the time."

"Sure. I know," said Frank, very much the man of the
world. "Well, one thing, with her away for a couple of
days, you'll have a chance to kind of pull yourself together. She couldn't have picked a better time."

"She certainly couldn't," said Voss sincerely. As Frank
stood up to leave, he added, once more conscious of his
own pathos, "Many thanks for bringing me the letter,
Frank. And for the moral support."

Things couldn't have gone more swimmingly, he was
thinking. With his mind clicking away in this admirable,
mechanical way, there was no reason why he shouldn't
breeze through the rest of the morning without turning a
hair. All it took was careful planning and a cool head. He
had the cool head, all right. And—thanks to Myrtle—the
withered heart that would nevertheless come back to life,
all in good time.

It was at this self-congratulatory moment that Frank
dropped his bomb. Casually; as an afterthought, a final
pleasantry that occurred to him when he was halfway out
to his car. "I suppose Myrtle took Pepper with her, didn't
she?" he called back. "Of course. I never knew her to go
half a block without that dog."

Voss himself remained intact. The world around him
reeled, and then, with a stately, slow-motion effect, it shat-

tered. Except for Frank, who still waited out there, smiling expectantly.

"Oh, yes." Voss's voice rang, remote and dreamy, in his own ears. "Of course she took Pepper. Myrtle never goes anywhere without Pepper."

"In his traveling case, I suppose? Only dog in the country with his own specially built traveling compartment." Another cheery wave, and Frank was gone.

It was incredible. Only gradually was Voss able to grasp the magnitude of his blunder, the treachery of his own mind, seemingly so faultless in its operation, which had remembered every other detail and had forgotten—of all the ignominious, obvious things   Pepper.

For Pepper and Myrtle were devoted to each other. She referred to herself as his "Muvver." He was a small, beagle-type dog, a cheerful extrovert whose devotion to Myrtle did not prevent him from indulging in an occasional night out, and he had chosen last night for one of these escapades.

Voss closed his eyes. The veranda seemed to echo, as it had last evening, with Myrtle's strident summons: "Here, Peppy, Peppy!" But they had waited in vain for the sound of Pepper tearing through the shrubbery and up the driveway, for his joyful voice proclaiming that he was home. Ordinarily, Myrtle would have kept on calling, at intervals, until Pepper showed up—as he always did, sooner or later—looking ashamed and proud in equal parts. Ordinarily, it wouldn't have mattered that he was still not back.

But there was nothing ordinary about last night and this morning. That was just the point: Voss had to make this extraordinary, deranged, secret stretch of time *seem* ordinary. He had to. And it was impossible, because all his calculations had been made minus Pepper.

A current of panic ran through him. He willed himself to stand still and think. Now was no time to lose his head, or to dissolve in futile self-recrimination. He must think, the way he had thought last night, with that beautiful, unhurried precision . . .

Pepper at large, perhaps galloping around the neighborhood calling attention to himself, was a shocking hazard. But to call the little beast would only advertise more fatally the fact that he was not where he ought to be, and furthermore that Voss knew it.

There was nothing to do, then, but wait.

He rubbed his clammy hands against his pajama pants. His knees threatened to buckle under him. But it was somehow unthinkable to sit down. He stood in the middle of the veranda, staring at the screen door, where the bougainvillea climbed, trying to get in. It was the personification of Myrtle, that burgeoning vine. Its harsh purplish flowers were her color, and the way it swarmed over everything, its boundless vulgarity—it was Myrtle to the life.

There was nothing to do but wait . . .

Then all at once Pepper was there. He barked, in an apologetic way, as if he were anxious to make it clear that he was only suggesting—but no means demanding—that he be let in. And when Voss tottered to the screen and opened it, the dog swaggered in with an uneasy attempt at bravado.

Trembling all over, Voss collapsed in one of the wicker chairs. He could hear the little dog clicking off in search of a more demonstrative welcome. And in spite of all he could do, memory re-enacted for him last night's whole flawless (almost) project, after— Well, just after. It had seemed to work itself out with such magical accuracy. First of all, the heaven-scent circumstances of Myrtle's visit to her sister, who lived (bless her heart) in an inland town, the road to which was infrequently traveled, curving, and in spots precipitous. Ideal for Voss's purposes. Who was likely to be abroad at three thirty in the morning to see him, either when he left the house—with Myrtle's body and the bicycle bundled in the back seat of her car—or when he returned, alone on the bicycle?

The answer was, no one. He had had the whole moonless, empty world to himself; he had managed the crash—like everything else—with dreamlike precision.

And when Myrtle's body and her car were found smashed to bits at the bottom of the gorge, who was going to pry too much? Accidents happened all the time, and Myrtle was a notoriously rash driver.

He had thought of everything, including Myrtle's suitcase which, obligingly enough, she had already packed, and the new hat she had brought for her trip. It had a red veil, not quite the same shade as the flower trimming. Trust Myrtle. He had been very proud of remembering about the hat.

Only he had forgotten Pepper. She never went anywhere without him; she would as soon set out stark naked as without Pepper. She did not trust him to ride on the seat beside her; the possibility that something in the passing scene might prove too much for his inquiring temperament terrified her. So she had had a special traveling case built for him. The case, with Pepper inside, was placed on the floor of the front seat, during even the shortest trips.

When not in use, the case was stored in a corner of the garage. That was where it was now, along with Voss's own car, the one he used to drive back and forth to work. If only, last night, he had happened to glance in that particular corner . . . He must get rid of it. And he must get rid of Pepper.

At least Pepper was here, under his control, no longer prancing around in public. Perhaps he had already been noticed? Perhaps, Voss answered himself grimly. In which case it would simply be his word against someone else's. All right, his word. But there was no way whatever to account for a hale and hearty Pepper here in the house, or for the telltale case, sitting undamaged in the garage. Voss recalled his own remote voice, replying to Frank: "Oh, yes. Of course she took Pepper." That was his story, and to make it stick, both Pepper and the traveling case ought to be in the car at the bottom of the gorge.

Well, he could get them there. He had his own car. He saw, with a flash of excitement and renewed hope, that there was time, that he still had a chance. A much chancier chance than the one he had taken last night, when no one had been around to notice his coming and going. It was broad daylight now. Even so, he would be safe enough, once he (and Pepper, and the case) got on the road that led to the gorge. Getting there was the tricky part; to reach the turn-off he would have to drive through one stretch of the American colony—dark and silent last night, but buzzing with activity now that morning was here. Someone would be sure to see him. Not that that was necessarily fatal. The point was that someone would be sure to hear Pepper, who invariably barked his head off the minute he was put in his case, and kept it up until he reached his destination. No, it was a risk that simply could not be taken. Pepper must be disposed of, silenced forever, before he set off on his final trip.

How to do it? This was the problem, stripped to its basic bones.

As if on cue, Pepper appeared in the doorway between the veranda and the living room. His expression was one of friendly inquiry. If this turned out to be a game of hide and seek, his manner seemed to convey, then they could count on him; he was always ready for fun and games; if, on the other hand, his favorite human being had actually gone away and left him—

Well, Pepper was no dog to brood. You would never catch him stretched out on somebody's grave, or refusing to eat and moping himself away to a shadow. Love came easy to this small, sturdy, lively little creature.

Voss eyed him, and Pepper, mistaking speculation for interest, trotted over, all sociability. My God, thought Voss, he'd even get attached to *me*, given time. Which of course was precisely what Pepper was not going to be given. He did not know this, however. He did not know that Voss's heart had all but withered, that he was not yet capable of the tiniest flicker of sympathy for any living thing. In cheerful ignorance, the dog sat down beside Voss's feet— tentatively, with his tail thumping and his spotted head cocked upward. He seemed to be smiling.

"Go away," said Voss coldly.

Pepper could take a hint; still smiling amiably, he ambled over to the living-room door.

A gun would be the easiest way. One neat shot—it

would sound like a car back-firing, in case anyone happened to hear it—and a quick, unobtrusive burial. No problem there, with a body as small as Pepper's. But Voss did not own a gun.

Well, there was gas. Except that there wasn't. Everything here was electric.

Where did you stab a dog? That is . . . Voss glanced toward the door, where Pepper sat, alert for the smallest sign of encouragement. His anatomy must be roughly like that of a human being. But somehow his front legs became, in Voss's mind, a hopeless complication. Pepper wasn't large, but he was strong and wiry. And he loved life; he would hang on to it with all his might.

Voss turned away from Pepper's trustful gaze, and, as he turned, his eye fell on the bougainvillea. One strand had thrust its way inside the screen door, probably when he let Pepper in; it swung there, searching for a toe-hold. He went over, shoved it out savagely, and hooked the screen door against it.

From time to time Pepper left his post to make another fruitless tour of the house. After each trip he looked a little less debonair, a little more anxious. Now he pattered over to Voss's side and uttered a series of barks. Not loud, but insistent.

He would have to be kept quiet until the method of permanent disposal had been decided upon. Food would do it. Voss stood up. Here at least was something he could handle. And anyway, Pepper, being condemned, was entitled to a hearty breakfast. The dog bustled out to the kitchen ahead of Voss, all eagerness and good humor again.

The business of opening a can of dog food and filling Pepper's water bowl was calming. But Voss was startled to see that it was now nine thirty; he should have been at the office an hour ago. He phoned at once, with the first excuse that occurred to him.

His secretary, a flip type, said sure, she understood about his headache, and had he tried tomato juice? Or a hair of the dog?

He had a perilous impulse to laugh and laugh. "I'll see you after lunch," he said icily, and hung up.

Meanwhile, Pepper, full of peace and breakfast, had retired to his favorite spot under the dining-room table for a nap. His round stomach rose and fell rhythmically. Now and then his forehead puckered, or his paws flicked busily, in pursuit of a dream-rabbit. Watching him, Voss felt a drowsiness, almost like hypnosis, creeping over him.

The jangling of the telephone jerked him to his feet, wild-eyed and suddenly drenched in cold sweat. After three rings, however, he had collected his wits and was able to answer in a normal, deliberate voice.

"Is that you, Voss? Is something wrong? Why aren't you at the office?" Myrtle's sister sounded flurried. But then she always did.

She always interrupted, too. He had barely begun to explain about his headache when she broke in. "But Voss, what I call about—what's happened to Myrtle? I thought she was going to get an early start, I've been expecting her for hours."

"You mean she's not there yet?" He paused, just long enough. "But I don't understand it. She left here before six—"

"Before six! But it's ten thirty now, and it's only a three-hour drive—at the very most!"

"I know," he said, aware that the slight edge of irritation in his voice was a convincing touch: worry often made people snappish. "She certainly should be there by now. I don't understand it. I'd better— What had I better do? I can check with—"

"Now keep calm. There must be some simple explanation."

"I don't know what," he said bleakly. "Thank God you called me. I'll get in touch with Frank Dallas right away. He'll know what to do. In the meantime, if you hear anything—"

"I will. Of course I'll call you." Her voice quavered.

This was according to schedule. He had expected the call from Myrtle's sister; the only change was that his next move—to report his problem to good old Frank—must now be delayed until Pepper was dead and at the bottom of the gorge.

Pepper strolled in, pausing at the doorway to yawn luxuriously and stretch each leg in turn. The sight of him chilled Voss; he had a moment's sharp, appalling view not only of his own peril but of his own irresponsibility in the face of it. How could he have let so much of the morning slip by in weak hesitation? What kind of tricks was his mind playing on him, that he could draw an easy breath with Pepper still here to blow his story to smithereens?

It's Pepper or me, he thought. Life or death. Dog eat dog.

In a frenzy now that time was so short, he rushed to the sideboard in the dining room and snatched the carving knife from the drawer. Pepper capered at his heels, making little jumps toward his knee. How easy it would be to grab him by his muzzle, force his head back, and, quickly, with one stroke of the knife . . .

Only not in here. In the kitchen. Tiles, instead of rush matting.

But at that moment it came—the phone call that exploded what was left of his original carefully planned schedule. It was Frank, and his voice was even heartier than usual, in a transparent effort to hide his concern. "Look, Voss, I just had a long-distance call from Myrtle's sister. Seems Myrtle hasn't shown up yet . . ."

Damn the woman, damn her! But damn himself, too, for not foreseeing that she would jump the gun and call Frank herself, instead of leaving it to him. He made a desperate snatch to salvage what little he could. "I know. I've been trying to get you, but your line was busy."

"Now don't get in a sweat, Voss. Like I told her sister, there are any number of simple explanations. Pepper might have gotten car-sick. He does sometimes, you know. I'll get right on it and call you the minute we've found out."

Abandon the idea of getting Pepper and the traveling case out to the gorge. Scrap it—there was no time. There was just time, now, to kill him, hide his body and the case temporarily, and hope that his absence in the wreckage might at first be overlooked. Then later . . .

It came to him then—the best way, the obvious method that he should have thought of right away. He could put Pepper to sleep, the way a veterinary would. Giddy with relief, Voss hurried into the bathroom and flung open the door of the medicine chest. Both he and Myrtle had prescriptions for sleeping pills. A handful of those . . .

There was one lonesome capsule rattling around in his own prescription bottle. Myrtle had evidently packed hers. They were nowhere to be found. It was hopeless, but he could not bring himself to stop searching. Not until the phone rang.

This time Frank's voice, drained of its usual heartiness, was all hushed gravity. "Voss, I'm afraid you've got to prepare yourself for some bad news . . . There's been an accident, a bad one . . . I'll be with you in ten minutes, old man."

Ten minutes, and Pepper still here to give the lie to the whole "accident" story. For his presence would surprise Frank. It would set him to wondering, set him to investigating what wouldn't bear investigating. Pepper stood at Voss's knee, the question—"What can I do for you, sir?"—on the tip of his cordial pink tongue.

"You can die," whispered Voss.

Ten minutes left—probably only nine by now. Voss cast an agonized glance around the room, with its jumble of tawdry color and design, its clutter of Myrtle's gimcracks.

The paperweight was right there on the table beside him. Heavy; a solid, ugly chunk of onyx that fitted suggestively in his hand. One stunning blow aimed at the brown spot between Pepper's ears, and the rest would be easy.

Clasping the paperweight, Voss sat down and patted his lap invitingly. "Here, Peppy," he said.

Pepper leaped up at once; he was used to being held and petted. Snuggling the little dog's head in the crook of his left arm, Voss slowly raised the paperweight, poised it, focusing eye, hand, and will for the one smashing blow.

But he could not bring himself to do it. Now, at this untimely, this fatal, moment, he felt his withered heart stir and come to life—as it should have done for Enid.

His arm sagged; the paperweight thudded to the floor. He grabbed Pepper's warm, sturdy body between his two hands and glared down into the trustful eyes. He did not really like the foolish, friendly creature any more than he ever had. But it was as if he were holding here, in Pepper's compact person, an engine of life. It set up in him a responsive current, melting away the numbness, throbbing all through him in a triumphant flood of warmth.

Yes, triumphant—although he was lost and he knew it, although he could hear the sound of Frank's car already turning into the driveway.

His hands tightened convulsively on Pepper, who had heard too, and was struggling to free himself. Then Voss gave a helpless laugh—or maybe it was a sob—and let go.

Bursting with his tidings of welcome, Pepper rushed out to the veranda. After a moment Voss followed him to the screen door and waited there—waited for Frank.

The Last
<< of the Rossiters >>
by
Thomas Walsh

THERE WAS NO explaining the thing. It simply acted out of itself in some way, flashing into life at the first moment of contact between them, swift as a thunderbolt and far quicker than tinder to match. They had absolutely no previous knowledge of each other, and in consequence there was no basis for even the most instinctive of animal reactions; and yet faster than thought it was there between them, and they each knew that it was. The man hated the dog. The dog hated the man.

The man, however, immediately glossed over the knowledge since later on, in all likelihood, that would be advantageous to him. The dog, compelled to act with honest and primitive simplicity, could not. At once he jumped up on the porch, all four legs stiffened out, uttered a low ominous growl of warning at the man, and bared his teeth.

"Now, Rummy," the girl said, anxiously hurrying forward to him. "Of all things! Now you stop that right away. What in the world is the matter with you?"

For her, although still watching the man, Rummy wagged the end of his tail slightly. He was a big and powerful Labrador Retriever, black as night all over save for handsome and lustrous brown eyes, and now those eyes fastened themselves on the man with an unmistakable challenge of the most direct and ominous intensity. He growled once more.

"Perhaps we startled him," the man said, trying casually to pass it off, but wary enough to stop right where he was and to remain there until everything had been put under control. "And he wouldn't have liked that. He wouldn't have liked that at all. Now take it easy, old boy. Dreaming of a nice juicy T-bone, were you?"

The girl, still openly flustered, got hold of Rummy by the collar and led him inside. Then she came back with an evident and uncomfortable flush on her cheeks.

"I'm so sorry," she tried to explain. "Most times he's awful gentle in spite of his size. I can't think what in the world could have got into him."

"No harm done," the man said—narrow sleek head, clipped British moustache, neatly aristocratic sharp features. "They all know they have a job to do and they get rather annoyed when they happen to fall down on it. Blow to their self-pride, you know. That's what irritates them."

"Yes, I imagine so," the girl said. She was a young girl, no more than 18 or 19, with a rather sturdy figure—which Harling Rossiter had always admired in women when they were that age—light brown hair, gawkily awkward way of managing herself, fair enough legs. Tonight she wore a cheap white dress, a little too tight for her—invitingly so?—and stood with a certain uneasy self-consciousness beside the porch glider, not knowing, obviously, whether or not to ask him to sit down; one of the Rossiters, after all, real quality folks in these parts. "But next time," she added, innocent and upset enough to betray herself without realizing it, "I know he'll have better manners for you."

And "next time" could only mean that she was already hoping for next time. But never frighten them off, Harling Rossiter had learned years ago. That would be stupid, especially when they were as young, lonely, innocent, and naive as this one appeared to be. Go slowly and carefully—and act just as shy. Therefore he only paused briefly at the top of the porch steps, hat in hand.

"Oh, I wouldn't worry about that," he said. "Just delighted to give you a lift home from the movies this evening. It wasn't a bad film at all, was it?"

"I really liked it," the girl said, still facing him with that rather attractive young awkwardness of hers. "But then I like Robert Redford so much, actually. Don't you?"

And probably, Harling Rossiter thought, she had a picture of Dear Robert up in her bedroom; just that age.

"First time I saw him," he remarked smoothly. The movies tonight had been an escape from pure boredom— but now, he saw, a fortunate boredom. A little rain coming down after the show; the sturdy figure in the tight dress before him; and his car handy. So—"And first time I've seen you. New in town?"

"Well, three months," she admitted, grateful for the way he led the conversation. "I used to live on a farm over in Taylor's Corner, if you know where that is. I just got my job here in the bank last winter, after Mama died."

Taylor's Corner was a much smaller town than even Marlowe Falls, hardly more than a general store, a gas station, and perhaps a dozen or so decrepit wooden houses. So Marlowe Falls, he realized, with its movie theater, its two restaurants, and its old country inn, must be almost a metropolis to her; and Harling Rossiter with his English brogues, his hound's-tooth sports jacket, and the carelessly knotted gold scarf around his throat was not too bad a comparison even with Dear Robert Redford.

But that first night he did not push it—a long dull summer was coming up—or dull until now. He walked down her porch steps rather well satisfied with himself. You never really knew, of course, not until you had tried, but it seemed easy enough to him—just little by little now, step by step.

There was only one jarring note. When he turned at the picket fence to smile at her and to lift his hat courteously, he could see Rummy back of the screened door, with the same ominous glare still fixed on him, and a sudden betraying flash of the strong white teeth under it.

Rotten miserable cur, Harling Rossiter thought angrily; ought to have a bullet put into its head. He had never liked dogs, and dogs had never liked him. But it had been a queer thing with this one. It had very nearly attacked him.

As if it knew, somehow; as if it could see everything in Rossiter's head, and right from the start. Yet on the whole he was well contented with himself and drove home looking forward to an enjoyable summer.

Alice Ferguson—that was her name. Not an unattractive little thing and thankfully with an experience of life limited as yet to Taylor's Corner. In short, the kind of sweet Alice in *Ben Bolt* who would soon weep with delight when Harling Rossiter gave her a smile and tremble with fear at his frown. For a week then he did not call her, so that she would be properly anxious. But when he did, and when he heard the quick happy catch in her voice, he understood that it was already just about a *fait accompli.*

Harling Rossiter himself did not work at anything. The Rossiters were an old family in Marlowe Falls, in past years the most prominent family, and there was still the big old colonial house out in the good section of Lake Avenue. But that was about all that was left. No longer a regular cleaning woman, a maid, and Hardy the chauffeur, and no longer two or three cars out in the garage. Last year, too, when Harling Rossiter, the last Rossiter of all, had to come home from Europe, it had been necessary to sell the summer place out on the lake to raise tax money, and now, the last of the last, there were only a few thousand dollars left in the town bank.

Eventually, therefore, something would have to be done, but as yet Harling Rossiter had no idea what the something would turn out to be. It was only when Elizabeth Henderson came back to Marlowe Falls as a lonely, recently bereaved, and still rather horse-faced young widow, that a possible solution presented itself. He could always tell about women, and he remembered that years ago Elizabeth Henderson could have been his simply for the asking.

Then why not now? The Hendersons were another old family in Marlowe Falls, suitable even for a Rossiter alliance, and Grandfather Henderson had invested wisely and widely in the stock market way back in the thirties, at depression prices. The rumor in town went that he had left Elizabeth about $2,000,000, and by August, when Harling Rossiter began to think seriously about it, horse face or no horse face, he found himself considerably irritated at having promised sweet Alice so much.

It had proved necessary, however. She had never been with a man before, and although Harling Rossiter did not reproach himself for that fact, taking it as a not unflattering compliment, certain loving assurances had to be given. But come August his usual weariness and boredom were beginning to set in, and by making deliberately cutting remarks about certain manners and crude habits of speech, Harling Rossiter tried to persuade himself that the affair would die a natural death.

It proved not to be that simple and uncomplicated. On the night he decided to break it off with Alice once and for all, since Elizabeth might hear something, he was informed that she could not let him go, and for the best possible reason. She would not agree to a weekend in New York, with all her expenses paid and nothing asked of her but an overnight visit to a certain clinic that Harling Rossiter knew. She wept at first. She wept wretchedly and endlessly. No, she said, not that, never that. He had said he loved her. He had sworn he did. So marriage was necessary now. There was nothing else for him to do. He had promised!

They were on a lonely dirt road back in the woods near Dark Pond where for some time they had been in the habit of parking while on the way home, and all at once Alice stopped that silly weeping of hers and faced up to him with a resolution and defiance that Harling Rossiter could almost admire in her. Good farm stock had its points occasionally. Even the tone of her voice changed, as if understanding him at last—what he had wanted from her, all he had wanted from her—and she answered him back with cold flashing anger.

"I know what it is," she almost spat out at him. "It's that old hag of a Henderson woman. She has money, hasn't she? So if you can only get rid of me now—well, you won't! I'm not going to let you. I'll tell her about us. I'll tell her the whole thing!"

"Oh?" he said, looking carelessly past her into dark woods, into silent and lonely woods. "I should think you'd have a little more pride, Alice, if you're still incapable of behaving with even a pretense of decent manners. Or is it the country yokel in you—to grovel and humiliate yourself for a lady's sympathy? Because she's a lady, at any rate, where you aren't—and never will be. This summer we both had a little fun together, and that's all. Now it's over. Why can't you accept it? Why continue to be as tiresome as you are now?"

But he had pushed her a little too far. He wanted to hurt, and he had hurt. She brushed the last angry tears from her eyes and got out of the car.

"Now where?" he inquired pleasantly, to hurt a second time. "I'd say it's a little late for you to walk all the way home, Alice. You should have done that the first time you ever came up here with me, back in June. Or didn't you want to, then?"

A ghostly September moon revealed itself back of the clouds. When she turned, it showed her expression as scornful as his, as hating as his—which he had not expected. A faint uneasiness stirred in him. Was she serious? He also got out of the car, but she moved quickly away from him.

"I'll have the child," she said, lips curled. "Your child. I'll have it just out of spite, you dirty rotten low skunk, you. Then see if she marries you, when everybody in town knows—but I think not. She's too decent a person. She isn't your kind."

"But you are?" Harling Rossiter drawled. "Why, I never even suspected, dearest. Is that what you mean?"

"No, not quite—" and with a childish defiance in her to face whatever she had to face now, even if all alone and no matter the cost. "Maybe you're Lake Avenue and I'm Taylor's Corner—but I wouldn't lower myself to spit on you after this. Skunk, skunk! Rummy knew what you were the first instant he set eyes on you, where I didn't. You'll even promise love, won't you, to get what you want. You promised it to me, and you'll promise it to her—for the money. Only you'll never get it and I'll see that you won't. Don't touch me!"

But he made no attempt to, not at that moment.

"St-st-st," he said. "You're perfectly right about Lake Avenue and Taylor's Corner. I'm glad you realize it finally. Now just use your head and marry someone your own kind. And let me marry mine."

She ran forward then and slapped him. She slapped him twice, and something very odd happened. It was not the pain, it was partly the blind fury at Taylor's Corner slapping Lake Avenue and partly the realization that Elizabeth Henderson had certain high and old-fashioned standards of conduct. She had always cringed from cheap gossip, and despised meanness in anyone. Which meant, if she ever was told about this—

He reached out and got hold of Taylor's Corner by the two arms, shaking her violently.

"You'll tell no one anything," he gritted. "You'll do as I say! You'll go down to New York next week and you'll—"

But at that she did something even more childishly foolish. She threw back her head and laughed at him. She laughed triumphantly. At that everything shifted in Harling Rossiter, blindly and desperately, and before he quite realized it, he had taken hold of her by the throat. And no longer was it a body seductively desirable to him; he now thought of it with loathing and hatred, as something that had dared to put itself in his way, something unspeakably common, ugly, and revolting.

He shook it again, but she stood like a stone, still facing him, still laughing at him. It was not to be endured, not from a common little farm chippie out of Taylor's Corner. If she was stupid enough to—

And she was. They stood face to face like that, her expression stony and unafraid, a venomous triumph in her eyes.

"Never, never!" she screamed. "She'll never marry you,

and you know she won't. Take your hands off me. I'm warning you. Rummy!"

It was not an idle threat. In nice weather she always let the damned hound loose before leaving the house, and if it was anywhere near Dark Pond tonight, and if it heard her voice calling— It was necessary to shut off the voice, and he did. His fingers tightened as if of themselves, without the slightest direction on his part, and tightened still more.

She made a few choked sounds and began kicking at him, but a sudden naked fear in her eyes sent an emotion of serene and absolute power flooding through him over Alice, and even over everyone else in the world. He got her back against the car, held her free of the ground there, and bent over her. Perhaps a minute or so passed. Then he straightened.

He discovered that his legs were shaking. He discovered that he had got his handkerchief out and was wiping his face. He put both hands down on the hood, spreading them wide, dropped his head toward them, shook his head, and shook it again. "Alice?" he whispered finally, when he could whisper; but only to make sure. "Alice?"

There was no answer. He had not really expected one. So? So things to do. He got her back into the car, and glared one way along the dirt road, then the other. But there was no one, all clear—and now the rest of it to be done. How?

But that proved simple enough. There was a marshy spot near this side of the pond and an old spade in his car with the box of sand he kept there for winter driving. He was just taking the spade out of his trunk when the dog came.

It came silently at him from out of the trees like a black ghost, from whatever distance it had to cover after it heard the girl calling. It came with a wolfish glitter of eyes and white teeth, the front paws extended, and it came straight for his throat. Only at the last possible instant was he able to get the wooden haft of the spade between them to thrust it off.

When it recovered and came at him once more, still with that deadly swiftness and silence, he smashed down at it with the metal blade, and smashed again and again and again. Then he kicked it off the bank into Dark Pond and waited until he had made sure it did not come up.

He dug the grave then and got it occupied. Everything in? Yes—hat, gloves, purse, scarf. He smoothed over the grave and drove back to the state road. No one saw him, and when he got home the gray September mist over the trees had transformed itself into a sudden and torrential downpour. He was very glad it had. It would wash any possible traces of mud from his car—and they could do marvelous things, it came to him, with their scientific laboratories these days. Nothing to worry about now—just quick, quick, and careful, careful.

In the house he stripped himself to the skin, grinning jumpily, and burned every stitch of the clothes he had been wearing. After that he scraped up the ashes with scrupulous care and flushed them away in the downstairs toilet. He brushed his shoes for at leave five minutes, with particular attention to the crevices around the heels and soles, and washed off the outsides of them with warm water.

Done then? Yes, all done; mistress and dog. Still, he woke up twice that night in the small hours and each time found that he was making a terrified low whimper deep in his throat. It was not caused by Alice, however. It was, rather, a nightmare that Rummy was coming at him again, its white teeth bared, its eyes glittering.

But when he woke up the next morning there was bright sunshine after the rain; his car looked spotless, and when he called Elizabeth Henderson about eleven o'clock to inquire about a spot of golf, the offer was accepted happily and at once. He had better show himself out and around over the weekend, with not a worry in the world so far as a country clod like Chief of Police Frank Culkin would never determine.

It was over and done. Never again would he have to bother his head about it.

She was not missed until Monday when she did not

show up for her clerical job at the State National Bank. But it was rather late Tuesday night, about 9:30, before Chief Culkin stopped by on Lake Avenue with a few questions.

It was a hot night, and at Culkin's suggestion they sat out on the back porch, which was fully screened. Yes, Harling Rossiter declared manfully there—he'd had three days to go over the thing again and again, and to decide what he had to admit, because it could be proved against him, and what he must not. Saturday night they had dined together at a French restaurant near Lake Champlain, but then on the way home she had started quarreling with him.

"You know," he explained, while mixing a friendly drink for them, "I only felt sorry for the girl—no family at all, and only a child, really—so we had dinner together a few times. That was the whole thing. Why"—man-to-man honesty, both hands outflung for a moment in the most self-explanatory manner possible—"I never so much as kissed her good night, Chief. My word of honor. And now no one's seen her around since Saturday night, you say? I wonder why. I admit she might have developed a silly kid's crush on me. But that's no reason—"

"Hard to say," Culkin put in. "At that age." He was a big burly man with a long dour face and heavily lidded gray eyes, and now without touching his drink the eyes moved a little in Harling Rossiter's direction, though still warily lowered. "Apparently she hasn't been home in three or four days, or since Saturday, at any rate, and even her dog Rummy is gone. Did you take him along with you out to dinner?"

"Why, no," Harling Rossiter answered, as if rather surprised by the question. "I'm afraid Rummy never quite cottoned to me, Chief. But I believe she let him out into the woods before we left. She usually did, when she knew I was coming over that night."

"What time did you bring her home on Saturday?"

"Oh, lord," Harling Rossiter said, in a tone of fond but somewhat petulant helplessness. "That silly kid. But I—well, I didn't bring her home, as a matter of fact. I stopped to get some cigarettes at a drugstore in Plattsburg, and when I came out again she was talking to some young fellows in another car. Then she got in with them and called out to me that they were giving her a ride home. I wouldn't have to bother. They were rather fresh and insolent youngsters. Pop, they called me—if you can imagine it. Pop."

"How many young fellows? Did you recognize them? Were they from town here?"

"I don't know—" eager to help now, but of course helpless. "All I can tell you is that they were driving an old black Chevrolet sedan. Two or three of them—but nobody I knew. Just young and smart, Chief—and I believe maybe just two of them. I can't even tell you the license number. I simply paid no attention to it."

"Then more's the pity," Culkin told him. He was brooding out at the woods, fingers steepled, and he had not yet touched the friendly drink that had been prepared for him. "Then we might have had some kind of a lead. As it is—or wait a minute. Is that a dog out there by your back fence? Is that Rummy?"

Harling Rossiter's heart jumped—catching horribly, then twisting horribly. Because, turning his head in the direction indicated, he caught sight of something black, quick, and furtive, something that reflected into the porch light a snarl of white teeth and over that the flaming glitter of two savage, hate-filled eyes. It was there only for a breath, then it was gone, but it was long enough to make Harling Rossiter drop his whiskey glass.

"By God!" Culkin said, getting up quickly. "Was it Rummy, do you think? Did you get any kind of a look at it?"

They went down to the lawn and there Culkin got out a flashlight. "And what's this?" he demanded, bending over for something. "A blue and white scarf, it looks like. Would it be the girl's, do you think?"

There was light on the porch behind Harling Rossiter. There was safety back there, a door to be locked. But there was something else now—a road to be followed, a road he had himself created, and with no hesitation at all.

"I don't know," he got out. He was staring at Culkin in the lawn shadows, and Culkin was staring at him, he could be certain of that. An ominous chill breeze stirred, and—and a patter of invisible feet, was it? "She had at least two or three scarves, Chief, and that could be one. I just can't say."

"Damned queer," Culkin muttered, and glanced around edgily. "And where the hell did the dog get to? Here, Rummy, boy."

There was no answer. Under the trees there was only a silence like death itself.

"Well," Culkin said at last, stuffing the scarf into his pocket, "I think I'd better hand this thing over to the State Troopers in Plattsburg soon as I can now. I don't much like the look of it, Mr. Rossiter, sir. All dirty and stained, did you notice—but they might be able to analyze the spots up there and tell where they came from."

Harling Rossiter, fixed smile on his lips, waved assent. Harling Rossiter nodded. Then he had to go back all alone into the house, just the one dim lamp on the porch, and the lonely woods all around. For perhaps five full minutes he stood motionless by the screen door, with a slight but uncontrollable shiver of his whole body every few seconds. Could it be possible? Could that damned hound have actually . . .

Of course it could! How many stories had he heard of a dog's devotion to a master or mistress? Of a dog that settled itself on a loved one's grave somewhere and never left no matter what inducement was offered? Or a dog forgotten and left behind when its family moved, and who, months and months later, was found to have traveled hundreds and even thousands of miles to track down its owner in a strange city it had never seen before? There had been no way for them to know what had happened and why they had been abandoned—and yet they had known! Their love had been the driving force, but hatred might also serve. And that damned hound had always hated him! So could it be that even in death . . .

Or wait up now! Say that he had not killed it Saturday night, but had only thought he had. What then? It might have floated up into the bank shadows where he did not see it, then lay there for the last couple of days, doggedly regaining its strength. Sometime today it might have blinked its eyes open, crawled up the bank, and then over to the grave of Alice. There it could have pawed at the soft ground—why in God's name had he picked soft ground?—until the body was at least partially uncovered.

After that it would have thought of help, of human help, and to get it might have torn that blue and white scarf from her dead hand. Harling Rossiter had bought it for her.

And then? Then back to town, obviously, to get the help it needed and could not itself give. Or to accuse him, was that it? To prove it beyond any question? Certainly it had been her scarf, and even more certainly it had been laid here at his own doorstep only a few minutes ago, right here in his own yard. Could instinct do that? Could black hate do it? It had been done, no matter what.

And perhaps in a few hours now, at the State Troopers' laboratory up in Plattsburg, the experts might be able to decide where the stains of mud had come from—from somewhere around Dark Pond. So he must act. There was no time to lose. He must be the first one there!

He drove into town, circling around in several different streets to make sure no one was following him, and then he drove out to the dirt road, still watching his rear-view mirror every few seconds. It was still all right; no one at all was there—and Frank Culkin by now would be half-way to Plattsburg. So boldness and resolution had won for him, and the help of a moon that was coming up a bit later tonight, and in even a more ghostly fashion.

There were white streamers of mist under the trees, and a beating hush that seemed deeper and more threatening, as if alerted now, than any hush that Harling Rossiter had known until this moment. Also, not long after he left his car and had begun to trot forward breathlessly, there was something else. Or did he only imagine the almost inaudible patter of other feet off in the woods behind him? Not human feet—and not even living, perhaps?

All he knew was that they seemed to keep a steadily fixed pace. They stopped when he stopped. They went when he went. Damn hound! It knew everything he knew, everything he thought, and it was leading him on. But there was no turning back now. He had to go on. He had to find out. He had to make sure!

He heard someone else sobbing aloud in wild terror, and he felt someone else stagger and then fall down in the dirt road at full length. Harling Rossiter lay quiet for a moment, to listen for Rummy again—and there was nothing. Then he got up, plunging forward thankfully—and there it was. Always behind him, never to be shaken off: the hound. He sobbed again, plunged ahead even more drunkenly, and came to the pond.

But there even the dim moon tormented him. Heavy clouds shut it off. All he could distinguish was a glitter of stagnant water below, when a slight breeze came and the September mist parted sluggishly to each side. Yes, here—and he crawled forward the last few steps on his hands and knees.

Yes, right here. A big rock on one side, a clump of thin white young birch on the other. So under him now, just in between those two markers—and thank God the moon came out again as suddenly as it had dropped from sight moments ago.

No disturbance, apparently. No arm or leg showing, no bit of white dress, no tip of shoe to be seen anywhere at all. Thank God! Everything was still as carefully concealed as he had left it on Saturday night. He laughed foolishly to himself and even squatted back on his heels like a small child. So all his terror was for nothing! He clapped his hands, at the same time lifting his head up quickly and gleefully—and when he did so he saw the hound.

It was just behind him. It stood there silent as death, all black, with long legs and powerful shoulders, and with a wolflike tongue lolling out as if hungrily. It did not move.

It could not be heard breathing. It just stood there, and the hush around Harling Rossiter froze into glare ice.

He wanted to get up. He could not. He put both hands out, to fend off, and shook his head. Then at last, lifting its nuzzle skyward, the dog howled. It was a long howl from deep in its chest, as if gloating and exultant, as if savagely vindictive, as if ferociously triumphant at last. Under the great circle of the sky it was like a summons, pitilessly unforgiving, that rang out over the hushed darkness and stillness of the whole earth. Arrow-straight it pierced into the heart like a sinister and icy foretoken of death waiting—and it was answered.

Because other sounds approached now, quite audible sounds. A voice murmured and a second replied to it. Harling Rossiter pushed himself up on both hands, with the expression of a dazed and even lunatic cunning on his face, and from under the trees a powerful flashlight glittered, blinding him. Rossiter flung up an arm to shut it off, and in the blessed dark again, heard one more voice.

It was Chief Culkin's.

"Somewhere right here," he was saying. "Maybe right there where he's kneeling, Lieutenant. I'd take my oath this is the place, all right. It just has to be. Buster's treed him for us!"

"No, no," Harling Rossiter babbled, foolishly appealing now with both palms. "You don't understand, Chief. Listen to me!"

"Why?" Culkin interrupted brutally and contemptuously. "You damned silly fool! You did just what we were hoping you'd do. It was only necessary to snap a beeper onto your car and then have Buster here follow you along out of sight the way he's been trained to do. I knew, wherever the body was, we'd never find it any way else in God's world, not up here in all these Adirondack woods, not unless you yourself led us to it. Try that soft spot just under him, Harry. He's a Rossiter, you know. He wouldn't like to work with his hands too much."

"No, no—" but desperately sprawling forward to protect

with both arms the place Culkin had indicated. "You can't, Chief. You mustn't. There's nothing here! Only—"

"Only a scarf," one of the troopers behind him yelled out. "Only something that looks like a girl's dress. Come on, Al. Let's put our backs into it now. She's here!"

"A scarf?"—and Rossiter's head twisted around to confront Culkin. "But it can't be. You're making them lie to me. You put the scarf in your pocket. I saw you!"

"Yes, you did," Culkin said, roughly snapping the handcuffs on. "Bought it in town for her yourself, didn't you? Which the poor silly creature had to parade around before her girl friend down at the bank—while you weren't clever enough to think that maybe the Bon Ton had another scarf just like it in stock! That's the one her friend picked out for us, the one we had Buster drop on your lawn back there—when you turned white as a sheet. So I knew then, and particularly after we found poor Old Rummy slashed almost to ribbons in the pond here. Tried to protect her, did he? But either way there's no escape for you now, no escape at all. Because if you didn't bury her like this, how in the hell did you know just where to come? All right under your eyes, eh?—but under mine too. Now get him back to the car, a couple of you. I don't want to have even another sight of the man."

All this time the trained police dog had been watching them with great interest, one and then the other, its tail wagging amiably. But soon it gave a wide lazy yawn, inched its head up against the Lieutenant's leg for a rewarding pat of the hand, and got it.

"Good boy," Culkin also approved, with a second pat. "Just a little touch of black dye, which we'll have off of you in a few seconds, and you were almost a dead ringer for poor Rummy—in bad light, anyway. When we let him see you like that, only a glimpse, right after you apparently dropped the same scarf she was wearing that night, and that he'd bought for her himself, what the hell else could he do but what he did? My compliments, Lieutenant. You have a great little actor here."

Two other uniformed men pushed Harling Rossiter up

onto the path. "No, no," he kept whispering anxiously. "Wait a minute. You don't understand. No, no, no! You see—"

But it was no good; no good in the world. Guiding him on stolidly and silently before them, one at his right elbow, one at his left, neither of the troopers even bothered to answer the last of the Rossiters.

The Dog That
<< Came to the Funeral >>

by

John Collier

IT WAS AN hour or two after dinner on the day of the
General's funeral. The drawing room was large but ill-lit
and the fire smoked a little. Mrs. Bulteney was alone with
Harry Despencer, a lawyer who had charge of the affairs
of two or three of his cousins and second cousins, and who
rode to hounds three days a week. He was down there in
his legal capacity.

"I must say, Di, I wish you'd called in someone other
than Harding."

"Harding's all right. He's the doctor here. He set my leg
damned well when I came off Blazer."

"I know. But I wish you'd had someone else in."

"Why exactly do you wish that, Harry?"

"Well, the poor bloody old man! Everyone knows he's
drunk as a fiddler's bitch any time after ten in the morning."

"And a sober doctor might have pulled him through? Is
that what you think? Is that why you wish I'd called someone else in?"

"You know very well what I wish," said Despencer.

"I hope I do. Because it's going to come true. Isn't it?"

"It most certainly is."

"Then why think of anything else in the world?"

"One has to think sometimes of what people may say."

"We've thought of it. I'm sick of it. Now we don't need

57

to any more. Look, darling," said Mrs. Bulteney, "every-one knows about septic pneumonia. The penicillin works—or it doesn't work."

"Harding gave him penicillin? I didn't know he'd even heard of it."

"He's drunk, but he's not such a fool. I filled the hypo-dermic myself. He was a bit shaky, so I did it for him. Four times!"

"It didn't do him much good."

"No good at all, Harry. It might just as well have been tap water."

"Well, at least it gave him a sporting chance. I mean, it'd be a bit of a fly in the ointment if he'd died of any sort of neglect."

Mrs. Bulteney always had her servants knock before en-tering. The cook-housekeeper now knocked, and was told to come in.

"If you please, ma'am, is there anything else you re-quire?"

"Nothing at all. I think you might all go to bed. Good night."

"Please, ma'am, there's a poor dog out there at the back."

"A dog? What sort of dog?" asked Mrs. Bulteney.

"A cold one, ma'am, and a hungry one. Only we gave it a plate of scraps. Briggs thought if he might let it into one of the stalls, just for tonight. I mean, a night like this you don't hardly like to turn a dog out in."

"Proper wild goose weather!" the lawyer remarked.

"That's what it is, sir—a night for the geese. Briggs said—you know his way of talking, sir—what with the wind and the sleet, he said, you'd think the old Devil was standing astride the house, a-laying on to it with a cat o'nine tails."

Mrs. Bulteney's voice took on an edge of impatience. "Parfit, I asked you what sort of a dog it was. Do you know one breed of dog from another? Or don't you?"

"Well, I must say, ma'am . . ." Mrs. Parfit was a woman of character, but she was exceeded in this respect by her

mistress, who had the additional advantages of great
size, great beauty, and great arrogance. "No special breed,
ma'am. Just one of them middle-sized, black, shiny ones.
A good deal of the Labrador in him, I'd be inclined to
say, ma'am."

"Well, a dog's a dog, I suppose," Mrs. Bulteney conceded. "No sort of dog's been turned away from this house
on a night like this. But I don't want mongrels hanging
about the place with Christabel and Lady coming in heat
any minute. Give him a bed, and get him off first thing in
the morning. But make sure he goes. You understand me?"

"Yes, ma'am. Thank you, ma'am. Good night, ma'am.
Good night, sir."

"Good night, Mrs. Parfit," the lawyer replied. "I say,
Di, I wonder if that's the dog that came to the funeral."

"And supposing it is?"

"It must have followed us home."

"Obviously, if it's the same one. Of course it's the same.
What's the point?"

"No point. Idle remark," said Despencer. "I'm just as
glad it's got a bed for the night. Listen to the wind! I bet
the horses are snugger than we are. I'll say this for old
Gilbert—he let the house go to pot but you've still got the
best stables this side of Norfolk. You could say worse
things about a place."

"I'm glad you like the place, Harry. It's snug enough
upstairs. Do you want some more whiskey, or shall we go
up?"

They went up. Despencer's bedroom was in the left corridor at the head of the stairs; Mrs. Bulteney's was in the
big bay in the center. They both went into Mrs. Bulteney's
room. As soon as they had closed the door, they fell into
an embrace which was ravenous to the point of ferocity.
There was that about this savage love-making—if the
word can be applied to the congress of tigers—which indicated it was not occurring for the first time. It was less
observable, but no less true, that this violence was natural,
and a supreme fulfillment, to Diana Bulteney, and unnatu-

ral, an intoxication, though in a way all the more exciting
for that, to Despencer.

"Well, I suppose I'd better get back to my room," he
said.

"I don't think you really need to, Harry."

"I think I'd better."

"Come back a moment! Just a moment. Must it really
be six months?"

"Darling, you know just as well as I do," said
Despencer. "You can come up to town. Maybe we can go
abroad for a month."

"I don't think I like this place any more, Harry."

"Oh, that's just the funeral and the damned wind and
everything. You love it really; you always have."

"No! I'd like to sell out, pack up, and go to Italy or
somewhere tomorrow."

"You wouldn't get much hunting," Despencer reminded
her. "Besides, what do you get for a place like this in these
days? We've been into all that. We'll be all right here.
Couldn't be better, as long as we take our time and don't
put people's backs up. If I could get two or three more es-
tates to handle I could pay my shot."

"Who cares, you stuffy old lawyer, you!"

"I do, a bit. Not too much. But you've got a temper, you
know. I mean, a fellow likes to stand on his own feet."

"Good night! Kiss me first! Oh, Harry, you don't know
how different you are! Good night!"

Next day was clear, still, and frozen, as often happens
after the northeast gales in the coastal districts of Norfolk.
Hunting was out of the question so soon after the funeral,
but Despencer felt it was all right to walk round the
hedges with a gun. Mrs. Bulteney accompanied him. They
ate their lunch under a big ash on the edge of a wood.

"There's that cursed dog sneaking after us!" exclaimed
Mrs. Bulteney. "I gave word for Briggs to get rid of it first
thing this morning. You heard me yourself. One of these
days I'm going to sack the whole gang of them. Don't
throw food to it, Harry, the wretched thing gives me the
creeps."

"What's wrong with it? Perfectly ordinary sort of a dog."

"You didn't hear it howl in the night?"

"Not I, nor you either. With that wind, you wouldn't have heard a pack of wolves howling. What you heard was the wind in some chimney or other."

"I seemed to hear it under the wind," Mrs. Bulteney insisted.

"Definitely not," said the lawyer.

"Well, it kept me awake anyway. I can tell you I feel like absolute hell today, and I don't want that damned creature looking at me. I don't like its eyes."

"Perhaps they remind you of somebody else's eyes?"

"There you are! You see it too! They're the same. I saw it yesterday as soon as he came up to us. I don't like it." Mrs. Bulteney shivered.

"There's a lot of black, beady eyes in the world, and that sort of dog usually has them. I wouldn't let it worry you."

"Well, it does, and if it comes crawling after us any more, by God I'll take that gun and shoot the bloody thing!"

"Don't talk like that, Di! You know perfectly well you wouldn't. After all, a dog's a dog, you know."

"Yes, I suppose it is. Drive it off! Chuck a stone at it! Drive it away!"

The lawyer waved an arm. "Here, you! Clear off! Go on! Get out, I say! There you are, darling! He won't come back in a hurry."

However, the dog, though timid, was seen about the house late that afternoon. After dinner Mrs. Bulteney questioned her housekeeper.

"Parfit, is that dog finally got rid of, or not?"

"Well, ma'am, it's been chased off with a broom three times."

"Has it *stayed* off? That's what I'm asking you."

"I haven't seen it since the last time, ma'am. We was as hard with it as we could bring ourselves to be."

"Well, if it shows up tomorrow I want Briggs to get out

the Austin and take it into Norfolk. There's some sort of
lost animals' home there. I want that *done*, do you hear?"

"If it'll let us lay a hand on it, ma'am. It's got pretty shy
of us now we've been after it with brooms. And, I must
say, no wonder!"

"That's quite enough, Parfit. Go downstairs. I'll serve
the coffee myself."

"Very well, madam. Good night, madam."

"Brandy, Harry?"

"Thank you, yes. Easy though! My God, Di! Easy does
it!"

"Oh, come on! It'll cheer us up."

"I don't know that I want any cheering up."

"Then why sit there looking like a wet week?"

"Was I? Sorry! I was just thinking," he said.

"Thinking of what?"

"Look here, if we were going to throw everything over-
board and to hell with everybody, I wouldn't say a word.
But we're going to get married after a decent interval;
we're going to live here, and we want to stand well with
the neighbors, and we don't want any stink. You know
what backstairs gossip can be; we don't want any. You're
altogether unreasonably worked up about that dog. What's
more to the point, you're showing it."

"Well, if I can't have a nasty mongrel stray run off my
own place, when I've got two champion bitches coming in
heat any day, I'd like to know why, that's all."

"Di, you've been through a lot in the last few days. I
can understand, but they can't. All the same, they've got
eyes in their heads, and tongues too. They can spot a likeness just as well as you can. As a matter of fact, they've
spotted it already."

"How do you know?"

"I could hear them down in the yard when I was dressing," said Despencer.

"Your dressing room doesn't overlook the yard."

"All right then—when I was in the lavatory. Briggs and
the boy were down there; I suppose they'd just been chas-

ing it away. I heard Briggs say: 'Well, let's hope that's goodbye to the poor old General!' "

Mrs. Bulteney almost burst. "I think that's the damndest cheek I ever heard of in my life!"

"Oh, I don't know. You saw it; I saw it; why shouldn't they see it? I mean, when that dog put his head on one side and looked at us when we were having lunch, I'd have sworn it was old Gilbert himself. But the point is, these people read nothing but the Sunday papers, and you can be quite sure they know it wasn't any sort of a marriage, and . . . are you listening?"

"Yes, I'm listening."

"Well, the dog turns up on the very day of the funeral and you seem afraid of it; you can just imagine the sort of nonsense they could make up. And that sort of thing's no better for being nonsense, let me tell you. In fact, it's all the harder to nail down."

"I see." Mrs. Bulteney bit her lip. "I suppose you're right. It seems a bit strange to have to mind one's p's and q's in front of the servants, I must say. I didn't tell you, but last night the creature gave me a nightmare, and I couldn't sleep after it, and somehow I can't shake it off."

The lawyer looked thoughtful. "You know," he said, "a nightmare can weigh on you all the next day. Did I tell you that in the last few months I've had the same absolutely identical nightmare six times at least, probably more. I'm in one of those terrific great cars they're putting out now. Best-looking car you ever saw in your life. Cream-colored, open, buzzing along at a hundred miles an hour . . ."

"I wish you were with me, Harry."

"Oh, but, darling, I am, I assure you. Sorry! I didn't mean to interrupt."

"After you went last night," she continued, "after I'd heard the damned thing howling, I dreamt I was down there in the churchyard. I think I'd followed it down there, trying to kill it. Yes, that's who it was. And there it was on the grave, and I had to go up close, and it fixed its beady, black eyes on me, and by God, Harry, it *was* Gilbert! I tell you, Harry, I . . ."

"Keep your voice down, darling, for heaven's sake! I know what it is. You've got what they call a guilt complex. Now listen! Let me explain. I've read books on this Freudian stuff; a lot of it's awful rot but all the same there's something in it. They say when people wish other people were dead and all of a sudden they kick the bucket, the person—it's generally a kid but it can be anybody—he feels just as responsible as if he'd actually done 'em in. You see, it's all unconscious, so he can't be reasonable about it. So he gets the jimjams. Then the mind doctor gets to work, and tells him what's biting him, and he feels better."

"It's not like that," she objected.

"Of course it is. You've wished he'd die; I've wished he'd die. We've said as much to each other. It's only natural. If I'd had money enough there could have been a divorce, but as it was we were stuck. Now we both feel the same—glad as the devil and yet a bit sick inside, and of course you feel it more than I do."

"You think I'm making it up about that bloody dog?"

"I think you're making a hell of a lot out of a perfectly ordinary little coincidence. You want a good night's sleep, that's what it is. Got any pills in the house?"

"Sleeping pills? Yes, I have. Harding gave me some when I broke my leg. I didn't take them, though; I don't go in for that sort of thing."

"Well, take one tonight," he urged. "Get eight solid hours—no nightmares, no nonsense—and in the morning you'll laugh at the whole silly business."

"All right, Harry. Stay with me till I go to sleep, though, won't you?"

"Of course I will," he promised.

Perhaps Despencer should have taken a pill himself. At all events he experienced a return of the recurrent nightmare he had spoken of. Once more he was in that incredibly beautiful and powerful car, cream-colored or flesh-colored, open, and rushing along at a hundred miles an hour. Again he realized his foot was not pressing the accelerator. The car was going by herself, faster and faster, and there was no such thing as a brake. The wind rose to a menacing howl in his ears, and he tried to get out, but the seat held him. The seat gripped him, enfolding his loins in the close and fleshy grip of foam rubber that was somehow alive. And suddenly there was a loud crack, and he was wide awake.

The crack was something new in the dream. Perhaps it wasn't in the dream at all. Perhaps it had come from outside. The thought moved him before it made itself known to him; he was already on his feet, on his way to the window. His pajamas were wet through and it was abominably cold.

Outside there was a breath-taking stillness and moonlight as bright as ever he'd seen it. The rather ugly fir plantations were black blocks defining the circle, its center also black with a pyramid of conifers in which the drive ended in front of the house. The ground had that glitter which foretells a thick hoar-frost in the morning. It was incredibly beautiful but too disturbing to be altogether pleasant. There was a dark movement, then a flicker of light which could have been the moon on the barrels of a gun. Someone had passed from blackness to blackness across one of the rides that radiated between the encircling firs.

"If that fellow's after the birds," Despencer thought, "if that fellow fired a shot right under the very windows, all I can say is he's got a hell of a nerve. Perhaps I'd better wake Briggs."

He put on slippers and a dressing gown and set off on this errand. In the corridor, looking toward the stairwell ahead of him, he could see there was an unusual amount of light there, as though the moonlight, though more attenuated and ghostly, was leaking into the house. After a few more steps he saw the reason for this: Mrs. Bulteney's door was wide open and the light inside was nearly as bright as day. Looking in, he saw that her bed was empty; the sheets, thrown back, had in every fold the likeness of sculptured marble. He was reminded of a tomb he'd seen in Italy or somewhere.

This changed his mind about waking Briggs. He went down into the big hall and found that the outer door, though closed, was not completely shut. He put out his hand to open it but it moved of itself, like the car in his dream. He suddenly found himself face to face, very close, with Mrs. Bulteney. Her face was so streaked and cratered by the blue moonlight that he didn't recognize her at first. When he did, he realized she must have been deathly white underneath. She had a fur coat on over her pajamas and she was carrying a gun. She spoke quietly but in such a way that he thought her next words might be very loud indeed.

"I missed him!" she said.

"Come in, for God's sake, and don't make a noise! Let me put that thing down. Come up to your room!" He took her arm.

"Thirty feet! Clear as daylight! And I missed him! I never missed like that before."

"Just as well you did! Are you absolutely mad, Di? If you shoot a man like that, it's murder."

Diana Bulteney began to laugh. Her laugh had undergone exactly the same sort of change as her face. Moonstruck! thought Despencer, who was by no means given to fanciful expressions. At the same time he thought, "She weighs as much as I do; I can never carry her up."

He pulled at her coat and to his surprise and relief she yielded to the pull, not in the least responsively but as if she had abandoned her body to any force that might act on it. Now Mrs. Bulteney, more than anyone else in the world, had lived in and for her large and magnificent body, feeding it great lumps of raw sensation at its lightest demand. This drifting hulk, uncertainly and stumblingly following the rude pull on its fur exterior, seemed to have suffered the same lunar ruin as her face and her laugh. The laugh continued as they ascended the stairs, but fortunately seemed to have no sort of force or breath behind it. By the time they got into her room it had ceased.

He seated her on the bed and went to close the door. Turning back, he found her with her head sagging forward and her eyes almost closed. Then he remembered the sleeping pill.

"Di, it's that pill you took. You're drunk on it. I say, you're sure you really did miss that dog, aren't you?"

"I missed him. I might have known I would."

"You'd better lie down and sleep it off."

"He would have died if I'd given him both barrels pointblank."

"You're half frozen. You're out of your mind. Get into bed and I'll cover you up."

"You can't kill them and you can't chase them away." She moaned.

"All right. Don't worry. Just go to sleep."

"I went to sleep. It wasn't any good. I woke up and he was out there, right under the window, howling for me."

"Do you mean the dog?" He shook her. "Are you talking about the dog? Was it the dog you tried to shoot?"

"Damned silly thing to do! He's dead already. Know what he died of?"

"Do you mean Gilbert?" asked the lawyer. "Are you talking about Gilbert now? Here, wake up! Tell me!"

"Tap water, Harry. That's what I put in."

Her mouth moved as if she were going to laugh again, but before she could do so she was asleep, and she slept till the low winter sun fell on her face in the morning. Then she woke and rang the bell.

"Good morning, ma'am!"

"Good morning, Parfit. What time is it?"

"Just gone half-past ten, ma'am. Mr. Despencer said you weren't to be disturbed. He left this for you, ma'am."

"Left it? What do you mean? Where's he gone?"

"Up to town, ma'am. He had to go all of a sudden, so he left the letter."

*Di, I've absolutely forgotten what was said last night.
I do know, however, that no sort of life is possible for
you and me. I have to get out if it kills me.*
               Regretfully,
               Harry

"The dog's gone too, ma'am. Gone for good this time, you'll be glad to hear. A little boy came from Church Farm where the new people have moved in. No higher than that, ma'am, and frightened out of his life coming here. I think he had the idea we'd stolen his precious dog. The postman told him he'd seen it hanging about. I want my Blackie, he says, trembling all over. So off he went with his Blackie on a piece of string, happy as a sandboy!"

"Parfit, I don't feel well today."

"Why, I'm sorry to hear that, ma'am, I'm sure. Would you wish me to send for the doctor?"

"Dr. Harding? No. On the dressing table there, or in the bathroom, there's a little bottle of reddish sort of pills. Give it to me, will you? Thank you. Parfit, unless I ring, I'm not to be disturbed on any account whatever."

"Not even for a little luncheon, ma'am?"

"Not for lunch or dinner either. I want to sleep. I may sleep right through. You may come in at this time tomorrow morning. Not before. Do you understand?"

"Well, yes, ma'am, if you say so. I hope it'll make you feel better, ma'am."

≪ A One-Man Dog ≫

by

William Bankier

ELOISE CROUCHED ON the window-seat, watching her husband and his big black dog. Jethro Maxwell was stretched out on a lawn chair under a colorful umbrella. Born seventy-four years ago, he had never grasped the concept of casual clothes. Half in shade, half in sunlight, his lanky body looked tortured in a three-piece tweed suit, wing collar, bowtie, and high-topped oxblood boots.

She wanted him to die. Right now would be as good a time as any. Sunstroke would serve. It was no secret—he knew how she felt. But whenever she voiced her frustration, he seemed not to hear. She was reduced to the frantic imperative, "Get out of my life!"

It was the boredom of the status quo that made her want him gone. He was on his last legs, anyway, one foot in the grave. Long since retired from the real-estate business, Maxwell clung to passing-grade health, not well enough to be anything but a pest. The situation was untidy. A fiend for neatness, Eloise wanted to replace the worn-out relationship with pristine solitude.

The dog was worse than its master. Jethro insisted on letting it wander everywhere inside the house. Eloise would have relegated the brute to the garage. Its glossy coat shed constantly. She found a hair now on the paisley upholstery beside her. She plucked it with lacquered nails, opened the casement window, and dropped it outside.

69

Jethro inclined his head to the sound, but his eyes remained closed.

He said to the dog, "Think it's time for the mail, Mike?" The dog heaved itself up off the flagstones and padded out of sight around the corner of the house.

Was that not infuriating? There had been no obedience training, no "heel," no "sit." The old man simply spoke to the animal as an equal. It seemed to understand and it did his bidding. But nobody else's. Mike was a one-man dog, and Jethro Maxwell was that man.

"You're wasting the dog's time," Eloise said through the open window. She could remember evenings long ago when she and Jethro sat within reach of each other, drinking their sundowners, replaying the day, planning the evening. Now she stalked him from a distance. What had gone wrong? Nothing. Their life together was like a predictable play. The current hostility was merely the last few pages of a repetitive script. "There's no mail on Sunday."

"I'm expecting a letter from Sanford," the old man replied. "A response to something I sent him. He said he'd drive by today and drop it in the box."

"But he wouldn't come up to the house and see a person." Eloise was peeved. The lawyer was not her favorite individual, but his appearance would have been the excuse for a drink.

"Why should he?" Maxwell said. "If he wants *Who's Afraid of Virginia Woolf?* he can go to the theater."

The dog reappeared with a letter in its mouth. It was pleased with itself. Maxwell accepted the envelope and dried it on his sleeve. He opened it, read the contents, and tucked everything away inside his jacket pocket.

Now, as Eloise watched, he got to his feet—too quickly as it turned out. He staggered, grasping at the umbrella pole to keep from falling. He sat down and let his head hang between his knees. She felt some pity watching this demonstration of infirmity. The pump inside the frail chest was not as efficient as it used to be. Asking it to deliver blood all the way to a brain raised suddenly several feet higher was expecting too much.

Please, no stroke, Eloise said to herself. The only thing worse than the present situation would be an impaired Jethro dragging his paralyzed side from room to room, talking like a ventriloquist. And with faithful Mike dogging his footsteps. Let him go quickly, she prayed. An accident with the car would be ideal.

When he came inside, she said, "I'm having a drink." An ice cube discharged from chrome-plated tongs bounced inside a crystal glass. "Would a taste of bourbon lift you up?" She knew alcohol was against doctor's orders.

"Not for me. I nearly keeled over outside."

"Remember what I told you. When you're gone, the dog goes, too."

"I haven't forgotten your threat."

"So you'd better take care of yourself."

"I take care of everything." Maxwell sat in his wing-back chair. The dog lay down and put its chin on the polished toe-cap of the left boot. "I'll rest for a minute. Then I'll take Mike into the kitchen and feed him."

"I prepare meals in that kitchen. They don't allow pets in restaurants—why should I put up with one?"

"We'll be gone before you go in there."

"Shedding hairs and dropping fleas and spilling liver." They were both tired of the ancient argument, but Eloise could feel it erupting again. The words were like the hornets that came swarming out of their grey paper nest under the eaves on that summer afternoon when she was nine years old. There was no keeping them in. "I wish you'd get rid of that dog."

"Not again."

"We don't need a dog."

"You don't, but I do. He's my friend."

"I'm your wife."

"What's that got to do with anything?"

They were barking at each other. Despite her sense of shame, Eloise felt some satisfaction. It was as if the worn-out argument had shreds of comfort attached to it. Harsh words were better than no words at all. "You used to have time for me," she said.

"I have very little time," he intoned, "for anything." He got up and the dog followed him out of the room. "You know how it is, don't you, Mike. What's life like when you're old and tired?"

"Rough," said the dog.

Three years ago, when Mike first came aboard, Eloise had tried to win him over. But the animal wouldn't come when she called, he wouldn't pursue the ball she tossed across the lawn. It was a rubber ball pocked with tooth-marks from many retrievals in response to Jethro's command. "Damn it, I'm not trying to take you over," Eloise snapped at him that day. "*Be* his dog! But give me a moment of your time." The soulful face might have been carved out of ebony. The idea of shared allegiance was beyond Mike's understanding.

Last summer, K. J. Sanford came over for one of his rare visits. In the old days, when the Maxwell real-estate business was thriving and Jethro was in his litigious prime, the lawyer had plenty to do. Now the war was over so there wasn't much to bring the old men together. On the occasion of that visit, Sanford spotted the dog crossing the lawn. "Hey, boy! Come on, doggie!"

"He won't pay any attention," Eloise said. Jethro was inside the house recharging the visitor's glass.

"I like dogs. Come on, boy! What's his name?"

"Mike."

"Here, Mike! Come on, Mike!" Sanford struggled out of his chair. He was a Jethro Maxwell clone, bleached and dried and destined to live another twenty years. He whistled and clapped his hands. "Come on, boy! Here, doggiedoggiedoggie!"

Mike continued on inside through the patio doors, deaf head swinging. There was satisfaction for Eloise in that. Minutes later, Maxwell was back with two drinks. As he handed one to the lawyer, he saw his wife's empty glass. "Did you want something?"

"I've had enough."

"Where's Mike?" He raised his voice. "Come on, Mike!"

The dog loped out onto the patio and presented himself to the old man.

Remembering all this, Eloise wandered down the dark corridor into the kitchen. Here, the last light of day was pouring in through leaded panes. Mike was wolfing his meal. Jethro was crouched close by, watching. From the doorway, Eloise asked, "How much longer?"

"Finished in a minute."

"I mean us."

"What about us?"

"This limbo. Our cold war. How much longer does it go on?"

"Not much longer," the old man said. "Trust me." He glanced over his shoulder and the malevolent look he cast her way was so inappropriate that Eloise told herself it must have been a trick of the light.

Early mornings were chilly this time of the year. Eloise stood at the top end of the steeply sloping driveway. Bundled in a raincoat, she was smoking a brown cigarette. There was no need for her to be outside, she had told the detective all she knew.

But she didn't want to go inside the house. After all the frustration, it was fulfilling to see Jethro's body lying halfway down the slope with the car fifty feet past him on level ground. He was dead. A neighbor had noticed the body at seven o'clock when he came out to pick up his newspaper. When the doorbell rang and she hurried outside and ran across the lawn to lean over him, she had said, "Who did this?" Nobody could answer that question.

The medical examiner finished his work and was now talking to the detective. They were standing near the car. But Jethro Maxwell was not alone. The black dog sat like a statue beside the corpse. It was hard to tell what Mike was thinking. The animal's head was turned to the hori-

zon. For all Eloise knew, it was considering the dog equiv-
alent of "Who did this?"

Eloise shivered. She needed more clothes on. She went
inside and dressed herself in slacks and thick socks and a
woolly sweater. She was making coffee when she thought
of K. J. Sanford. The lawyer ought to be told. She picked
up the telephone. It was still early, but waking up the old
coot would be a pleasure.

"K.J.? It's Eloise. I'm fine, but Jethro isn't. Somebody
drove over him in our car. Crushed his chest, stopped his
heart. Right outside the house in the driveway. The detective thinks I did it. —No, he hasn't said so, but I can tell
what he's thinking. Cherchez the wife."

Sanford said he would be right over. "Don't say anything, Eloise," he warned her. "About you and Jethro and
your relationship."

"It could be taken down and used against me?"

"Exactly."

She carried a mug of steaming coffee to the detective.
He took a sip and said, "Mmm." It was the nicest sound
Eloise had heard in weeks. His name was Stokes and he
looked like an accountant in his blue pin-stripe suit and
rimless glasses. "You must be cold," he said.

"I was before. You don't even have a coat on."

"I like early mornings. I run at five o'clock. Before the
sun comes up."

"That's admirable."

"Best time of the day. Keeps the mind tuned, even more
than the body."

"My husband gets up early. To walk the dog." She saw
two men approaching with a stretcher. "Used to get up."

Stokes said, "I must ask you some questions."

"I know."

They were taking Jethro's body away. The dog didn't
move. Its eyes were turned to the pale sky.

"You don't have to answer them."

"So I've been told."

"Is that his dog?"

"His alone. It would never come for me or anybody else. Only for my husband."

"Time of death is set at around four A.M. Where were you?"

"Asleep in bed." Eloise was high on her husband's demise. The light-headed sensation was making her behave without inhibition. "I have no alibi. I don't mind telling you I wanted him dead. I'm glad it happened."

Their eyes met and held. Stokes seemed to come to a conclusion. His method in new cases was to trust his instinct early on.

A shiny black car, much like the murder weapon, rolled onto the drive. K. J. Sanford climbed out and joined the couple near the house. He refused coffee. He said to the detective, "If you're in charge, I'd better give you this." He handed over a sealed envelope. "Jethro filed this document with me a couple of weeks ago. He seemed to be afraid for his life. He said it was to be given to the police if he died under suspicious circumstances."

It was a note in Jethro Maxwell's handwriting. Stokes read it aloud. "My wife intends to murder me. She has said so more than once. She not only wants me gone, she means to get rid of my dog. If I should be killed, Eloise Maxwell is the guilty party." There was his signature— then: "P.S. See that Mike finds a good home."

With a wry smile, Eloise extended her wrists. "Is this when you snap on the cuffs?"

"Not just yet." Stokes walked down the steeply sloping driveway to where the car was standing. First he peered in through the open window on the driver's side. Carefully, using his handkerchief, he opened the door and studied the steering wheel. Then he knelt down and ran his hand over the brake pedal. Standing up, he examined the palm of his hand. Nodding to himself, he walked back up the slope.

"This isn't a case of murder," he said. "This was suicide, carefully planned to cast suspicion on Mrs. Maxwell."

"How do you figure that?" asked Sanford.

"Dog hairs on the brake pedal." He presented his hand.

"The gear shift is set in neutral. Here's what must have happened. The deceased brought his dog inside the car and placed the animal with its weight against the brake pedal. He told it to stay there. Then he went and lay down in front of one of the wheels, far enough down the slope to let the car pick up speed. Finally, he called his dog. It jumped out through the open window, the brake was released, the car rolled down the slope, and the old man's chest was crushed."

After a lengthy silence, K. J. Sanford said, "Sounds like Jethro to me."

Eloise let the earth turn until the sun was low and the afternoon cooled off, then she brought her drink onto the patio and sat in one of the recliner chairs. While Jethro was alive she had believed she couldn't be lonelier. Now he was gone and it was as if part of her inner self had been pulled out through her skin. Years ago, she had watched somebody thrust a sharp implement into a melon, twisting it to withdraw a red, wet plug. Her present situation was far worse than solitude. She had not anticipated such pain.

Something touched her hand. She glanced down, blinking to clear the tears. The black dog was beside her chair. He opened his mouth and something bounced on a flagstone. It was his wornout, misshapen, tooth-ravaged rubber ball.

≪ Money on the Snow ≫
by
Ennis Duling

IDA PRATT PICKED up the phone as her brother Cliff ran down the hall in his pajamas. "Fire department," she said.

She wasn't actually in the fire house—a two-bay garage near an abandoned freight depot—but was in her own home standing beside a framed, hooked-rug scene of a sailboat.

A gravelly voice said, "There's a chimney fire at Art Herbert's. The flames are shooting ten feet above the roof." There was a click and the caller was gone. All over town, for the next few minutes, volunteer firemen were stumbling out of bed and reaching for their phones while Ida repeated the information over and over, adding directions to Herbert's, just as if there were someone in town who didn't know old Art or his ramshackle house on the Lake Road. By the time she was done, Cliff was dressed and out the door.

She was surprised to see it was only three A.M.—lonely nights in January seemed endless. She glanced out the kitchen window at the thermometer next to the clear plastic bird feeder that was attached to the window with a suction cup. Ten degrees below zero.

She put on long johns, red flannel hunting pants, and a bulky sweater. People in town liked to tease the firemen:

"Ida and her coffee wagon beat you there every time, don't they?"

Ida was tall and thin, thirty-two and unmarried. In high school, where she had been captain of the girls' basketball team, she had picked up the nickname "Elbows." It had something to do with how she'd spring in the air after the ball and land with her feet planted and her elbows out. She'd always hated the name but had done nothing about it but blush. Other girls had bodies with curves, she'd decided. She had bony elbows.

Men didn't pay her much attention except the brotherly kind. As far as she could tell, no one ever stopped to wonder what she was doing standing out in below-zero weather heating up coffee. Wouldn't your sister do that sort of thing for you?

Only one man had recently treated her any differently, and that episode had depressed her for days.

Ida had been in Art Herbert's house two Sundays earlier to serve the sick old man a supper cooked by her church group. She hadn't realized he was bedridden until she had arrived.

His room had an odor like the smell copper pennies leave on your hands. Sitting up in bed, his mouth full of turkey, he said, "Can't trust anyone in this town. I trust this dog here and that's it." He reached across the bed and fed a piece of meat to a shaggy mutt whose white muzzle showed his age. "And you know what? He agrees. Old Sam don't trust but one or two people himself."

When he was done eating, Art Herbert gently lowered Sam to the floor. "It's cold in this room, Ida."

"I'll get you an extra blanket and put some wood in the stove before I go."

"I mean a body gets cold in a way blankets don't touch." Then he reached between the mattress and the box springs and pulled out a wad of money, tattered and limp with age.

The money didn't surprise her especially, nor did the proposition. People said Art Herbert had money. You could hear people claim he had two thousand dollars jammed in a cookie jar in the kitchen, five thousand under his mattress, twenty thousand in a duffel bag in the closet. You could hear almost any figure you wanted to for his net worth, but you could also hear he didn't have one cent in the bank. Rumor had it that Dr. Martinson, Reverend Richards, and bank president Hatcher had made a joint call on Art to convince him to deposit his thousands. They had been unsuccessful—or so people said.

"Bet you didn't know I had this, did you?" he said to Ida, shaking the money. "Poor old Art, people say."

Without a word, she gathered the church's plates and silverware.

"I don't plan to part with any of it to just anyone," he said. "But you're kind and good-looking, even if you are a mite skinny."

She reached out and touched his stubbled face gently. "I'm sorry, Mr. Herbert. I really am."

Sam was seated by the bedroom door, and as Ida walked toward him, he bared his brown teeth soundlessly and slipped behind her. Silently he followed her down the hall. At the front door Ida looked back up the steps. Sam was on the landing watching her with his tail between his legs.

And now Art Herbert's chimney, maybe his house, was on fire.

When she got to Herbert's, the pumper and the water truck were already there. The air was so clear the stars seemed a short distance above the brick chimney, from which shot a volcano of fire and black smoke. The lights were on in Art's room, but there was an orange glow behind all the windows. She noticed Sam crouching off by himself under the runningboard of his master's old pickup.

Ida watched her brother and Junior Abrams, owner of Abrams Energy Supply Company, smash the pane of glass in the front door. They switched on a light and darted into the black smoke. Worried about Cliff, Ida ran across the road and stood in the foot-deep snow. Firemen put a ladder up against the house and climbed to Art's window, which, for some reason, was already open.

There were flames by then, and the house looked as if it were lit up for the holidays.

Cliff and Junior Abrams staggered out, coughing. "We don't see him! There's no going up the stairs," Junior said.

The man on the ladder yelled down, "He's not in his room, either. Get a hose up here."

Ida glanced down for a second, then knelt and picked up a five-dollar bill. The ground under Art's window was littered with money. The firemen were trampling it into the snow.

Ida gathered a handful of cash as if she were picking fallen apples from under a tree. She set out a can for it on the tailgate of her jeep and, turning back to her coffee-making, brought a pot of water to the boil.

The boys were too busy with the fire, which had appeared through the roof near the chimney, to worry about the money. But she knew they'd start bringing the cash over when things settled down a bit.

Fred Newell was the first to the coffee wagon. He stuffed a fistful of money in the can. "I reckon I just paid you fifty bucks for a cup of coffee, Elbows."

He was a thin-faced man, about Ida's age, who seemed swallowed up in his black fireman's coat and hat. Ida always figured he was in the fire company because Junior Abrams, his former boss, encouraged his employees to join. Now that Newell was laid off and collecting unemployment, Ida wondered why he didn't quit.

Newell peeled off his gloves and blew on his hands while Ida poured the coffee. "You hear he's dead?" he said.

"Mr. Herbert?"

"Yeah, Junior put a ladder up against the back of the house and looked through into the upstairs hall. Art's body was lying on the floor. When Junior broke the window, he was almost blown off the ladder by the heat. Old man Herbert was gone a long time ago. No way to save him."

"How awful!"

"Yeah. You know we tried to warn him. You don't

know how many times Junior and me came down to tell him to get his chimney cleaned, maybe stop burning wood and spring for an oil burner. I told Junior it was a waste of time talking to that skinflint. The only thing he loves is that damned dog. That's what I said."

The roof was completely ablaze by then, and crews of firemen were spraying the barn and outbuildings to keep them from catching fire from the showers of sparks.

"The old fool had it coming," Newell said, "though I don't want to talk ill of the dead. I bet he hadn't had that chimney cleaned in three or four years. Said he couldn't afford the fifty bucks! The creosote could have built up two inches thick inside. Get a good fire going and whoosh! There'd be no stopping it. And that chimney was none too good. No liner or anything. It just let the fire out."

"You think he got up in the middle of the night and lit a big fire in the woodstove," Ida said, trying to think of something other than Art Herbert's body in the upstairs hall.

"Probably has to get up once or twice in the middle of the night—sick old man like that most likely has trouble in the waterworks—and threw all the wood he could in the stove, opened the damper wide, and went back to bed. Like I said, whoosh! Once the creosote in the chimney started burning, the house was as good as gone. We ain't doing no good here. Damn fire department might as well stayed in bed."

"Maybe you could help save the barn," Ida said sharply.

"Yeah. I guess someone inherits." He threw the rest of the coffee on the snow. "They should make you fire chief, Elbows. You'd keep everyone in line."

An hour later the town's only police car pulled off the road next to her. Matt Jensen, the chief of the three-man force, got out and spoke to her over the top of the car.

"Good evening, Ida, or morning or whatever it is." He was several inches shorter than Ida and a little paunchy. His red and blue ski cap was pulled down so low it nearly covered his bushy eyebrows. Ida knew something of his life and would have happily known more. Divorced, Matt Jensen spent every day off with his children, who lived with their mother somewhere in New Hampshire. "I heard there's money all over the place," he said.

"I have some of it here." She held up the can.

Matt smiled sadly. "I can picture him in his nightshirt, standing in the open window, baling out money. How much do you think there is?"

"Lots. The boys have been bringing it over by the handful. I bet there's a couple thousand, maybe more."

"Strange way to die. He was so busy saving his money, he didn't bother to save himself until it was too late. Smoke inhalation must be a terrible way to die."

"Can I get you a cup of coffee, chief?" Ida asked.

"I don't think I've done much to deserve a break," he said. "Sitting in a heated car with the blinker going while the boys put out the fire hardly qualifies me."

"Modesty will get you a doughnut as well," Ida said.

A station wagon pulled off the road a short distance away. Bill Herbert, a middle-aged man in a wool suburban coat and a Tyrolean hat, jumped out and rushed up to Matt.

"How much of Uncle Art's money have you found, Chief Jensen? I expect you to protect it."

"I have some bad news for you about your uncle, Mr. Herbert," Matt said solemnly.

Bill Herbert's face was unmoved so far as Ida could tell. "He *is* dead then?"

Matt nodded and Ida stared at the ground.

"I guess I should be grief-stricken or something," Bill Herbert said in the silence. "He was my uncle, even though he wouldn't do a thing for me. I'm sorry to hear of anyone's death."

Ida thought of offering coffee and then realized how out of place it would sound.

Matt spoke. "Ida thinks she might have a couple of thousand in the can."

"What happened to the rest of it? I know for a fact Uncle Art was worth forty or fifty times that much. I think he insulated the walls with cash."

"Burned," Matt said softly.

"All of it?"

Without answering, Matt looked over at the house. Only the chimney and a few heavy timbers remained standing as the firemen continued to wet down the smoking wreckage.

"So he took it with him after all," Bill Herbert said.

"I doubt he looked at it that way," Ida said.

Bill Herbert crossed the road and stood on the glacier of frozen black water that had flowed from the hoses across Art's yard. If there was any money there, it was locked in water until spring.

Ida watched him walk toward a shed near the barn. Like a ghost Art's dog slunk into the darkness at his approach.

The sky was lightening a little when Ida spoke with Matt again. He was standing off by himself, his arms folded as if they were resting on his stomach. "You look like you're on a serious mission, Ida," he said.

"I guess I am, chief," she said. A minute before she had switched on the light inside her jeep and fiddled with her hair in the rear view mirror. Hopeless, she'd decided. And she wasn't sure what neat hair had to do with what she'd come to say. "I don't think this was an accident," she said so quietly she wondered for a second if Matt had heard her.

"It's never really an accident when someone's careless with fire," Matt said heavily.

"I mean it was murder."

"That's what I thought you meant. I don't need this. The town doesn't need it."

He sounded annoyed, and Ida wished she hadn't spoken. She always claimed to detest gossip. Sometimes she'd bang a cup of coffee on the counter of the Colonial Diner, which she owned and ran with her brother, and say to a customer, "That's just the kind of mean gossip I won't allow in my restaurant." People joked about her attitude, she suspected. She was probably an object of more than a little gossip herself.

And now she had accused someone in town of murder.

"Come on, let's go sit in my car," he said. "I better hear this, much as I don't want to."

He turned on the ignition. "We'll have some heat in a few minutes. Now what's your thinking?"

Ida stared out the frosted window at the black shape of an elm tree. "The dog was outside," she said.

"My experience with dogs is they always have to go out at the wrong time—certainly in the middle of the night."

"But the only light was upstairs."

"You lost me, Ida."

"Art Herbert loved that old dog. It's ten degrees below zero. If he had let him out, he would have stayed downstairs with him. Another light would have been on."

"So?"

"So another person was in the house. He let the dog out."

"And from that you've built a murder case! I don't want to be hard on you, Ida, but listen to some facts. First, the fire was certainly a chimney fire. You saw the flames shooting out of the chimney. I'll make sure the fire marshal checks it, but that's how it started."

"Couldn't you start a chimney fire by stuffing cardboard or paper in the stove and opening the damper?"

"Maybe," Matt said, "but that doesn't mean it happened. And I've got a second and a third. What about all the money on the snow? You mean someone murdered Art while he was throwing money out the window?"

"I think the murderer threw the money out the window."

"Whatever for?"

"So no one would think it was murder," Ida said. "He killed Mr. Herbert, stole as much money as he could, threw a few thousand out the window, and then started a roaring fire in the stove. Maybe he even splashed some gasoline around inside the house to help the fire along. My guess is that he called the fire department so everyone could see it was an accident."

"Who did call in the fire?"

"He didn't say. He hung up right away."

"That's not strange," Matt said. "You'd be surprised

how many anonymous calls we get at the police station. Even in a town this size, there are people who won't give their names. But I've got to admit your theory could have been the way it happened."

"You don't mean I'm convincing you?"

"I said *could*! Little green men *could* have set the fire. You've got nothing but a could. There are no witnesses."

"Except the dog," Ida said.

Matt slapped the steering wheel and laughed. "What are we going to do, put the dog on the witness stand? 'Please sink your teeth into the leg of the person who murdered your master, Mr. Dog.' "

"But the dog wouldn't do that. He likes the murderer. I've been watching him off and on all night. Whenever anyone gets near him, he runs off. No one could have caught him inside the house to throw him out. He must have followed someone he trusted to the door, and the friend let him out and then killed Mr. Herbert."

"What are we going to do, lead the dog around town and see whose hand he licks?"

"We don't have to do that, Matt."

The sun hadn't come over the horizon yet, but it was light enough to see Sam standing loyally next to Junior Abrams. Junior—who had visited Art many times and whose business was in such bad shape he was laying men off—reached down and stroked Sam's head with his gloved hand.

"I'll give his name to the State Police," Matt said. "It may be a little early to be sure, but I think you just solved a murder."

"I'm a good guesser," Ida said. Looking at Junior Abrams and the dog, she suddenly felt like crying, but she wasn't sure why. For some hopelessly sentimental reason, she thought—because a man who loved dogs was also a murderer; because an old man hoarded money, forgot to live, and then died; because she was alone.

Matt reached out and touched her arm. "Life's never easy," he said.

≪ A Dog's Life ≫
by
Ray Davidson

"HERRINGBONE TWEEDE—I mean, Harrington Tweede," Herringbone intoned at his speaker phone. He spoke absently at first, his attention still focused on the funnies in the L.A. *Times*. Then he flushed and corrected himself apologetically.

A rich, offensive chuckle assaulted his ear from the phone's speaker. "I prefer blue serge myself," a husky bass voice said, "but 'chackin ah sun gowt.' "

Tweede sighed. "Nobody pronounces it that badly, Paul," he said. "You're putting me on."

"The basis of all true friendships," Paul Holroyd replied, his voice oozing righteousness.

"Are you calling to practice mauled French at me?"

"Of course not. This is official business," Holroyd said.

Paul Holroyd was with the LAPD, "on the administrative side." He and Tweede had met over food (which was one thing neither of them ever made fun of), found their tastes congenial (without any pun intended), and had become friends. It was an unlikely association. H. Tweede, ex-reporter and current private investigator, was small, thin, intelligent, shy, pleasantly homely, and gentle. Holroyd was large, inclined to surplus weight, boisterous, fleshy-featured, and rude as the devil. It must have been the shared intelligence or an attraction of opposites, Tweede thought.

"You do find missing, er, persons, don't you?" Paul
asked.

"I've found a few. Usually, though, it's just a dodge to
gather divorce evidence. But you know all this. You want
me to find someone?"

"Exactly. I want you to find Greta."

"Greta? Not Greta Garbo, I hope."

"I'm sending over a file."

"But Paul, why me? Your people have got resources I
can't even touch. And who's ..."

"I'll explain this evening at Dingo's. You'll be there?"

"Sure, Paul, but ..."

"Gotta go, Herringbone. See you."

Tweede sighed again and switched off the phone. He
tended to sigh a lot during his conversations with Holroyd,
sometimes with forced patience but almost always with a
measure of friendly tolerance. The trouble was, he liked
Paul Holroyd.

The file arrived a half hour later, delivered by a uniformed employee of the city who glanced blankly around
Tweede's shabby office and departed mystified. Tweede
opened the envelope and extracted its contents. An eight
by ten glossy slipped to the floor facedown.

"Greta Gorgeous Countess St. Germaine," the name
across the top of the file read. He stooped, retrieved the
photo, and stared at the delightfully pug-nosed visage of a
magnificent female boxer, clipped ears erect, the mischief
of innocent youth in her eye.

"You want me to find a dog?" he asked Holroyd over
coffee and Danish at Dingo's late that afternoon.

"You read the file?" Holroyd mumbled through a
mouthful of pastry. Tweede nodded. "Then you know this
isn't just an ordinary dog," Holroyd continued, swallow-
ing. "That bitch is worth three months of my salary."

Tweede winced. "Keep it clean, Paul," he murmured.

"For your information, Herringbone, 'bitch' is the technical term dog fanciers use ..."

"I know, but you're not a dog fancier."

Holroyd had the grace to look slightly abashed. He shrugged. "Anyway," he went on, "it's a valuable dog and its owners are friends of mine. This is the fourth time she's disappeared. The first three times, it was only a day or two. This time, it's been two weeks."

"Paul, how am I supposed to find a dog that's been missing two whole weeks?" Tweede asked.

Holroyd had just taken another bite of Danish, so there was a slight delay until he reduced it to manageable proportions. "Same way you find humans, I guess," he mumbled.

"Dogs don't have driver's licenses and credit cards," Tweede pointed out. "Anyway, if she's been kidnapped—I mean dognapped—she won't be running loose. She could be anywhere."

"You've got a 'last address,' haven't you?" Holroyd asked testily. "And a description. Even a picture! What more do you want? Look, Sylvia expects me early tonight. I gotta go."

He rose, patting his lips with a little paper napkin and completely missing the cluster of frosting grains at the corner of his mouth.

"This is asking a lot," Tweede said.

"That's what friends are for," Holroyd replied, grinning now that he was sure Tweede would do it.

"I usually work for a fee," Tweede remarked bitterly at the big man's retreating back. Holroyd paused and turned.

"Didn't I tell you?" he asked innocently. "I guess I forgot. There's a two thousand dollar reward for information leading to recovery. I'll see that you get it. Good coffee, dolly," he added to the waitress at the counter as he passed.

The waitress, whose name was Irene, said, "Yeah," without looking up from the *Inquirer* spread out on the counter in front of her.

Tweede sighed and drank his coffee. Holroyd had eaten all the pastries.

•   •   •

Following Holroyd's implied suggestion—he would have started there in any case—Tweede began by visiting Greta's owners, a Mr. and Mrs. Harvey (and Sheila) Bettinjohn. They lived in a stratum of life with which he was not even remotely familiar. For example, the guard at the electronically controlled gate, a quarter of a mile from their Orange County home, phoned up to confirm before admitting Tweede's battered Volkswagen to the grounds.

"I really do not understand it," Mrs. Bettinjohn said. "She's usually an affectionate and obedient bitch. A bit playful, of course, as boxers are, but she seemed quite content. We've given her everything she could possibly want."

"Mr. Holroyd says she has disappeared before," Tweede prompted.

"She has," Mr. Bettinjohn said. "But you must understand, officer, that dogs do sometimes go off on their own."

"Males, yes," Tweede said, ignoring the "officer." If Holroyd hadn't told them who he was, it wasn't up to him to spill the beans. "I thought, though, it was not so usual in the case of females."

"Males more often, certainly, but, er, females occasionally."

"You don't confine her, then?" Tweede asked.

"She has the run of the house and estate," Mrs. Bettinjohn said. "Within reason, of course."

"We have noticed one thing," Mr. Bettinjohn said slowly. "I don't really know if it means anything but, well, you must judge for yourself. Each time before she disappears, she seems quite uncharacteristically excited."

"She's a playful dog," Mrs. Bettinjohn objected.

"No more than other boxers her age," her husband replied. "Each time before she leaves, she runs about, whines, practically climbs up in your lap."

"Your lap, Harvey," Mrs. Bettinjohn said. "Certainly not mine."

"Of course not, my dear. She wouldn't dare."

Mrs. Bettinjohn looked daggers at her husband for a

moment, then shrugged. Men were, after all, completely impossible to understand and not worth the trouble at that.

Tweede hastened to intervene. "Anything happen to bring these attacks on? Anything unusual?" he asked.

Bettinjohn shook his head. "Nothing unusual," he said.

"You dropped that book, Harvey," his wife murmured.

"Come now, Sheila. What could dropping a book have to do with the dog running away?" he objected. Women were apparently no more comprehensible than men.

She had meant to nettle him. Now she had to defend her comment. "Well, Greta always has been sensitive to loud noises. I know it startled me. In fact, I felt quite faint for a moment."

"You've never felt faint in your life," Harvey said. "Anyway, my dear, it isn't 'germaine.' " He smiled a smug, self-satisfied little smile, but Tweede doubted if Mrs. Bettinjohn had caught the pun.

"Then there's really nothing more you can tell me about the dog's disappearance?" he asked.

Bettinjohn shrugged. "I'm afraid not, officer. She gets excited, she goes out, she disappears."

"Where did you get the dog, Mr. Bettinjohn?" Tweede asked.

"From a breeder in Glendale, a Miss Fedders."

"We've called her, of course. She hasn't seen Greta," Mrs. Bettinjohn added.

"Still . . ." Tweede murmured his goodbyes. Neither of them saw him to the door. There are limits, Tweede supposed.

The Two Fedders Kennels were not easy to locate. He might have passed the house a dozen times without seeing the modest little sign or realizing it was more than just another well-kept residence along a suburban street. The grounds behind the house were surprisingly extensive, however, and even more surprisingly wooded. The kennels and runs were large and clean.

"Yes, of course I remember Greta," Miss Fedders said, "and I don't understand it. She certainly didn't use to run off. An affectionate, obedient dog, well-trained, and not the least neurotic."

"Neurotic?" Tweede was intrigued.

"These highly inbred dogs are quite frequently quirky, you know," Miss Fedders explained. "Easily upset, intelligent but emotional. They're just like people in some ways. But Greta isn't like that at all—oh, she's intelligent, but quite placid for a boxer. Of course she's spayed. That helps."

Tweede frowned. "Doesn't that detract . . ."

". . . from her value? Not as much as you'd think," Miss Fedders said. "It's the males that earn the money. Of course she'll have no litters, but Mr. and Mrs. Bettinjohn didn't want to breed her. They just wanted a dog and, of course, it had to be one they could brag about. I'm sorry, but she has not shown up here."

"The picture you've given me isn't quite the same as the one Mr. and Mrs. Bettinjohn gave," Tweede said. "They described her as excitable and lively."

"It's probably a relative thing, Mr.—Tweede, is it? Boxers on the whole are an inquisitive, friendly breed. They like people and tend to seek attention. Greta is less active than the average, but someone who doesn't know dogs . . ."

"How long has she been, uh, neutered?" Tweede asked.

"I have no idea."

"But didn't you . . ."

"Oh, no! Greta isn't one of my dogs," Miss Fedders said. "I took her on a year ago from a Mr.—what was his name, now? Greenmeadows? Wait, I'll look it up." She departed toward the house while Tweede allowed a large, rust-brown male boxer to lick his hand through the mesh of the run fence.

"That's enough, Roscoe," Miss Fedders said cheerfully when she returned. The dog trotted obediently off. "It's Goodpasture. Mr. Clarence Goodpasture in Brentwood."

Tweede considered. "Tell me, Miss Fedders, how would a dog like Greta respond to a sudden loud noise?"

"Most dogs wouldn't like it," Miss Fedders replied

promptly. "It's a regularly used trick of training. I use a rolled-up newspaper slapped against the side of my leg. Of course, some dogs are less bothered than others. Greta, now! As I said, placid. I noticed that she seemed more intrigued by the slap of the paper than alarmed. But thunder sent her cowering. She doesn't like thunder. A lot of dogs don't."

"Do you have an address for Mr. Goodpasture?" Tweede asked.

She gave it to him and he departed, followed by a single, sharp bark of farewell from Roscoe.

"So you needn't pursue the matter further," Mrs. Bettinjohn said. Tweede had called to report his progress, only to find that Greta had come home again. "She's dreadfully thin and was quite dirty, but she's unharmed."

Tweede caught himself about to ask where she had been.

"I asked her where she had been, but of course she couldn't tell me," Mrs. Bettinjohn continued, laughing archly. "So I suppose we'll never know. We do thank you for your trouble, and we'll tell Mr. Holroyd how kind and helpful you've been."

"Thank you." Tweede hung up. Then, driven by a nagging intuition, he went out to Brentwood and rang the Goodpasture doorbell. There was no electronic gate with a guard, but the house might have held a small regiment in comfort. The Bettinjohns were new money and trendy architecture. Goodpasture was old money and solid, uncompromising Victorian, or perhaps Edwardian, substance.

Mr. Goodpasture received him diffidently.

"My mother gave her to me," he said. "But really, after Mother moved back to Marreneck, I simply couldn't keep her. She needed exercise and attention, and I—it was just too exhausting."

Mr. Goodpasture looked as though anything beyond a deep breath would be too exhausting. In fact, he looked positively ill. His cheeks were hollow and his eyes tired and sunken. Tweede felt a strong impulse to lead the man to a sofa and ply him with restoratives. He repressed it. When not ill, Goodpasture was evidently a good-looking man. His features were small and neat and regular. His short hair was thick, about halfway between blond and brown, and rather tightly curled so that it stood out all over his head in a kind of miniature African halo.

"And you haven't seen her recently?" Tweede asked.

"Oh, is that what it's all about? No, not since the dog lady came and got her. She wouldn't come back here anyway. She was really Mother's dog—that is, she belonged to me but she seemed to think Mother belonged to her, if you know what I mean. After Mother went back east again, she didn't seem very happy here."

"Tell me something," Tweede urged. "Was Greta a very excitable dog?"

"Oh, no! She's—at least, she was—very placid. Playful, sometimes, but not excitable. Seldom barked unless it was to come in or go out, you know."

"Were there things she was frightened of?"

"Not that I remember. She was curious. I remember she spent about twenty minutes exploring a horse once that someone had ridden over here—a friend of mine, actually. He has since married and moved away somewhere. The horse was a lot more nervous than Greta was."

"Then things didn't startle her?"

"Things?"

"Oh, a cat jumping out . . ."

"She generally ignored cats."

". . . or loud noises?"

"Loud noises?" Goodpasture seemed faintly puzzled and very tired.

"Well, thunder, say, or a car backfiring," Tweede explained.

"Oh. No, not that I remember, Mr., er, Tweede, is it? You keep saying 'was.' Is Greta dead?" The idea seemed to distress him.

"Not that I know of," Tweede replied cheerfully. "She was alive this morning."

"Oh. Oh, that's good. I wouldn't like to think . . . But I thought you said she'd run away."

"Several times," Tweede said. "But this morning she came back."

"Oh. Then, why . . ."

"Why am I taking up your time like this? I'm curious about why she runs away. Her owners would like to know."

Goodpasture sighed. "She never used to," he said. "Maybe she doesn't like her new home. Anyway, it isn't that she comes back here. We haven't seen her at all."

"We?"

Goodpasture waved a hand vaguely toward the great outdoors to indicate the two acres or so of wooded park that surrounded the house. "There's a man who takes care of the grounds. His wife cooks and cleans. They live in town somewhere. If they'd seen her, I'm sure they'd have said something."

"Probably," Tweede agreed. "Well, thank you, Mr. Goodpasture."

"You're welcome, Mr., er, Tweede."

Tweede had left his car at the foot of the drive. Goodpasture watched him all the way down from the doorway, then nodded and fluttered a hand before Tweede drove off.

"You'd like to borrow Greta?" Mrs. Bettinjohn repeated. "I—I don't understand."

"It's just for a little experiment. We have a theory about why she runs away, but we need to test it," Tweede said.

Mrs. Bettinjohn glanced uncertainly at her husband.

"I don't see why not," Bettinjohn said. "It would be nice to know, Sheila."

Mrs. Bettinjohn shrugged. "Well . . ." she said doubtfully.

"I'll take very good care of her," Tweede assured her.

"I hope so," Mrs. Bettinjohn said. "Greta is a very valuable dog."

Greta, her back end wagging in lieu of tail, seemed

quite willing. She jumped into Tweede's VW without hesitation and sat in the passenger seat, looking about curiously at the traffic. Tweede drove to Brentwood, parked the car in a winding wooded street without sidewalks about a quarter of a mile from the Goodpasture house, and got out. Greta sat in the car, her head swiveling to keep him in view. Then, as he stood without moving behind the car, her attention wandered to a solitary pedestrian two or three hundred yards away in the opposite direction. Quietly, Tweede pulled a revolver from his pocket and fired one bullet into the earth at the edge of the pavement. The dog turned and looked at him, then began pawing at the door of the car. With some difficulty, Tweede climbed back into the driver's seat. The dog tried to slip past him, but he blocked her. He shut the door. Greta whined and pawed at the window, then tried to crawl onto his lap, but the steering wheel was in the way. She licked his ear, turned completely around a couple of times and gave one sharp, peremptory bark. Obediently, Tweede opened his door and stepped out, Greta crowding closely behind. Nose to the ground, she circled the car, found the spot where the bullet had plowed into the earth, and sniffed. Another two laps around the car and she began trotting off down the road toward the northwest. Tweede closed and locked the car and followed.

She set a good pace, indifferent to him and the rest of the world as well. A passing collie failed to divert her. Soon she swung off the street and headed across an open field. Tweede followed as well as he could. It was a good thing he had taken up jogging a year ago. He could never have kept up otherwise.

This part of the metropolitan area was unfamiliar to him. The winding street had confused him. He wasn't sure precisely which direction he was going. But Greta seemed to know. She trotted down a dead-end street and across another open field. The field ended in a fence and a wooded area—some pines and underbrush. Beyond, glimpsed vaguely through the trees, Tweede saw the roof of a large house. Greta had slipped through the fence, and into the brush. Tweede was about three minutes behind her. The fence proved awkward but passable. He hurried on into the brush.

At first, he was afraid he might have lost her, but a low whine, as though she were crying, led him. He emerged into a small open space among the trees and found her pawing at the ground. Having gotten where she intended to go, she took notice of him, came to him, and shoved her nose into his hand. Then she went back to the patch of weeds, pawed at it some more, and lay down, her muzzle resting on crossed forepaws. He circled the little glade. Her eyes and ears followed him. The earth was slightly depressed on the spot where she lay, but there was little evidence of its having been disturbed. Tweede sighed and wondered what to do. He went to the edge of the brush and looked at the house for a moment, trying to fix its shape on his mind. Then he returned and spoke softly to the dog.

"Come on, Greta, let's go home," he said, snapping his fingers. Obediently, the dog rose and followed him back the way they had come. He had only to say, "Heel!" and she walked sedately at his side, about a half pace behind him so that her head was even with his thigh. When they arrived back at the car, she climbed in and sat in the passenger seat, looking about like some dignified but lively dowager. He drove her back to the Bettinjohns. She seemed quite pleased to see them.

"Was your test successful?" Mr. Bettinjohn asked.

"I'm afraid so," Tweede replied. Thanking them again for Greta's help, he drove away.

Paul Holroyd was inclined to scoff, but mindful of certain times in the past when Herringbone's hunches or intuitions or whatever they might be called had proved to be more than fancy, he listened and considered a moment before he spoke.

"There are problems," he said. "But there are a few things we can do. A couple of official questions will help.

A little presumptive evidence, that's all we need. Of course, you could be all wet. The dog . . ."

"She was pretty sure, Paul. Straight to the spot."

"All right. I'll have the department ask around."

"It's the least you can do," Tweede said.

Holroyd finished the last Danish and wiped his mouth. "The Bettinjohns were quite complimentary about you," he said.

"They ought to be," Tweede replied. "I exercised their dog for a whole afternoon. I'll bet they don't."

"Tut tut, Herringbone. You sound snide and resentful. Something bothering you about the Bettinjohns?"

"I think it's that guard at the gate," Tweede said. "I'll bet he gets paid more in a month than I make."

"Oh, I'm sure he must," Holroyd agreed. "But you wouldn't like the work. Too sedentary. No chance for exercising. Quite dull."

"The money would be nice," Tweede observed wistfully.

"But can it buy happiness or peace of mind?"

"Mr. and Mrs. Bettinjohn . . ." Tweede started to say. Holroyd sniffed.

"Every day about three in the afternoon, Harvey Bettinjohn goes down to the Long Beach wharves and spends an hour watching the ships. He started as a stevedore, bought a boat of his own, and parlayed it into a fleet. Registered out of Puerto Rico. It's a wholly-owned container shipping line now. Twenty ships. But every day—or nearly every day—he goes down to watch the boats unload.

"Well, I got to get along. Sylvia's mother is visiting from Salt Lake and the old girl wants to go see the Mormon Temple lit up at night. See you. Good coffee for a change, dolly."

The waitress, whose name was Maria, acknowledged the compliment with a smile. She was new on the job and had not yet learned the inverse relationship between Holroyd's compliments and the presence of a tip beside the saucer. Tweede sighed and laid down two quarters. He hated to see new immigrants disillusioned so quickly.

Holroyd called two days later just before noon.

"You may be right," he said. "We got a negative reply."

"Is that enough presumptive evidence?" Tweede asked.

Holroyd hedged. "Well, it wouldn't satisfy the D.A., but Judge Rolfe is always willing to let us go out on a limb. Keeps hoping it'll break off. The limb, I mean. With us on it."

"I get the picture," Tweede said.

"So," Holroyd continued heavily, "I'm going to go along with you. I've got a nasty mind like you, I guess."

Late that afternoon, Tweede led Holroyd, a uniform, a curious dentist, and a pair of shovels to the little wooded patch in Brentwood. While Holroyd and the dentist watched, Tweede and the uniform began to dig in the spot where Greta had been lying. The soil was loose and the grave shallow. Within ten minutes they had uncovered the skeleton of a woman together with the rotting fragments of the dress and the corset she had been wearing. Patches of matted, dissolving hair lay about the skull. Her rings still gleamed against the dirty, yellowed bones of her fingers. The remains of a pair of sensible rubber-heeled shoes encased her mostly decomposed feet.

The dentist, looking green, bent and compared the exposed teeth with a chart he pulled from his pocket. "It matches," he said, after a brief examination. "I recognize some of my own work. This is Mrs. Goodpasture all right."

Holroyd left the uniform on watch beside the disinterred body. The dentist departed back the way they had come while Holroyd and Tweede crossed the backyard and made their way around to the front door. Tweede rang the bell.

"There's a woman who cooks and cleans," he explained.

"She must be out," Holroyd said after a time.

With one of those largely habitual, unpremeditated gestures we all make, Tweede tried the door. To his surprise it was unlocked and opened easily.

They found him in the bath, slumped beneath the red water so that only his eyes showed above.

"Dear Mr. Tweede (the letter said),

"I saw you looking out of the woods at the back of the house this afternoon, so I know you have found out. It was Greta, I suppose. I should have put her away, of course, but it seemed such a cruel thing to do. She loved Mother, but that really had nothing to do with it. I thought if I sold her through a breeder, that would end it.

"I'll never really understand why she loved Mother. Mother certainly didn't love her—only me. It was like being perpetually smothered with a pillow. I got so I couldn't breathe. I suppose I could have stood it, but when she began nagging at me to get married and father some children, it got to be too much. Day and night, she went at it. Finally, she decided we'd have to move back to New Hampshire, since I obviously didn't like any of the girls here. Actually, I do. I may even have fathered a child or two, I don't know. I just don't want you to get the wrong impression. But I don't want to get married. Really, all I want is a little peace and quiet and time to read. Women are so demanding. . . .

"I didn't realize Greta was in the room when I shot her—Mother, I mean. That was Thanksgiving Day a year ago. You asked if Greta were startled by loud noises. I could see you suspected even then. The gun certainly did startle her, but she seemed more alarmed when Mother lay there and wouldn't move. I had to coax her out and shut her in the pantry before I could move Mother to the woods. When I caught Greta the next day pawing at the ground where I'd buried Mother, I knew I'd have to get rid of her. I did like her, you know. She was a gentle dog and good company. I don't understand why she liked Mother more than me.

"I wrote this so there wouldn't be any misunderstanding. I did think I'd gotten away with it. I've handled Mother's money matters for years. I'm really quite good

*at that. She has no relatives. Her few acquaintances had
heard her say we were moving back east. There was no
one to miss her except Greta and I—or is it me? And it's
funny, but I do. I must be mad, but I do. Too late, of
course.*

"Yours,

"Clarence Goodpasture"

"What in hell made him think he could get away with
something as crude as that?" Holroyd growled when they
had finished reading the letter.

"But he did get away with it," Tweede objected. "You're
just piqued because it's one of those things you missed."

"And he'd have gone on getting away with it if I hadn't
got you looking for the dog," Holroyd said, his anger
evaporating. "I guess that evens things up, so what do you
mean, piqued?"

"Nothing, Paul," Tweede said. "I just wonder sometimes how many other cases there are like this one—cases
that we never find out about. Oh, sorry! Now, you're
piqued again. Hadn't you better call the squad?"

Holroyd grunted and turned away. Tweede followed.
There was nothing more he could do. Now it was up to the
LAPD. He walked to the door.

"Yeah, Brentwood," Holroyd was saying into the tele-
phone. "No, we don't need the team. Hey, hold on a minute,
Sam." He covered the phone with the palm of his hand.
"See you at Dingo's?" he called after Tweede. "I'm buying."

"Sure," Tweede called back. "What happened? You
come into money?"

"It's the least I can do," Holroyd said. "You didn't even
earn a fee on this. The Bettinjohns said to tell you since
the dog came back on her own . . ."

"Thanks, Paul. You've made my day," Tweede said.

"Well, it's a dog's life, you know," Holroyd called.

Tweede sighed and closed the door behind him. Some
days, he thought, it certainly was.

The Case of
<< the Lost Collie >>

by

M. M. LaCour

"MAKE YOU A deal? You take him in this time, and I'll take him in next time?"

"Make *you* a deal! You take him in this time and I'll clean the bathroom, which you've promised to do now for four days!"

Elly was being unnecessarily hard to deal with and outrageously unfair.

"If you take him in, I'll do the bathroom when we get back and scrub the kitchen floor."

"You take him in, Hec, and I'll do the bathroom, the kitchen floor, and change the oil in the car, which you promised to do last week."

I took a swallow of tea and gave Daug a dirty look over the top of my mug. "Will you vacuum, too?" What the heck, it was worth a shot.

"Hec!"

"All right, all right," I gave in graciously. "I'll take the ornery lump in to see the vet, but next time, Elly, it's your turn."

I swear to God, Daug looked like he was smiling.

Elly was smiling for sure. "Lest you forget, Hec, it was my turn the last three times. Anyway, after this trip, he'll only have to go in once a year for shots."

I sighed and looked out the picture window, sourly contemplating my defeat. Naturally, it was raining. I'd get

101

soaked; Daug would get soaked. Sometimes life was just not fair. But I'd do it, to please Elly. I'd take her dumb dog to the vet to get his shots.

Elly poured us both a fresh cup and added, "I'll ride in with you, but you'll have to take him into the examining room. After all, Hec, he *is* your dog."

On the way over, while Daug slobbered all over my rear seat, Elly speculated about why Daug always tried to eat Doc Melbourne on sight.

"Sometimes I think dogs just don't like certain people. You know how he barks at the UPS deliveryman. Do you think it's something they smell?"

"Last time we were there, Melbourne smelled all right to me."

Elly giggled. I love it when she giggles, just like a little girl. She'll be sixty-five come July, but she'll never lose that giggle, thank God. Of course she could afford to giggle; she wasn't going to be the one who'd have to hold down a hundred pounds of unmanageable animal while Melbourne tried to give Daug a shot.

"I know why he hates the vet," I said knowingly. "Do you remember the first thing Melbourne did when we brought Daug here the first time?"

"No, what?"

"Stuck that thermometer you know where."

"Oh my, you are a smart dog, aren't you!" she praised while shaking Daug's paw. "Now, let me see your teeth, that's a good dog, nice and clean. I can see your owners take good care of you." She handed him another piece of cheese. "I don't think we need to take your temperature, you look pretty darn healthy to me. Just one more little bitty thing we have to do, and that's give you a shot. Now, it's not going to hurt . . ." Before I could blink she'd whisked the needle in and out. "There, that wasn't too bad, was it." Then more cheese.

Daug was in heaven. I was in shock. Elly was standing in the examining room door smiling.

"I just can't believe it," I stammered. "He didn't growl once, he even got on the table for you. . . ."

She patted Daug on the head and smiled at me. "Doc told me how difficult Daug has been, just thought I'd try a new approach. "This is a nice looking dog. Is he papered?"

"No, he goes outside," I answered stupidly.

From Elly came, "He was a stray, but he does look full-blooded."

With a charming toss of the head, Lee Cronkite laughed. "That's what I meant, is he a full-blooded German shepherd? Going outside does help, though!"

I liked her. Quite a change from crotchety old Melbourne. I guessed her to be in her late twenties, early thirties. She reminded me a little of Elly's niece back in Chicago. Both were petite and perky, and both wore their hair in a short straight bob that framed round, scrubbed looking faces. Our new vet, though, was definitely cuter than Kate. Kate was on Elly's side of the family.

From the reception area came a plaintive, "Oh no! Not again!"

Before I could grab him, Daug shot off the table and past us into the waiting room.

"Not a cat!" I exclaimed, on the run after him.

It wasn't a cat but the most bedraggled, dirty, down and out looking collie I'd ever seen in my life.

"I could kill that man!" said Lee angrily from beside me. "I could just kill him!"

"Twenty-five years on the Chicago police force, and now look what I'm reduced to! Delivering filthy, lost hounddogs back home." I wasn't really mad; the skies had cleared and I enjoy driving around the back roads of Cedar Bend, exploring. That is, when I don't have to go down too many bumpy gravel roads.

"Look, Hec, a deer!" Elly exclaimed with delight.

Daug saw it, too, and let out with a bark right in my left ear. I looked in my rear view mirror. The runaway collie was content to lie stretched out across my rear seat. Fortunately, Lee had thoughtfully provided a blanket. The collie was probably the dirtiest dog I'd ever come across, even among the scavenging packs that occasionally wandered Chicago's back alleys.

"You'd think we were the humane society or something," I continued to grumble.

"Watch out for that hole in the road, Hec, and you know, dear, we didn't have anything else planned for this morning. Lee couldn't help it if Dr. Melbourne was out on a call."

"This is an awfully long way for that mutt to have come."

We'd already gone several miles southeast of town off Edgewick Road, out into what I called the super boonies. Could I have missed a turn? The towering evergreens were no help. They told no tales, close-mouthed as they were, keeping their secrets to themselves about who lived where, up what gravel road, at what unmarked fork.

"There's the mailbox, and there's the big cedar," I proclaimed with relief. "Must be that road to the right."

"There's another big cedar up farther, Hec."

"Elly, this is a forest."

"I guess it must be the place, but . . ."

I had started up the most godawful excuse for a road I'd yet had the pleasure of driving in the fair state of Washington. The recent rains had made the potholes muddy land mines. "No wonder you're so filthy," I said to the collie. Talking to animals is a disgusting habit I'd picked up from Elly.

That's when the shot whistled past my window.

Elly shouted, "What was that?"

"Get down!" I commanded, slamming on the brakes. Daug was barking his fool head off, and so was the collie. "Shut up!" I yelled at them both, and surprisingly they did.

Instinctively I reached for the area on my side where I'd carried a .38 for over twenty-five years. Nothing.

Then the second shot whistled over the top of our little Honda.

There we were, sitting ducks, with me retired and un-armed.

"Turn that heap around and get the hell out of here!" demanded a not-at-all-friendly male voice. It seemed to boom out menacingly from all directions.

In retrospect I must say Daug was fearless as he answered with an equally menacing, deep-throated growl.

As I ran my hand under the front seat, searching for the tire iron, I whispered "Stay down," to Elly and tried to figure out what the heck was going on.

"This here's private property. Turn around." I didn't like the edge of craziness in that voice.

"Hec, I'm scared."

"So am I."

Loudspeakers, I realized. Well, two could play at that game. Sliding over, keeping my head down, I stretched to reach under the rear seat and grab Tom's Christmas present to me, a bull horn. The Christmas before he'd given me a CB. It was a tricky maneuver and the collie didn't help matters by licking me in the face.

I managed to slide the bull horn out and up into the front seat with me. Then I grabbed the CB mike and tried to raise Clara. "Clara," I whispered into the mike. "Clara, this is Hector Hoggs. Get me Tom, right away. This is an emergency. Over."

No response.

I cursed.

"Clara," I tried again. "This is Chief Hoggs, Elly and I are out off Edgewick Road at Jack Simpson's place, and we're being shot at. Tell Tom to get the heck out here, and fast. Over."

Nothing. We were on our own.

I'd have to go for it. There's no way you can stay down in the front seat of a Honda and talk into a bull horn at the same time when you're five ten and nearly a hundred and sixty pounds, with a lot of that poundage gravitating in the gut area.

The loudspeakers blared again, "You've got twenty seconds before I turn that sardine can into spaghetti!"

Lowering the window, I raised my head, stuck the bull horn outside, and started talking all at the same time. "This is Chief Hector Hoggs." Didn't think it was necessary to mention that I was retired. "And I'm here on official business, Mr. Simpson. If you don't drop that gun and come out here right now, I'm going to have to put you under arrest." I didn't have the power to arrest anyone any more, but it was definitely worth a try.

I'd never heard a laugh like that. Maybe it was my imagination, but I sure thought the whole county quaked a little in response. Daug howled and the collie whimpered.

"You sure got nerve, give you that! Ain't blind, you know, you're that ole coot moved to town a couple of years back from Chicago. 'Case you ain't noticed, this ain't no Chicago."

So much for that bright idea.

"And don't you go calling me no Mr. Simpson, neither. Next time I gets me hands on that skunk, he's a dead man. Now turn that heap around and head out! Simpson's still on up the road a piece, and the only reason I'm a telling you that is you got that sweet li'l wife of yours in the car with you. Now get the hell off my property, and if you see that half-brained Scooter, tell him to stop stealing logs off my property!"

"Hec," Elly gasped, "I know who that is!"

At that moment I didn't care who it was. I just started the motor and backed out.

I guess if you concentrated on the pieces, like the pond doing what ponds do in the morning sun, the trees looking like trees do after having survived the rain and ending up in warmth, and Rattlesnake Ridge just standing there looking formidable, it was okay.

Add to that, though, a dilapidated trailer from the fifties, twenty-five or so mangy chickens, a collapsing corral that was barely able to contain two not too healthy looking horses, more rusting junk than you'd find in a commercial junkyard, and rotting timber odds and ends all over the place, you had the whole scene.

Elly actually seemed enthusiastic. "Oh, Hec, isn't this interesting!"

"Wait, Elly, don't get out yet. So far the natives haven't been that friendly." I didn't tell Elly, but as soon as we'd dropped that mutt off with the Simpson character, I planned to bring Tom back out with me and charge Simpson's shooting neighbor with assault.

She dropped her hand from the door handle. "You don't think . . ."

"Let me look around first."

"Be careful."

"Doesn't seem to be anyone around, Elly, except for all these animals." I let Daug and the collie out. Daug went straight for the chickens and the collie sat down by the car, apparently not greatly overjoyed about being home. "I think it's okay, you can come on out. I guess we should go knock on the door."

A single huge ginger cat lounged on the trailer's front porch, which was a piece of plywood sitting on two bricks. It seemed untroubled that some strange dog had set off chickens scurrying all over the place.

"Daug," I commanded irritably, "get over here and sit down." He obeyed, for once.

Undaunted, Elly marched right up to the door, giving the cat a kind word in passing, and knocked. "Yo-ho! Mr. Simpson!"

Nothing.

With a harder knock she tried again. "Mr. Simpson, we brought your dog back."

Still nothing.

"Maybe he's out back?" she cheerfully offered. Sometimes Elly's sense of adventure surprises me. Here we'd just been shot at on some stranger's property and were trying to deliver an obviously unwanted dog on some other stranger's property, and she was acting like it was fun.

"Elly, wait. . . ." Too late. Disgruntled, I followed her around as she wandered. Of course she had to stop and pat the horses and talk chicken talk to a few brave birds.

"These animals certainly aren't well taken care of, Hec. Now I see why Lee doesn't like Mr. Simpson. Oh, Hec, look at that old tractor!"

Sometimes I get irritable, like when I haven't had breakfast, have to take Daug to the vet, have to deliver runaway dogs, and get shot at.

"Elly, would you please forget the tractor. If you don't mind, could we please leave this mutt and go home. I would like to have breakfast before lunchtime."

"Now, Hec, you don't have to get crabby. It's just that Lee said Mr. Simpson is always here. Remember, she did say he was sort of a hermit?"

I remembered. "I guess you're right. We should look around a little."

"It's just like the one Grandma Jenkins used to have up in her orchard in Michigan! We kids used to love playing down there. And did it ever keep the apples crisp!" She was talking about the root cellar we'd found on the back side of the trailer.

"God, doesn't this man ever cut back the raspberries!" I grumbled, extricating myself from a killer vine.

"I wonder what Mr. Simpson keeps in his." Fearlessly, she was trampling through the bushes, headed straight for the two flat wooden doors of the root cellar.

"Elly! Will you please stop. This is private property. It's none of our business what Mr. Simpson keeps in his root cellar."

Hungry as I'd been, I decided to pass on breakfast. Wendell drove Elly home in my Honda. "Hec," Tom addressed me as we returned from his police jeep, "I've put a call in to Clara to get the guys out here. I don't think Jack got himself locked in there by accident, you know."

"Neither do I." A few year back I'd stopped smoking, for Elly's sake, but I sure wanted one then. "You still haven't told me how you knew we were here."

"Your call to Clara."

"Clara never answered my call."

"She can't answer if you're on the wrong channel, Hec. You just lucked out that she was monitoring the emergency channel when you got on the air."

"I was on the wrong channel?"

"Yep."

"Elly's never seen anything like this before, you know." The kid was looking a little ghastly himself. "To be honest with you, Hec, neither have I." Then, more like himself, " 'Course I haven't been around as long as some people I know."

"At least you know what channel the police band is," I returned sourly.

"Come on, Hec, don't be so hard on yourself. You know, for a man of your age you do all right."

I turned in time to see that good-natured grin plastered across that baby face, and I had to smile. Then, more in the way of our usual banter, "I think you're going to need some help on this one, kid. Somebody hit Simpson on the head and stuck that stick in the latch to make sure he couldn't get out. And given your lack of age and experience and all that, you might need some assistance from a wiser, more experienced gentleman."

"Just might. Want to come along with me to pay Holcombe a visit?"

"Nothin' would suit me better. I never did like being shot at; like it even less now."

"The right of private property is sacred to me, now you know that, Tom," pontificated Ty Holcombe over the top of a glass of sherry. "Pretty good stuff, huh, fellas?" he added with a lift of his crystal glass. "One thing I ain't got is education, but taste, now I know what's good, and this stuff's good."

He was right, it was good. So was everything else I'd seen so far. Top of the line, good quality, from the furniture to the Oriental rugs, from the crystal we were sipping the best sherry I'd ever tasted from to the electronic gadgetry visible everywhere. Loudspeakers had only been the tip of the iceberg.

"Private property's one thing." I was still hot about my Elly being shot at. "But shooting at innocent people is illegal, Mr. Holcombe."

He dropped his head and actually tried to look embarrassed. But I caught the fleeting twinkle in the scoundrel's eye as he said, "Shucks, Hec, I can call you Hec, can't I? Call me Ty. Tom can tell you, I wasn't really trying to hit you, just don't like nobody messing around my property. And you believe you me, Hec, if I'da known you had Elly with you, shoot, I woulda just used the speakers."

I bet. "Well, you nearly scared Elly half to death."

All around us the strains of Vivaldi could be heard. Don't know diddly about classical music, but I recognized the *Four Seasons* because it was Elly's favorite. I couldn't see the speakers, but I guessed them to be in every room of the house.

From Tom, "Chief Hoggs is right, Ty. You know this isn't the first time I've had a complaint. You just can't go around shooting at people."

"All right, all right!" He raised his hands in jovial surrender. "Cross my heart, Tom, won't do no more shooting till I find out who it is. Good enough?"

Tom looked at me.

Despite it all, I liked the man. There was something about him that reminded me of a big panda bear. He had piercing deep brown eyes set back in huge sockets framed with bushy eyebrows that almost went from end to end of his forehead. His chin was covered with a huge brown beard turning to grey, and his head was as bald as a crystal ball.

But I still remembered that crazed laugh and shots whizzing by my head. "Well . . . you know, Mr. Holcombe, you weren't as congenial an hour ago as you are now."

"I can come off pretty ornery, can't I!" he bellowed unself-consciously. "All an act, Hec, gotta keep my privacy, you know."

I took another sip of sherry; it *was* excellent. "You know Elly?"

"Who doesn't know Elly Hoggs!"

Tom shot me a wink. Smart-aleck kid.

Holcombe continued, "Sweetest li'l thing God ever sat on this green earth. Never forget that Christmas party she got going for the old folks in town, now that was some bash!

"Then that food drive she organized, helped a lotta folks in this river valley with that. Yep, that wife of yours is pretty well thought of out here. You are gonna tell her how sorry I am 'bout this morning?"

Grudgingly I nodded.

Tom cleared his throat. "Mr. Holcombe . . ."

"What's with the Mr. Holcombe stuff, Tommy boy? Hell, known you since you were just a twinkle in your rascally father's eye. Now . . ."

"Mr. Holcombe," Tom insisted sternly, "Jack Simpson is dead and we want to ask you a few questions."

" 'Bout time somebody put that no good excuse for a human being where he belongs. Feel sorry for Scooter, though." There was no surprise in Holcombe's voice, no sorrow, and no apology for saying what he felt.

I sat back and shut up. This was the kid's job, not mine. Being a cop as long as I had, you came across a lot of different types of characters, but as unique as we all like to think we are, you start seeing types after a while, not identical but the similarities begin to stand out more than the differences.

When I was at the 12th Precinct I worked with a captain who claimed he'd logged every type of personality that existed. Two hundred and ten, if I remember right. Captain Novakowski had never been to Cedar Bend.

"I gather, then, there was no love lost between you and Mr. Simpson?" Tom continued smoothly.

"Ha! Jack Simpson was the lowest type of varmint to walk the face of this earth. You know that, Tom. Bet you a dime to a dollar you won't find nobody in this here valley with a good word to say 'bout Simpson."

"Somebody bashed him in the head, threw him in his own root cellar, and stuck a stick through the latch so he

couldn't get out. That, Mr. Holcombe, is a little more serious than not having a good word to say about a man.
That's murder."

The light strains of *Spring* pleasantly filled the silence
as we sipped sherry and thought our own thoughts.

Then with the suddenness of a cobra strike Holcombe
asked me, "Want to buy a newspaper, Hec?"

"Clara," Tom said into his CB mike, "this is Sheriff
Rhodes. Did Wendell call in yet? Over."

"Is that you, sheriff?" responded the most awful, high-
pitched, nasal whine the human voice is capable of pro-
ducing.

Tom slowly counted to six before switching the mike
back on. "Yes, Clara, it's the sheriff. When I get on the radio and say this is Sheriff Rhodes, it means, Clara, that it's
Sheriff Rhodes."

"Well, you don't have to get snippy, now do you? Sheriff Tim never got snippy." The woman's voice was like
fingernails on a blackboard. Clara was good at her job, but
lousy as a warm, loving, human being. "As you know,
Sheriff Rhodes, it says right in the rulebook, make sure
you identify who you're talking to."

I had a smart-aleck remark in the offing, but seeing the
look on Tom's face I decided to keep my mouth shut.

"What it doesn't say in the rulebook, Clara," Tom responded, smooth as glass, "is that Sheriff Tim has retired
and no longer pays your salary."

"Wendell dropped Mrs. Hoggs at home, then went back
to where that no-good coot Simpson finally got what was
comin' to him." End of transmission.

"Simpson certainly was well liked," I mused out loud.

We were headed, I hoped, back to my house in Tom's
new police jeep. Fifteen grand of the taxpayers' money,
and it was the best. Top of the line CB, gun rack, leather
upholstery, and springs that made you forget you were going fifty mph down a gravel ditch called a road.

It was nearing lunchtime, my hunger was returning, and

I was getting a little peevish. "Could you please slow down!"

"I thought you were hungry."

"I would also like to be alive to eat my lunch."

"Am I invited?" Never known the kid to miss a free feed from Elly.

"Are you kidding? If Elly sees you pull up, there's no way you'll get away until she's stuffed you to the gills."

"I was counting on that."

It was almost eleven A.M., the sun was still out, and I tried to relax and enjoy the scenery. It'd taken a while, but I was getting used to trees instead of tenements and watching for deer running in front of your car instead of kids. "Who is this Scooter, anyway?"

"Scooter Simpson, Jack's nephew."

"He live out there? Elly and I sure didn't see any sign of life other than animal type." I took a hefty breath, letting the air out slowly, and leaned back in my seat. A lot had happened that morning. I needed time to digest it all.

Tom sighed wearily. "I don't like the sound of Scooter's not being around, Hec." Then, shaking his head for emphasis, "Don't like the sound of that one bit."

"You know this Scooter?"

"Everybody knows Scooter."

I didn't and said so.

Narrowly skirting a pothole the size of a Jacuzzi, he wised off, "If you'd get out more, like Elly does . . ."

"Are you or are you not going to tell me who Scooter is?"

When he didn't answer immediately, I turned to see his face had clouded over. Then, picking his words carefully, "Like I said, Scooter's Jack's nephew. If I remember right, Scooter is around twenty or twenty-one by now. He's, well, he's . . . I'm not sure what the right word is these days, but he's what I'd call retarded. Been that way all his life."

Somberly, matching his mood, I asked, "And you think Scooter killed his uncle?"

Another, heavier sigh. "With the way that jerk treated

him, wouldn't blame him one bit." Then, more to himself, "Poor kid."

Everyone who had known Jack Simpson had hated him. Real lovable guy. "What's so terrible about this Simpson that I haven't heard a kind word spoken about him yet?"

With a short, derisive laugh, Tom started counting on his fingers. "To start off with . . ."

"Would you please keep your hands on the wheel."

". . . the stingiest person I've ever known. Hated to pay for anything, and it wasn't because he didn't have any money, don't let that shack fool you. What got me most, though, was the way he treated Scooter. Hell, the kid's parents died when he was five; his mother was Jack's own sister. Only did enough for the kid to keep the state from coming and taking him away. Kept Scooter stuck out there in the sticks with him, doing all the work around that place. Never gave him a dime to spend, never tried to get him in any special classes, nothin'." Tom virtually spat those last words out.

"What about Lee? She didn't seem to be that fond of Simpson either."

I certainly didn't expect what happened next. The kid actually turned bright red. "You mean Lee the vet?"

"Yes, I mean Lee the vet. I told you that's how we ended up out there anyway."

Interesting turn of events, I thought. The kid's smitten.

"You saw those animals, man barely fed them. Humane society's been out there a couple of times, checking on the horses."

"What'll happen to them now?"

With a self-satisfied smile he informed me that he'd already instructed Wendell to make arrangements for the animals.

"By arrangements, you mean new homes, not . . ."

"Hec!" he admonished.

"Just checking."

We were back on the main road; lunch was near. The sun was actually warm on my face as it beat down through the window. Not a summer sun yet but in a few months ... "And," I abruptly broke our comfortable silence, "what did Holcombe mean about did I want to buy a newspaper? Is everyone in this valley as loony as Simpson and Holcombe?"

"Holcombe isn't loony, not by a long shot. One of the most successful businessmen in this area, at least he was. Nowadays he just sits around counting his money. You saw that house."

I was incredulous. "You mean he really does want to sell me a newspaper?"

"Sure sounded like it to me. Probably talking about the *Beacon*, not really a newspaper yet, more like a flyer. So far it's been coming out biweekly."

"Never heard anything more ridiculous, me running a newspaper."

Finally we were leaving Interstate 90, heading down Cedar Bend Road. Home was nearing. "What arrangements did you make about the collie?"

Elly would want to know.

"You mean the collie that was sitting in the back seat of your Honda?"

"No, he was out by the time you got there. The dirty, smelly one, the one we were delivering back for Lee."

"Like I said, you mean the one that was sitting in the back of your Honda when Wendell left to take Elly home?"

Lunch was delicious, as usual.

Wendell called just as we finished eating to inform Tom that Scooter had been picked up in Pierce County trying to hitch a ride. Lee had called Elly shortly afterward to ask how the collie was. She also asked if Tom was there. She didn't ask to speak to him, though.

By the time Elly had packed Tom off with a bag full of half the chocolate chip cookies she'd baked the day before for *me*, I was exhausted and said so.

"A nap, now?" Elly protested sweetly. "Who's going to give the collie a bath, then? I can't bring her in the house in the condition she's in."

Sometimes a man has to put his foot down. "Elly," I

said firmly, "we are not going to keep that collie. One dog is enough!"

Needless to say, I spent what was left of the afternoon bathing the collie, making her a cedar chip bed just like Daug's, and going into town to buy her a collar, a leash, and matching doggie bowls.

I'd seen those eyes before, questioning but not sure of the question or answer; unconsciously friendly and desiring to please but wary; hopeful but sure of disaster to come. And what did we do at the 12th when yet another set of those eyes presented themselves? We'd hustle them off to County, that's what we'd do. They had a special ward for those kinds of eyes. Out of sight in special wards, though, doesn't make you forget, no matter how hard you want to. I think there's a uniquely reserved place in your brain where you try to lock that stuff up. Most of the time that door stays closed, nice and tight, until . . .

"Nobody's going to hurt you, Scooter," Tom gently reassured those eyes. "I know you must be scared, but honest, we just want to talk to you, ask you a few questions. Is that all right with you?"

I like to tease Tom, call him the child-sheriff, wet behind the ears stuff, but the kid was all right.

The eyes grew less apprehensive. "You wanna ask Scooter questions?" You couldn't miss the wonder and amazement in his voice. Why would anybody think Scooter could answer anything about anything?

We were in Tom's cubbyhole of an office, not that great but better than interrogating him in a cell. Dressed in what Elly would have pronounced rags, his hair in a crewcut, his round, flat face smudged and dirty, Scooter sat stiffly on the edge of a wooden, slat-backed chair, anxiously turning those eyes back and forth between Tom, Wendell, and me.

"Just a few questions, Scooter," Tom patiently went on. "Okay?"

"Okay!" Scooter piped out with glee. "Scooter can answer questions!" Those eyes had begun to twinkle with delight.

"Why were you running away, Scooter?" Tom asked, pointedly but not harshly.

Scooter smiled joyfully. It was a question he could answer. "Scooter hates Uncle Jack. Scooter'll never see him again. Scooter's gonna get a job!"

Sympathetically Tom nodded encouragement. "Uncle Jack wasn't too nice, was he?"

"Scooter hated Uncle Jack! Never see Uncle Jack again."

"Don't you think Uncle Jack'll come looking for you, Scooter?"

With a broad smile, Scooter shook his head knowingly. "Uh-uh! Uncle Jack never come after Scooter again!"

There are moments that hang in time, pieces of life that are indelibly engraved on your brain. That was one of them.

The next words out of Tom seemed to come in slow motion, as if they knew the outcome and were in no hurry to get there. "Why won't Uncle Jack ever come after Scooter again?"

" 'Cause he's in the root cellar!" Then he began to sing softly to himself, "Scooter put Uncle Jack in the root cellar. Scooter put Uncle Jack in the root cellar, shame on Scooter, shame on Scooter!"

"You know, Hec, she's really a very smart dog." Elly continued to be undaunted by the nasty mood I was in.

"Good."

"And she and Daug seem to really like each other."

"Good."

I was in my favorite chair that looks out onto the river and the south face of Mount Si. It was another sunny morning, but as far as I was concerned it could just as well have been raining and overcast.

Elly, comfortably curled up on the couch, was crocheting a sweater, by the size of it, presumably for me. I hadn't gotten up enough nerve yet to tell her that I would never wear a sweater of that shade of yellow.

"I know what you're brooding about, Hec. But things really didn't turn out that bad for Scooter."

"Scooter didn't kill Jack Simpson."

"But nobody's blaming him, Hec. Tom's got him all settled in that nice animal preserve place with a job as a helper taking care of the animals and his own little trailer. And those people who run the place seemed awfully nice. It was like they really care about him. You don't need to feel sorry for Scooter."

"But he didn't kill Simpson. Maybe he did give the old man a hit on the head and push him in that root cellar, but the autopsy report said Simpson had only been stunned by that blow and ended up with a broken ankle. What he actually died of was hypothermia. What killed Simpson was that stick's being stuck in the clasp. Somebody knew Simpson was lying helplessly in that root cellar and took advantage of the situation to make sure he never saw the light of day again. And I don't care what the authorities believe. Scooter didn't do that. Scooter is not smart enough to have even thought to make that root cellar a coffin. Shame on Scooter all right, but shame on somebody else, too."

Probably thoroughly exasperated with me, Elly sighed. "I know you don't think he's guilty, that's what you told Tom and me over and over last night. But, Hec, if he didn't, who did? And, sweetheart, what difference does it make now?"

"It makes a difference to me," I stated flatly. "And I don't know who did it. Don't you understand, Elly, I don't know who did it, and that makes me thoroughly P.O.'d."

"You don't think it was Lee, do you? She's such a nice young girl, and I think she and Tom just might . . ."

"She hated his guts. And why did she ask us to take an animal back to the person whom she knew mistreated it? I know she said because the only other choice was to take it to the shelter and they'd probably put the mutt to sleep.

I guess I believe her. No, I do believe her. I don't think Lee killed Simpson."

"Holcombe?" she threw out, not missing a stitch.

"Hated Simpson, too. Crazy enough to think he could get away with it. But I don't think the method fits the man. If I read Holcombe right, he would have just blown Simpson away if he felt like it. Thing is, Elly, anyone who knew Simpson hated him. Makes for a lot of suspects."

"Are you going to buy the *Beacon*?"

"Are you kidding?"

Elly decided she wanted to grow cauliflower, brussels sprouts, and broccoli that spring. All the things I didn't eat. And wouldn't a cold frame be just the thing to get them started?

That's how I happened to be out in our front yard that morning trying to make the prefab, precut, easy-to-assemble job I'd bought go together.

Par for the course, nothing fit, and after two hours I'd managed one half of a frame that, according to the manufacturers, would take a two-year-old fifteen minutes to assemble. I decided to take a break before I burned the whole thing up.

A break for me means playtime for Daug. He brought me his ball, and I threw it. Elly had been right, the collie, which we hadn't named yet, was pretty smart. On seeing what was going on, she found a stick and brought it to me. I threw it in the water, and she was after it like a shot.

Between throws for those two mutts I tried to take my mind off Elly's unfinished cold frame and enjoy the spring morning. It was definitely okay, having retired in Washington, that is.

A little dull, but okay. Was buying a newspaper what I needed? What the heck did I know about running a newspaper? Diddly, that's what.

Then Daug dropped a rock in my lap, fortunately for me between my legs. "No rocks!" I demanded. "You hardly have any teeth left now." He sulked off.

Finally I went back to the cold frame, and after an eternity more of cursing, it was standing. All I needed to do was add the latch. Latches I'd had experience with and finished that up without a hitch.

"Elly!" I called proudly toward the house. "Elly, come on out and see your cold frame." Not half bad, I said to myself.

Her reaction when she got out there was worth waiting for.

"Hec, it's fantastic!"

I put my arm around her and we sat down on the grass and admired my handiwork.

Elly was all smiles. I liked that. It almost made up for the fact that cauliflower loomed in my future.

Daug was back with the ball; Elly threw it for him. I looked around for the collie, expecting that a stick would be next.

A stick *was* next, she had it in her gracefully pointed snout.

But instead of bringing it over to Elly or me, she pranced as proudly as could be over to Elly's new cold frame and stuck the stick, neat as a pin, through its latch.

≪ Beast at the Door ≫
by
Donald Olson

OLD MRS. WEYBURN died at seven-thirty that evening, quite unexpectedly despite her precarious condition. The family and Dr. Catesby were summoned, and after a decent interval, her services no longer required, Lucy packed her bag and returned in her car to the secluded brick house on Barberry Road where she and her husband had lived ever since Clifford had assumed an assistant professorship in the natural-sciences department of the University.

It was dark when she arrived. Lights burned in the living room and kitchen and in Clifford's laboratory, which was actually a small greenhouse at the rear of the attached garage. Clifford's car, however, was not there, although the sound of a Haydn quartet coming from the stereo as Lucy entered the house suggested he would soon be back. Lucy was glad. Mrs. Weyburn's death had come as a shock. Lucy had grown fond of the old lady in the three days she had attended her, a job she had undertaken as a favor to Dr. Catesby when the regular nurse-companion had been called away by an illness in her own family. Lucy herself had done only intermittent nursing since she and Clifford had moved to the city.

Lucy changed out of her uniform and returned to the kitchen, where she discovered with a smile that Clifford hadn't bothered to wash the dishes after his evening meal before leaving the house. From the number of dishes, it was evident he hadn't dined alone. The remains of two salads and a scarcely touched salmon loaf stood on the counter along with a wedge of cheese and an empty soup can. Lucy swept the lettuce into the disposal and was about to do the same with the salmon, but then wrapped it in tinfoil instead and deposited it in the freezer. She herself loathed salmon, but she hated to waste good food even though Clifford refused to eat leftovers—one of the caprices Lucy had learned to live with over the years, obliging her to practice various forms of domestic deception. Clifford was an only child, and more than once Lucy had accused him of having been a very spoiled child.

She had just finished putting everything away and tidying the kitchen when she heard a sound at the front door. Removing her apron, she went to investigate, but when she switched on the light and looked out there was no one there. She opened the door and looked down to find a dog crouched almost at her feet. A black dog of indefinable breed, perhaps part shepherd, part setter. At sight of her the animal retreated, growling.

"Now where did you come from?" Lucy said, scanning the road for the dog's owner. Barberry Road was a favorite area for dog-walking—a few houses and an abundance of trees and shrubbery. She saw no one. The dog cowered a few feet away, uttering a low whining sound.

"Go home, boy. Go on. Go home now."

The dog didn't move. Lucy shut the door and switched off the light. She was fond of dogs but the sight of a black one whining in the night less than an hour after she had been in the presence of death mildly unnerved her. She wished Clifford would come home.

She had been watching television for over an hour when she heard his car pull into the garage and the door swing shut. A moment or so later, she heard water running in the lavatory off the kitchen. Clifford came out with a glass of water in his hand. He was wearing jeans and the old college sweatshirt that made him look more like an ex-basketball player than a rising academic, even at thirty-seven. "What are you doing home?" he asked.

She laughed. "Well, thanks."

He bent to kiss her. "I didn't expect to see your car in the garage. You weren't supposed to be home until Sunday night. What happened?"

"Mrs. Weyburn died tonight."

"Sudden, wasn't it?"

"Very. Her heart gave out. So where have you been?"

He looked down at the glass in his hand. "Are we out of aspirin?"

"There should be some upstairs. Headache?"

"A real piledriver."

"I asked you where you'd been."

He glanced beyond her into the kitchen. "I drove Crandall home."

"*Herbert* Crandall? What induced you to invite *him* to dinner? I thought you detested him." The two men were presently competing for an important departmental promotion.

"He wanted to talk about the seminar agenda. I didn't feel in the mood to eat alone so I invited him over."

"Is there any word yet about the appointment?"

"Not for another week, at least." He wandered into the kitchen. "You needn't have cleaned up after me. I was going to do that when I came home."

"Well, now you can sit down and relax instead. You look tired. I'll get you an aspirin."

"What did you do with the salmon?"

"Tossed it out, of course. I wouldn't *dream* of serving you leftovers. Why, are you still hungry?"

He shook his head. "Crandall seemed to like it, but I didn't eat any. Only a little salad and cheese. No appetite."

"You haven't been eating properly for days. No wonder you're having headaches." She felt sure he was more worried about the appointment than he let on. She fetched him the aspirin and then took another look outside. "He's still there."

"Who is?"

"The dog."

"We don't have a dog."

"We do now, it appears. There's been one out there ever since I came home. A black one. He rather spooked me—because of Mrs. Weyburn, I suppose."

Clifford came to look over her shoulder. "Maybe he's a stray. He'll be gone in the morning." He yawned. "Too early for bed?"

Lucy smiled engagingly. "Is it ever?"

She checked the doors and turned out the lights before following him upstairs. Presently, in bed, she whispered: "Did you miss me?"

"Frightfully."

"I missed you. It seemed funny sleeping alone."

"I know what you mean."

"I won't be lured away again. Not for a while anyway. I've more than enough volunteer work to keep me busy."

"Good," he murmured sleepily, his back to her.

"Darling, is everything okay?"

"Sure. Why not?"

"You seem a little tense tonight. Is it the appointment?"

"It's on my mind, sure."

"Crandall may have superb credentials," she reminded him, "but you did say he has a reputation for being a bit erratic."

"Prone to tipple, you mean. That won't affect the outcome. He's a first-rate teacher."

"I know, but you said the board is ultra-conservative when judging a man's personal character."

Her hand, lightly caressing his muscled shoulder, drew no response. With a faint regretful sigh, she moved away. In bed, as elsewhere, she had learned to govern her instincts by her husband's unpredictable moods. A familiar reverie lulled her to sleep—the fading but still active hope that they might still have a child.

When he came down to breakfast Lucy said, "That dog, he's still out there."

Clifford walked to the door and looked out. When he re-

turned to the kitchen he wore a petulant, somber frown.
"Have you ever seen him around here before?"

"No. He must be a stray, as you said. He looks well fed,
though." Clifford sat and proceeded to eat his breakfast in
silence. "What'll we do if he just stays here?" Lucy asked
him.

"He won't if you don't feed him." When she didn't answer, he looked at her warningly. "And for God's sake,
don't."

"No, of course I won't."

When Lucy returned from doing the marketing, the dog
was still there. As soon as she had put the groceries away
she walked back through the garage and tried to approach
the animal. Instantly he rose, tail drooping, teeth exposed
in what seemed a half-hearted snarling grimace. Lucy
stooped down, extending her hand beckoningly.

"Don't be so standoffish, boy, I'm not going to hurt
you." The dog regarded her warily, causing Lucy to wonder if he had been abused and run away from home. But
why choose this house? She was quite sure he was wearing a collar, but whether it bore any identification she
didn't quite dare investigate.

Clifford's first words on entering the house that evening
were: "I didn't expect to come home and find that beast at
the door."

Lucy ignored the note of reproof, what she called his
you've-burned-the-toast-again tone, and merely remarked
that she'd been too busy to notice whether the dog was
there or not.

"Then you didn't feed him?"

"Of course not," she laughed. "And don't scowl at me
like that. It's not my fault he's still there."

Clifford strode to the door, flung it open, and glared at
the dog curled up under the magnolia bush with a ferocity
of expression that might have daunted a far more savage
animal.

"I think he's adopted us," said Lucy.

"We'll see about that." Clifford stalked into the kitchen and came back carrying a dishpan full of boiling water. Lucy cried out in alarm. "What are you doing?"

"What's it look like? Open the door."

"Cliff, you can't. That's brutal."

Cradling the pan in one arm, he pulled the door open himself, stepped out, and flung the hot water toward the dog. Lucy was glad to see most of it fell short of its target.

"Damned cur," Clifford muttered. "That's all we need. Some stray mongrel messing up the lawn."

"Darling, don't get so upset. Maybe there'll be something in the lost-and-found ads tonight. He must have an owner."

"*Had* an owner, more likely. Who dropped the brute off here."

There were a number of lost-dog ads in the paper that night but none resembling *their* dog.

Clifford dropped the paper and said, "Very well, this is what I want you to do. Call the Animal Control Unit of the Police Department first thing in the morning. Tell them to pick that dog up before I get home tomorrow, or else I'll— I'll give him something more than a hot shower."

Lucy felt, but dared not say, that he was using the dog as a release for some deeper tension she strongly suspected arose from his concern over the impending departmental appointment. All she did say was that she thought he was overreacting. "The poor dog hasn't done anything to you, darling. The way you're carrying on, one would think he'd taken a bite out of your leg."

"Well, he could. He could be rabid. Now you be sure to call them, understand?"

"Yes, master, I understand."

Lucy started to dial the number of the Animal Control Unit the following morning, but then instead, inspired by some spirit of defiance she couldn't have explained, she opened a package of frankfurters, stepped out onto the lawn, and flung one to the dog, who didn't hesitate to snap it up and wolf it down.

Idiot, she reproved herself. That was a dumb thing to do. And then, perversely, she called out to the dog: "Now go away! Go home! You can't stay here!"

Not surprisingly, the dog responded to this equivocation by loping toward her and nuzzling the hand that reached out to stroke his head.

Clifford called from the University at three that afternoon. "Did you call them?"

"I was going to but the dog disappeared," she lied. "I would have felt like a fool if they came way out here for nothing."

That evening Clifford came storming into the house as if primed to do battle with a legion of raging mastiffs. "I thought you said he'd gone!"

Lucy smiled innocently. "Hasn't he? He must have come back."

A grim smile formed on Clifford's handsome face. "Never mind. I'll take care of this myself, once and for all."

"What are you going to do?"

"I said never mind."

He swung around and headed for his lab. Lucy waited a few moments and then followed him. Her hand flew to her throat when she saw what he was doing.

"Cliff, what's that for?"

"Your pet's dinner."

"*My* pet?"

"You've been feeding him, haven't you?"

"Don't be silly."

"Don't lie to me, Lucy. No dog is going to hang around a strange house if he isn't being fed."

She put her hand on his arm. "Darling, please be reasonable. Would it be such a bad idea to keep the dog? He'd be company for me while you're away."

"You know my answer to that."

"What are you putting in that meat?"

"A little flavoring."

She knew he used poisons in his botanical experiments. She felt a sick chill. "Cliff, you're *not* going to feed that poor animal poisoned meat. That's barbarous."

"Any better ideas?"

"I told you. Let me keep him. He needs a home."

He looked at her with smug disdain. "I suspected as much. You *have* been feeding the brute. If you can't have a child you'll at least have a dog, is that it?"

"Oh, Cliff, what a rotten thing to say."

"Don't tell me you don't think it's my fault. All that talk about seeing a doctor. You think you fooled me? Well, for your information, my love, there's nothing wrong with *me*. If we haven't had a child, you can blame yourself."

"That's ridiculous," she retorted. "I said perhaps *we* should see a doctor. I never said it was your fault."

"You didn't have to. I could tell what you were thinking."

"Then you're smarter than I am. I can never tell what *you're* thinking. Not lately. You go off into these moods when I haven't the dimmest idea what's on your mind. More and more, you've been shutting me out. I thought it was because you're worried about the appointment. Now I'm beginning to wonder."

Such an uncharacteristic show of defiance surprised him as greatly as it did her. "What's that supposed to mean?" he snapped.

"It means I'm getting a bit fed up with your selfish lack of consideration. Darling, I love you dearly, but I do get a little weary of having always to be the one to yield. Is it so wrong for me to want a child even if you don't? I had a good career back East. But did I object when you wanted to come out here? Did I say no when you practically demanded that I stay home and not work regularly? We go where you want to go, see the people you want to see. Do what you want to do. You were spoiled all your life and you expect me to go on spoiling you, catering to all your whims. There's no reason on earth why we shouldn't keep that dog."

"We can't afford to feed a dog."

"Oh, that's *funny*. We could feed five dogs on just the leftovers you're too finicky to eat."

He uttered a recriminatory laugh. "What have leftovers got to do with anything?"

Thinking of that perfectly good salmon loaf he believed she had thrown in the garbage, she could have cried out of sheer exasperation. "Nothing!" she said hotly. "Everything! But if you think I'm going to stand here while you poison a helpless, homeless animal you're very much mistaken."

With that she reached out and swept the plate of hamburger off the work table into the dustbin.

Clifford slept in his study that night and when Lucy came down in the morning to prepare breakfast, he was already gone. A note lay on the kitchen table: *Darling, please forgive me. I didn't mean to behave like an ogre.*

The note only added to the pangs of contrition to which she had awakened. Clifford's attitude about the dog was childish, of course, but no less extreme than her own outburst of frustration. What did she really have to complain about? Cliff had always been a good husband, she had a beautiful home and almost everything she could reasonably desire, and if she had been an unduly submissive wife whose fault was that but her own?

She called the Animal Control Unit as soon as she had finished breakfast. Less than an hour later the van arrived and she explained to the officer how the dog had been camped on their doorstep since the evening of the sixteenth. The animal offered no resistance as he was lifted into the van and borne away.

Shortly after noon the doorbell rang.

"Mrs. Phelps?"

"Yes."

The man produced his identification. "Detective John Gourley, Police Department. May I speak with you a moment, please?"

Curious and even a trifle alarmed, Lucy invited him into

the house. He produced a notebook and pen. "Our Animal Control Unit picked up a dog here this morning. I believe you called them?"

"I did. But why—" And then suddenly she remembered something Clifford had said. "Oh, dear. The dog—*was* he rabid? Had he bitten someone?"

The detective shook his head. "You told the officer this morning that you didn't know who owns the dog. Is that correct?"

"No, of course we didn't know the owner. We'd have called him if we had."

"Her, Mrs. Phelps. The dog's owner is a woman named Joyce Madison. Is the name familiar?"

Lucy frowned. "No. Should it be?"

"Not necessarily. I thought it might be since she works in the administration office at the University. Your husband teaches there, does he not?"

"He does, but I don't recall his ever mentioning anyone with that name. Of course, Clifford doesn't know all the clerical personnel."

"The point is, Mrs. Phelps, a neighbor of Miss Madison saw the young woman leave her house—she lives alone—on the night of the sixteenth. The dog was with her. They both walked away and apparently that was the last anyone recalls seeing either. Until the dog was picked up this morning."

Lucy failed to grasp the significance of what he was telling her. "You're saying the dog belongs to this Madison woman? It's strange, I agree, that he kept hanging around here, but neither I nor my husband are acquainted with either the woman or her dog. I mean, neither one has ever been *here* before."

"Yet the dog was here and refused to leave."

Lucy smiled. "I'm afraid that was my fault. My husband advised me not to feed him but I did. Once."

"And you're positive your husband has never mentioned knowing Miss Madison?"

"Quite positive." Suddenly she saw the direction in which the man's remarks were leading. "Oh, but see here,

I hope you're not implying that this woman *did* come here. That's absurd."

"May I ask what kind of car your husband drives, Mrs. Phelps?"

"Of course. A Ford station wagon."

"The reason I asked is that we've been told Miss Madison was occasionally visited by a man who drove a station wagon."

"That may be, but it certainly wasn't my husband."

"Well, thank you for your time, Mrs. Phelps. I'll stop by the University and have a word with your husband. I'm sure he'll be able to verify what you've told me."

Despite the absurdity of the detective's insinuations, his visit left Lucy in a state of anxiety that nibbled away at her self-assurance no matter how many times she told herself it was all a stupid misunderstanding. The mere idea of Clifford being involved with another woman was ludicrous. He was anything but the philandering type, if for no other reason than that the faintest breath of scandal would ruin his chances of advancement at the University.

Still her mind kept drifting back to the evening of Mrs. Weyburn's death. She remembered the clutter of food and dishes in the kitchen when she arrived home, yet she could recollect nothing in Clifford's manner to indicate the slightest sense of guilt or mendacity. That he might have lied about Herbert Crandall having been his dinner guest was beyond serious consideration. Nonetheless it wasn't a strong enough conviction to prevent her, late in the afternoon, from picking up the phone and calling Gwendolyn Crandall.

"I happened to find it when I was vacuuming the dining room. I thought it might be Herbert's."

"Herbert's? Oh, no. That's impossible. Herbert never uses a lighter. Only matches. Besides, Herbert hasn't been in your house since the night you had us all for cocktails, months ago."

"Oh, I thought Cliff said something about Herbert being

here on the sixteenth. For dinner. I was away on a case at the time."

"You must have misunderstood, Lucy. Certainly not on the sixteenth. That was our anniversary and he took me out to dinner."

Clifford arrived home displaying a jauntiness of manner which somehow conflicted with the look in his eyes. Lucy asked him at once about the detective's visit.

Cliff made a dismissive gesture. "Yes, he stopped by for a few minutes. Have you ever heard of anything more preposterous? Some woman vanishes and her dog is found skulking about our property. Therefore I must have known the woman."

"Did you?" she asked in hardly more than a whisper.

"No. Not really. I knew who she was."

"And that she'd disappeared?"

"There's been some talk about it. I never pay attention to campus gossip."

"You never mentioned it to me."

"No reason to."

"That detective. He said a man visited her, in a station wagon."

His gaze, dull but reproachful, focused on her for the first time. "Darling, I hope you don't think *I* ever visited her."

Lucy was the first to look away. "Cliff, you may as well know. I called Gwendolyn Crandall. She said her husband wasn't here on the sixteenth. Who *was* here that night?"

What happened then was more of a shock to Lucy than when she had walked into Mrs. Weyburn's bedroom and found the old lady dead. For now it was as if the life force, in the space of an instant, had drained out of Clifford's body as well. His shoulders sagged; his facial muscles seemed to collapse: as if suddenly blinded, he groped for the arm of a chair and crumpled into it.

"Cliff! What is it?"

He didn't look up. His voice was as empty of expression as his ashen face. "She hounded me, darling. I only spoke to her a few times and she—she developed some sort of idiotic crush on me. She kept sending me notes. She waylaid me when I left the campus. I told her to leave me alone. I told her I wasn't interested. She started to threaten me. She said she was pregnant and was going to tell the dean I was responsible. It was stupid, but I did go to her home a couple of times, just to try to reason with her. She wouldn't listen to me. That night she showed up here. I was just sitting down to dinner. I tried to be polite. I even invited her to join me. I pleaded with her and I think I finally got through to her. At least she promised to stop annoying me. She left right after dinner. God knows what happened to her after that."

Suddenly his head snapped up and he stared at her with a look of thickening horror. "My God, darling, do you think she might have—might have done something to herself?"

His confession stunned Lucy, yet his air of woeful consternation brought her to her knees beside his chair. She took his hands in hers and tried to reassure him even though her own thoughts were a muddle of uncertainty.

"The dog. Was he with her?"

"Yes. She left him out front."

"And when she went away, why didn't she take the dog with her?"

"I know. That's what's been driving me out of my mind ever since that night. She must have ordered him not to follow her. And that could only mean she must have planned— But she couldn't have. She wouldn't have. Not over some silly schoolgirl infatuation."

"But, Cliff, where did *you* go that night?"

He ran a hand roughly through his hair. "I honestly don't remember. I had to get out of the house. I went for a long drive."

"You told all this to the detective?"

"I had to. There was no point in lying to him. If he thought I was trying to hide the truth, you can imagine what he might have suspected."

"Then don't worry." She kept pressing his hands. "You

don't think this might hurt your chances for the appointment, do you? I mean if it all comes out?"

He heaved a long, despairing sigh. "The appointment. God, I've scarcely given a serious thought to that for days."

"Well, try not to worry about it. She's bound to show up. If she'd done anything to herself, they would certainly have found her by now." She searched his eyes. "I wish you'd told me about this right from the start."

He regarded her with a melancholy look. "Would you have believed me? That I was innocent? That I'd never encouraged her?"

"Do you have to ask? Darling, let's not talk about it any longer. Go and wash up. I had a bowl of soup while I was waiting for you. Your dinner will be ready when you come down."

She tried to behave as if everything was as usual as he sat down to eat, but Clifford seemed as oblivious of her presence as he was of the food she had placed before him. Gently, she encouraged him to eat. Seconds later he suddenly dropped his fork, his hand clawed at his chest, and with a look of excruciating agony he pitched forward across the table.

Only after that first paralyzing shock did she realize with intuitive certainty what she had done—and what he had done. Unable to move, she stared with dreadful comprehension at the croquettes on his plate. The croquettes she had made from the leftover salmon he had served his guest on the night of the sixteenth.

<< A Dog in the Daytime >>
by
Rex Stout

I DO SOMETIMES treat myself to a walk in the rain, though I prefer sunshine as a general rule. That rainy Wednesday, however, there was a special inducement: I wanted his raincoat to be good and wet when I delivered it. So, with it on my back and my old brown felt on my head, I left Nero Wolfe's brownstone house on West 35th Street, Borough of Manhattan, and set out for Arbor Street, which is down in Greenwich Village.

Halfway there the rain stopped and my blood had pumped me warm, so I took the coat off, folded it wet side in, hung it on my arm, and proceeded. Arbor Street, narrow and only three blocks long, had on either side an assortment of old brick houses, mostly of four stories, which were neither spick nor span. Number 29 would be about the middle of the first block.

I reached it, but I didn't enter it. There was a party going on in the middle of the block. A police car was double-parked in front of one of the houses, and a uniformed cop was on the sidewalk in an attitude of authority toward a small gathering of citizens confronting him. As I approached I heard him demanding, "Whose dog is this?"

He was referring, evidently, to an animal with a wet black coat standing behind him. I heard no one claim the dog, but I wouldn't have, anyway, because my attention was diverted. Another police car rolled up and stopped behind the first one, and a man got out, nodded to the cop without halting, and went in the entrance of Number 29.

The trouble was, I knew the man, which is an understatement. I do not begin to tremble at the sight of Sergeant Purley Stebbins of Manhattan Homicide West, but his presence and manner made it a cinch that there was a corpse in that house, and if I demanded entry on the ground that I wanted to swap raincoats with a guy who had walked off with mine, there was no question what would happen. My prompt appearance at the scene of a homicide would arouse all Purley's worst instincts, and I might not get home in time for dinner, which was going to be featured by grilled squab with a brown sauce which Fritz calls *Venitienne* and is one of his best.

Purley had disappeared inside without spotting me. The cop was a complete stranger. As I slowed down to detour past him on the narrow sidewalk, he gave me an eye and demanded, "That your dog?"

The dog was nuzzling my knee, and I stooped to give him a pat on his wet black head. Then, telling the cop he wasn't mine, I went on by. At the next corner I turned right, heading back uptown. A wind had started in from the west, but everything was still damp from the rain.

I was well on my way before I saw the dog. Stopping for a light on Ninth Avenue in the Twenties, I felt something at my knee, and there he was. My hand started for his head in reflex, but I pulled it back. I was in a fix. Apparently he had picked me for a pal, and if I just went on he would follow, and you can't chase a dog on Ninth Avenue by throwing rocks. I could have ditched him by taking a taxi the rest of the way, but that would have been pretty rude after the appreciation he had shown of my charm. He had a collar on with a tag and could be identified, and the station house was only a few blocks away, so the simplest way was to convoy him there. I moved to the curb to reconnoiter, and as I did so a cyclone sailed around the corner and took my hat with it into the middle of the avenue.

I didn't dash out into the traffic, but you should have

seen that dog. He sprang across the bow of a big truck, wiping its left front fender with his tail, braked landing to let a car by, sprang again and was under another car—or I thought he was—and then I saw him on the opposite sidewalk. He snatched the hat from under the feet of a pedestrian, turned on a dime, and started back. This time his crossing wasn't so spectacular, but he didn't dally. He came to me and stood, lifting his head and wagging his tail. I took the hat. It had skimmed a puddle of water on its trip, but I thought he would be disappointed if I didn't put it on, so I did. Naturally, that settled it. I flagged a cab, took the dog in with me, and gave the driver the address of Wolfe's house.

My idea was to take my hat hound upstairs to my room, give him some refreshment, and phone the ASPCA to send for him. But there was no sense in passing up such an opportunity for a little buzz at Wolfe, so, after leaving my hat and the raincoat on the rack in the hall, I proceeded to the office and entered.

"Where the deuce have you been?" Wolfe asked grumpily. "We were going over some lists at 6 o'clock, and it's a quarter to 7." He was in his oversized chair behind his desk with a book, and his eyes hadn't left the page to spare me a glance.

I answered him. "Returning that fool raincoat. Only, I didn't deliver it, because—"

"What's that?" he snapped. He was glaring at my companion.

"A dog."

"I see it is. I'm in no temper for buffoonery. Get it out of here."

"Yes, sir, right way. I can keep him in my room most of the time, but of course he'll have to come downstairs and through the hall when I take him out. He's a hat hound. There is a sort of problem. His name is Nero, which as you know means 'black,' and of course I'll have to change it. Ebony would do, or Jet, or Inky, or—"

"Bah. Flummery!"

"No, sir. I get pretty darned lonesome around here, especially during the four hours a day you're up in the plant rooms. You have your orchids, and Fritz has his turtle, and Theodore has his parakeets up in the potting room, so why shouldn't I have a dog? I admit I'll have to change his name, though he is registered as Champion Nero Charcoal of Bantyscoot."

It was a fizzle. I had expected to induce a major outburst, even possibly something as frantic as Wolfe leaving his chair to evict the beast himself, and there he was gazing at Nero with an expression I had never seen him aim at any human, including me.

"It's not a hound," he said. "It's a Labrador retriever."

That didn't faze me, from a bird who reads as many books as Wolfe does. "Yes, sir," I agreed. "I only said hound because it would be natural for a private detective to have a hound."

"Labradors," he said, "have a wider skull than any other dog, for brain room. A dog I had when I was a boy, in Montenegro, a small brown mongrel, had a rather narrow skull, but I did not regard it as a defect. I do not remember that I considered that dog to have a defect. Today I suppose I would be more critical.... When you smuggled that creature in here did you take into account the disruption it would cause in this household?"

It had backfired on me. I had learned something new about the big, fat genius: he would enjoy having a dog around, provided he could blame it on me and so be free to beef when he felt like it. As for me, when I retire to the country I'll have a dog, and maybe two, but not in town.

I snapped into reverse. "I guess I didn't," I confessed. "Okay, I'll get rid of him. After all, it's your house."

"I do not want to feel responsible," he said stiffly, "for your privation. I would almost rather put up with the dog than with your reproaches."

"Forget it." I waved a hand. "I'll try to—myself."

"Another thing," he persisted. "I refuse to interfere with any commitment you have made."

"I have made no commitment."

"Then where did you get it?"

"Well, I'll tell you."

I went and sat at my desk and did so. Nero—the four-legged one—came and lay at my feet with his nose just not touching the toe of my shoe. I reported the whole event, with as much detail as if I had been reporting a major case, and when I had finished Wolfe was, of course, quite aware that my presentation of Nero had been a gag. Ordinarily, he would have made his opinion of my performance clear, but this time he skipped it, and it was easy to see why. The idea of having a dog that he could blame on me had got in and stuck. When I came to the end there was a moment's silence; then he said:

"Jet would be an acceptable name for that dog."

"Yeah." I swiveled and reached for the phone. "I'll call the ASPCA to come for him."

"No." He was emphatic.

"Why not?"

"Because there is a better alternative. Call someone you know in the Police Department, anyone, give him the number on the dog's tag, and ask him to find out who the owner is. Then you can inform the owner directly."

He was playing for time. It could happen that the owner was dead or in jail or didn't want the dog back, and, if so, Wolfe could take the position that I had committed myself by bringing the dog home in a taxi and that it would be dishonorable to renege. However, I didn't want to argue, so I phoned a precinct sergeant I knew. He took Nero's number and said he would call me back. Then Fritz entered to announce dinner.

The squabs with that sauce were absolutely edible, as they always are, but other phenomena in the next couple of hours were not so pleasing. The table talk in the dining room was mostly one-sided and mostly about dogs. Wolfe kept it on a high level, no maudlin sentiment. He maintained that the Basenji was the oldest breed on earth, having originated in Central Africa around 5,000 B.C., whereas there was no trace of the Afghan hound earlier than around 4,000 B.C. To me, all it proved was that he had read a book.

Nero ate in the kitchen with Fritz and made a hit. Wolfe had told Fritz to call him Jet. When Fritz brought in the salad he announced that Jet had wonderful manners and was very smart.

"Nevertheless," Wolfe asked, "wouldn't you think him an insufferable nuisance as a member of the household?"

On the contrary, Fritz declared, Jet would be most welcome.

After dinner, feeling that the newly formed Canine Canonizing League needed slowing down, I first took Nero out for a brief tour and then escorted him up the two flights to my room and left him there. I had to admit he was well-behaved. If I had wanted to take on a dog in town it could have been this one. In my room I told him to lie down, and he did, and when I went to the door to leave, his eyes, which were the color of caramel, made it plain that he would love to come along, but he didn't get up.

Down in the office Wolfe and I got at the lists. They were special offerings from orchid growers and collectors from all over the world, and it was quite a job to check the thousands of items and pick the few that Wolfe might want to give a try. I sat at his desk, across from him, with trays of cards from our files, and we were in the middle of it, around ten thirty, when the doorbell rang. I went to the hall and flipped a light switch and saw out on the stoop, through the one-way glass panel in the door, a familiar figure—Inspector Cramer of Homicide.

I went to the door, opened it six inches, and asked politely, "Now what?"

"I want to see Wolfe."

"It's pretty late. What about?"

"About a dog."

It is understood that no visitor, and especially no officer of the law, is to be conducted to the office until Wolfe has been consulted, but this seemed to rate an exception. I considered the matter for about two seconds, and then swung the door open and invited cordially:

"Step right in."

• • •

"Properly speaking," Cramer declared, as one who wanted above all to be perfectly fair and square, "it's Goodwin I want information from."

He was in the red-leather chair at the end of Wolfe's desk, just about filling it. His big, round face was no redder than usual, his gray eyes no colder, his voice no gruffer. Merely normal.

Wolfe came at me: "Then why did you bring him in here without even asking?"

Cramer interfered for me: "I asked for you. Of course, you're in it. I want to know where the dog fits in. Where is it, Goodwin?"

I inquired innocently, "Dog?"

His lips tightened. "All right; I'll spell it. You phoned the precinct and gave them a tag number and wanted to know who owns the dog. When the sergeant learned that the owner was a man named Philip Kampf, who was murdered this afternoon in a house at Twenty-nine Arbor Street, he notified Homicide. The officer who had been on post in front of that house had told us that the dog went off with a man who had said it wasn't his dog. After we learned of your inquiry about the owner, the officer was shown a picture of you, and said it was you who enticed the dog. He's outside in my car. Do you want to bring him in?"

"No, thanks. I didn't entice."

"The dog followed you."

I gestured modestly. "Girls follow me, dogs follow me, sometimes even your own dicks follow me. I can't help—"

"Skip the comedy. The dog belonged to a murder victim, and you removed it from the scene of the murder. Where is the dog?"

Wolfe butted in. "You persist," he objected, "in imputing an action to Mr. Goodwin without warrant. He did not 'remove' the dog. I advise you to shift your ground if you expect us to listen."

His tone was firm but not hostile. I cocked an eye at

him. He was probably being indulgent because he had learned that Jet's owner was dead.

"I've got another ground," Cramer asserted. "A man who lives in that house, named Richard Meegan, and who was in it at the time Kampf was murdered, has stated that he came here to see you this morning and asked you to do a job for him. He says you refused the job. That's what he says."

Cramer jutted his chin. "Now. A man at the scene of a murder admits he consulted you this morning. Goodwin shows up at the scene half an hour after the murder was committed, and he entices—okay, the dog goes away with him. The dog that belonged to the victim and had gone to that house with him. How does that look?" He pulled his chin in. "You know the last thing I want in a homicide is to find you or Goodwin anywhere within ten miles of it, because I know from experience what to expect. But when you're there, there you are, and I want to know how and why, and what, and I intend to. Where's the dog?"

Wolfe sighed and shook his head. "In this instance," he said, almost genially, "you're wasting your time. As for Mr. Meegan, he phoned this morning to make an appointment and came at eleven. Our conversation was brief. He wanted a man shadowed, but divulged no name or any other specific detail, because in his first breath he mentioned his wife—he was overwrought—and I gathered that his difficulty was marital. As you know, I don't touch that kind of work, and I stopped him. My bluntness enraged him and he dashed out. On his way he took his hat from the rack in the hall, and he took Mr. Goodwin's raincoat instead of his own. Now, Archie, proceed."

Cramer's eyes swiveled to me, and I obeyed: "I didn't find out about the switch in coats until the middle of the afternoon. His was the same color as mine, but mine's newer. When he phoned for an appointment this morning he gave me his name and address. I wanted to phone him to tell him to bring my coat back, but he wasn't listed, and Information said she didn't have him, so I decided to go get it. I walked, wearing Meegan's coat. There was a cop and a crowd and a PD car in front of Twenty-nine Arbor Street, and as I approached another PD car came, and Purley Stebbins got out and went in, so I decided to skip it, not wanting to go through the torture. There was a dog present, and it nuzzled me, and I patted it. Then I headed for home."

"Did you call the dog or signal it?"

"No. I was at Twenty-eighth Street and Ninth Avenue before I knew it was tailing me. I did not entice or remove. If I did—if there's some kind of a dodge about the dog—please tell me why I phoned the precinct to get the name of his owner."

"I don't know. With Wolfe and you I never know. Where is it?"

I blurted it out before Wolfe could stop me: "Upstairs in my room."

"Bring it down here."

I was up and going, but Wolfe called me sharply: "Archie!"

I turned. "Yes, sir."

"There's no frantic urgency." He said to Cramer, "The animal seems intelligent, but I doubt if it's up to answering questions. I don't want it capering around my office."

"Neither do I."

"Then why bring it down?"

"I'm taking it downtown. We want to try something with it."

Wolfe pursed his lips. "I doubt if that's feasible. Mr. Goodwin has assumed an obligation and will have to honor it. The creature has no master, and so presumably no home. It will have to be tolerated here until Mr. Goodwin gets satisfactory assurance of its future welfare. Archie?"

If we had been alone I would have made my position clear, but with Cramer there I was stuck. "Absolutely," I agreed, sitting down again.

"You see," Wolfe told Cramer. "I'm afraid we can't permit the dog's removal."

"Nuts. I'm taking it."

"Indeed? What writ have you? Replevin? Warrant for arrest as a material witness?"

Cramer opened his mouth, and shut it again. He put his elbows on the chair arms, interlaced his fingers, and leaned forward. "Look. You and Meegan check, either because you're telling it straight, or because you've framed it. But I'm taking the dog. Kampf, the man who was killed, lived on Perry Street, a few blocks away from Arbor Street. He arrived at Twenty-nine Arbor Street, with the dog on a leash, about 5:20 this afternoon.

"The janitor of the house, named Olsen, lives in the basement, and he was sitting at his front window when he saw Kampf arrive with the dog and turn in at the entrance. About ten minutes later he saw the dog come out, with no leash, and right after the dog a man came out. The man was Victor Talento, a lawyer, the tenant of the ground-floor apartment. Talento's story is that he left his apartment to go to an appointment, saw the dog in the hall, thought it was a stray, and chased it out. Olsen says Talento walked off and the dog stayed there on the sidewalk."

Cramer unlaced his fingers and sat back. "About twenty minutes later, around ten minutes to 6:00, Olsen heard someone yelling his name, and went to the rear and up one flight to the ground-floor hall. Two men were there—a live one and a dead one. The live one was Ross Chaffee, a painter, the tenant of the top-floor studio—that's the fourth floor. The dead one was the man that had arrived with the dog. He had been strangled with the dog's leash, and the body was at the bottom of the stairs. Chaffee says he found it when he came down to go to an appointment, and that's all he knows. He stayed there while Olsen went downstairs to phone. A squad car arrived at 5:58. Sergeant Stebbins arrived at 6:10. Goodwin arrived at 6:10. Excellent timing."

Wolfe merely grunted.

Cramer continued: "You can have it all. The dog's leash was in the pocket of Kampf's raincoat, which was on him. The laboratory says it was used to strangle him. The routine is still in process. I'll answer questions within reason. The four tenants of the house were all there when Kampf arrived: Victor Talento, the lawyer, on the ground floor; Richard Meegan, whose job you say you wouldn't take, second floor; Jerome Aland, a nightclub comedian, third floor; and Ross Chaffee, the painter, with the top-floor studio. Aland says he was sound asleep until we banged on his door just before taking him down to look at the corpse. Meegan says he heard nothing and knows nothing."

Cramer sat forward again. "Okay, what happened? Kampf went there to see one of those four men, and had his dog with him. It's possible he took the leash off in the lower hall and left the dog there, but I doubt it. At least, it's just as possible that he took the dog along to the door of one of the apartments, and the dog was wet and the tenant wouldn't let it enter, so Kampf left it outside. Another possibility is that the dog was actually present when Kampf was killed, but we'll know more about that after we see and handle the dog. What we're going to do is take the dog in that house and see which door it goes to. We're going to do that now. There's a man out in my car who knows dogs." Cramer stood up.

Wolfe shook his head. "You must be hard put. You say Mr. Kampf lived on Perry Street. With a family?"

"No. Bachelor. Some kind of a writer. He didn't have to make a living; he had means."

"Then the beast is orphaned. He's in your room, Archie?"

"Yes, sir." I got up and started for the door.

Wolfe halted me. "One moment. Go in your room, lock the door, and stay there till I notify you. Go!"

I went. It was either that or quit my job on the spot, and I resign only when we haven't got company. Also, assuming that there was a valid reason for refusing to surrender the dog to the cops, Wolfe was justified. Cramer, needing no warrant to enter the house because he was already in, wouldn't hesitate to mount to my room to do his own fetching, and stopping him physically would have raised some delicate points. Whereas breaking through a locked door would be another matter.

I didn't lock it, because it hadn't been locked for years and I didn't remember where the key was, so I left it open and stood on the sill to listen. If I heard Cramer coming I would shut the door and brace it with my foot. Nero, or Jet, depending on where you stand, came over to me, but I ordered him back, and he went without a murmur. From below came voices, not cordial, but not raised enough for me to get words. Before long there was the sound of Cramer's heavy steps leaving the office and tramping along the hall, then the slam of the front door.

I called down: "All clear?"

"No!" It was a bellow. "Wait till I bolt it!" And after a moment: "All right!"

I shut my door and descended the stairs. Wolfe was back in his chair behind his desk, sitting straight. As I entered he snapped at me: "A pretty mess! You sneak a dog in here to badger me, and what now?"

I crossed to my desk, sat, and spoke calmly: "We're 'way beyond that. You will never admit you bollixed it up yourself, so forget it. When you ask me what now, that's easy. I could say I'll take the dog down and deliver him at Homicide, but we're beyond that too. Not only have you learned that he is orphaned, as you put it, and therefore adopting him will probably be simple, but also you have taken a stand with Cramer, and of course you won't back up. If we sit tight, with the door bolted, I suppose I can take the dog out back for his outings, but what if the law shows up tomorrow with a writ?"

He leaned back and shut his eyes. I looked up at the wall clock: two minutes past 11. I looked at my wrist watch: also two minutes past 11. They both said six minutes past when Wolfe opened his eyes.

"From Mr. Cramer's information," he said, "I doubt if that case holds any formidable difficulties."

I had no comment.

"If it were speedily solved," he went on, "your commitment to the dog could be honored, at leisure. Clearly, the simplest way to settle this matter is to find out who killed Mr. Kampf. It may not be much of a job; if it proves otherwise, we can reconsider. An immediate exploration is the thing, and luckily we have a pretext for it. You can go to Arbor Street to get your raincoat, taking Mr. Meegan's with you, and proceed as the occasion offers. The best course would be to bring him here; but, as you know, I rely wholly on your discretion and enterprise in such a juncture."

"Thank you very much," I said bitterly. "You mean now?"

"Yes."

"They may still have Meegan downtown."

"I doubt if they'll keep him overnight. In the morning they'll probably have him again."

"I'll be hanged." I arose. "No client, no fee—no nothing except a dog with a wide skull for brain room." I went to the hall rack for my hat and Meegan's coat, and beat it.

The rain had ended and the wind was down. Dismissing the taxi at the end of Arbor Street, I walked to Number 29, with the raincoat hung over my arm. There was light behind the curtains of the windows on the ground floor, but none anywhere above, and none in the basement. Entering the vestibule, I inspected the labels in the slots between the mailboxes and the buttons. From the bottom up they read: Talento, Meegan, Aland, and Chaffee. I pushed Meegan's button, put my hand on the doorknob, and waited. No click. I twisted the knob and it wouldn't turn. Another long push on the button, and a longer wait. Nothing doing.

I considered pushing the button of Victor Talento, the lawyer who lived on the ground floor, where light was showing; instead, I voted to wait a while for Meegan, with whom I had an in. I moved to the sidewalk, propped myself against a fire hydrant, and waited.

I hadn't been there long enough to shift position more than a couple of times when the light disappeared on the ground floor of Number 29. A little later the vestibule door opened and a man came out. He turned toward me, gave me a glance as he passed, and kept going.

Thinking it unlikely that any occupant of that house was being extended the freedom of the city that night, I cast my eyes around, and, sure enough, when the subject had gone some thirty paces a figure emerged from an areaway across the street and started strolling after him. I shook my head in disapproval. I would have waited until the guy was ten paces farther. Saul Panzer would have made it ten more than that, but Saul is the best tailer alive.

As I stood deploring that faulty performance, an idea hit me. They might keep Meegan downtown another two hours, or all night, or he might even be up in his bed asleep. This was at least a chance to take a stab at something. I shoved off, in the direction taken by the subject, who was now a block away. Stepping along, I gained on him. A little beyond the corner I came abreast of the city employee, who was keeping to the other side of the street, but I wasn't interested in him. It seemed to me that the subject was upping the stroke a little, so I did, too, and as he reached the next intersection I was beside him.

I said: "Victor Talento?"

"No comment," he said, and kept going. So did I.

"Thanks for the compliment," I said, "but I'm not a reporter. My name's Archie Goodwin, and I work for Nero Wolfe. If you'll stop a second I'll show you my credentials."

"I'm not at all interested in your credentials."

"Okay. If you just came out for a breath of air you won't be interested in this, either. Otherwise, you may be. Please don't scream or look around, but you've got a homicide dick on your tail. He's across the street, ninety feet back."

"Yes," he conceded, without changing pace, "that's interesting. Is this your good deed for the day?"

"No. I'm out dowsing for Mr. Wolfe. He's investigating a murder just for practice, and I'm looking for a seam. I thought if I gave you a break you might feel like reciprocating. If you're just out for a walk, forget it, and sorry I interrupted. If you're headed for something you'd like to keep private, maybe you could use some expert advice. In this part of town at this time of night there are only two approved methods for shaking a tail, and I'd be glad to oblige."

He looked it over for half a block, with me keeping step, and then spoke: "You mentioned credentials."

"Right. We might as well stop under that light. The dick will, of course, keep his distance."

We stopped. I got out my wallet and let him have a look at my licenses, detective and driver's. He didn't skimp it, being a lawyer.

"Of course," he said, "I was aware that I might be followed."

"Sure."

"I intended to take precautions. But I suppose it's not always as simple as it seems. I have had no experience at this kind of maneuver. Who hired Wolfe to investigate?"

"I don't know. He says he needs practice."

He stood sizing me up by the street light. He was an inch shorter than I am, and some older, with his weight starting to collect around the middle. He was dark-skinned, with eyes to match.

"I have an appointment," he said.

I waited.

He went on: "A woman phoned me and I arranged to meet her. My wire could have been tapped."

"I doubt it. They're not that fast."

"I suppose not. The woman had nothing to do with the murder, and neither had I, but of course anything I do and anyone I see is suspect. I have no right to expose her to possible embarrassment. I can't be sure of shaking that man off."

I grinned at him. "And me, too."

"You mean you would follow me?"

"Certainly, for practice. And I'd like to see how you handle it."

He wasn't returning my grin. "I see you've earned your reputation, Goodwin. You'd be wasting your time, because this woman has no connection with this business, but I should have known better than to make this appointment. It's only three blocks from here. You might be willing to go and tell her I'm not coming. Yes?"

"Sure, if it's only three blocks. If you'll return the favor by calling on Nero Wolfe for a little talk. That's what I meant by reciprocating."

He considered it. "Not tonight. I'm all in."

"Tomorrow morning at eleven?"

"Yes, I can make it then."

"Okay." I gave him the address. "Now brief me."

He took a respectable roll of bills from his pocket and peeled off a twenty. "Since you're acting as my agent, you have a right to a fee."

I grinned again. "That's a neat idea, you being a lawyer, but I'm not acting as your agent. I'm doing you a favor on request and expecting one in return. Where's the appointment?"

He put the roll back. "Have it your way. The woman's name is Jewel Jones, and she's at the southeast corner of Christopher and Grove streets, or will be." He looked at his wrist. "We were to meet there at midnight. She's medium height, slender, dark hair and eyes, very good-looking. Tell her why I'm not coming, and say she'll hear from me tomorrow."

"Right. You'd better take a walk in the other direction to keep the dick occupied, and don't look back."

He wanted to shake hands to show his appreciation, but that would have been just as bad as taking the twenty, since before another midnight Wolfe might be tagging him for murder, so I pretended not to notice. He headed east and I, west, moving right along.

I had to make sure that the dick didn't switch subjects, but I let that wait until I got to Christopher Street. Reaching it, I turned the corner, went twenty feet to a stoop, slid behind it with only my head out, and counted a slow hundred. There were passers-by—a couple and a guy in a hurry—but no dick. I went on a block to Grove Street, passed the intersection, saw no loitering female, continued for a distance, then turned and backtracked. I was on the fifth lap, and it was eight minutes past 12, when a taxi stopped at the corner, a woman got out, and the taxi rolled off.

I approached. The light could have been better, but she seemed to meet the specifications. I stopped and asked, "Jones?" She drew herself up. I said, "From Victor."

She tilted her head back to see my face. "Who are you?" She seemed a little out of breath.

"Victor sent me with a message, but naturally I have to be sure it reaches the right party. I've anteed half of your name and half of his, so it's your turn."

"Who are you?"

I shook my head. "You go first, or no message from Victor."

"Where is he?"

"No. I'll count ten and go. One, two, three, four—"

"My name is Jewel Jones. His is Victor Talento."

"That's the girl. I'll tell you." I did so, giving a complete version of my encounter with Talento, and including, of course, my name and status. By the time I finished she had developed a healthy frown.

She moved and put a hand on my arm. "Come and put me in a taxi."

I stayed planted. "I'll be glad to, and it will be on me. We're going to Nero Wolfe's place."

"We?" She removed the hand. "You're crazy."

"One will get you ten I'm not. Look at it. You and Talento made an appointment at a street corner, so you had some good reason for not wanting to be seen together to-night. It must have been something fairly urgent. I admit the urgency didn't have to be connected with the murder of Philip Kampf, but it could be. I don't want to be arbitrary. I can take you to a homicide sergeant named Stebbins and you can discuss it with him, or I'll take you to Mr. Wolfe."

She had well-oiled gears. For a second, as I spoke, her eyes flashed like daggers, but then they went soft and appealing. She took my arm again, this time with both hands.

"I'll discuss it with you," she said, in a voice she could have used to defrost her refrigerator. "I wouldn't mind that. We'll go somewhere."

I said come on, and we moved, with her hand hooked cozily on my arm. We hadn't gone far, toward Seventh Avenue, when a taxi came along and I flagged it and we got in. I told the driver, "Nine-sixteen West Thirty-fifth," and he started.

"What's that?" Miss Jones demanded.

I told her, Nero Wolfe's house. The poor girl didn't know what to do. If she called me a rat, that wouldn't help her any. If she kicked and screamed, I would merely tell the hackie, Headquarters. Her best bet was to try to thaw me, and if she had had time for a real campaign—say four or five hours—she might conceivably have made some progress, because she had a knack for it.

There just wasn't time enough. The taxi rolled to the curb and I had a bill ready for the driver. I got out, gave her a hand, and escorted her up the seven steps of the stoop. I pushed the button, and in a moment the stoop light shone on us, the chain bolt was released, and the door opened. I motioned her in and followed. Fritz was there.

"Mr. Wolfe up?" I asked.

"In the office." He was giving Miss Jones a look, the look he gives any strange female who enters that house. There is always in his mind the possibility, however remote, that she will bewitch Wolfe into a mania for a mate. I asked him to conduct her to the front room, put my hat and the raincoat on the rack, and went on down the hall to the office.

Wolfe was at his desk, reading; and curled up in the middle of the room, on the best rug in the house, was the dog. The dog greeted me by lifting his head and tapping the rug with his tail. Wolfe greeted me by grunting.

"I brought company," I told him. "Before I introduce her I should—"

"Her? The tenants of that house are all men! I might have known you'd dig up a woman!"

"I can chase her if you don't want her. This is how I got

her." I proceeded, not dragging it out, but including all the essentials. I ended up, "I could have grilled her myself, but it would have been risky. Just in a six-minute taxi ride she had me feeling—uh, brotherly. Do you want her or not?"

"Confound it." His eyes went to his book and stayed there long enough to finish a paragraph. "Very well, bring her."

I crossed to the connecting door to the front room, opened it, and requested, "Please come in, Miss Jones." She came, and as she passed through gave me a wistful smile that might have gone straight to my heart if there hadn't been a diversion. As she entered, the dog suddenly sprang to his feet and made for her, with sounds of unmistakable pleasure. He stopped in front of her, wagging his tail so fast it was only a blur.

"Indeed," Wolfe said. "How do you do, Miss Jones? I am Nero Wolfe. What's the dog's name?"

I claim she was good. The presence of the dog was a complete surprise to her. But without the slightest sign of fluster she put out a hand to give it a gentle pat, and then went to the red-leather chair and sat down.

"That's a funny question right off," she said. "Asking me your dog's name."

"Pfui." Wolfe was disgusted. "I don't know what position you were going to take, but from what Mr. Goodwin tells me I would guess you were going to say that the purpose of your appointment with Mr. Talento was a personal matter that had nothing to do with Mr. Kampf or his death, and that you knew Mr. Kampf either slightly or not at all. Now the dog has made that untenable. Obviously, he knows you well, and he belonged to Mr. Kampf. So you knew Mr. Kampf well. If you try to deny that, you'll have Mr. Goodwin and other trained men digging all around you, your past and your present, and that will be extremely disagreeable, no matter how innocent you may be of murder or any other wrongdoing. You won't like that. What's the dog's name?"

She looked at me and I looked back. In good light I

would have qualified Talento's specification of "very good-looking." Not that she was unsightly, but she caught the eye more by what she looked than how she looked. It wasn't just something she turned on as needed; it was there even now, when she must have been pretty busy deciding how to handle the situation.

It took her only a few seconds to decide. "His name is Bootsy," she said. The dog, at her feet, lifted his head and wagged his tail.

"Good heavens," Wolfe muttered. "No other name?"

"Not that I know of."

"Your name is Jewel Jones?"

"Yes. I sing in a night club, but I'm not working right now." She made a little gesture, very appealing, but it was Wolfe who had to resist it, not me. "Believe me, Mr. Wolfe, I don't know anything about that murder. If I knew anything that could help I'd be perfectly willing to tell you, because I'm sure you're the kind of man who understands, and you wouldn't want to hurt me if you didn't have to."

"I try to understand," Wolfe said dryly. "You knew Mr. Kampf intimately?"

"Yes, I guess so." She smiled, as one understander to another. "For a while I did. Not lately—not for the past two months."

"You met the dog at his apartment on Perry Street?"

"That's right. For nearly a year I was there quite often."

"You and Mr. Kampf quarreled?"

"Oh, no, we didn't quarrel. I just didn't see him any more. I had other— I was very busy."

"When did you see him last?"

"About two weeks ago, at the club. He came to the club once or twice and spoke to me there."

"But no quarrel?"

"No, there was nothing to quarrel about."

"You have no idea who killed him, or why?"

"I certainly haven't."

Wolfe leaned back. "Do you know Mr. Talento intimately?"

"No, not if you mean—of course, we're friends. I used to live there. I had the second-floor apartment."

"At Twenty-nine Arbor Street?"

"Yes."

"For how long? When?"

"For nearly a year. I left there—let's see—about three months ago. I have a little apartment on East Forty-ninth Street."

"Then you know the others, too? Mr. Meegan and Mr. Chaffee and Mr. Aland?"

"I know Ross Chaffee and Jerry Aland, but no Meegan. Who's he?"

"A tenant at Twenty-nine Arbor Street. Second floor."

She nodded. "Well, sure, that's the floor I had." She smiled. "I hope they fixed that rickety table for him. That was one reason I left. I hate furnished apartments, don't you?"

Wolfe made a face. "In principle, yes. I take it you now have your own furniture. Supplied by Mr. Kampf?"

She laughed—more of a chuckle—and her eyes danced. "I see you didn't know Phil Kampf."

"Not supplied by him, then?"

"A great big no."

"By Mr. Chaffee? Or Mr. Aland?"

"No and no." She went very earnest: "Look, Mr. Wolfe. A friend of mine was mighty nice about that furniture, and we'll just leave it. Mr. Goodwin told me what you're interested in is the murder, and I'm sure you wouldn't want to drag in a lot of stuff just to hurt me and a friend of mine, so we'll forget about the furniture."

Wolfe didn't press it. He took a hop. "Your appointment on a street corner with Mr. Talento. What was that about?"

She nodded. "I've been wondering about that—I mean, what I would say when you asked me—because I'd hate to have you think I'm a sap, and I guess it sounds like it. I phoned him when I heard on the radio that Phil was killed, there on Arbor Street. I knew Vic still lived there, and I simply wanted to ask him about it."

"You had him on the phone."

"He didn't seem to want to talk about it on the phone."

"But why a street corner?"

This time it was more like a laugh. "Now, Mr. Wolfe, *you're* not a sap. You asked about the furniture, didn't you? Well, a girl with furniture shouldn't be seen with Vic Talento."

"What is he like?"

She fluttered a hand. "Oh, he wants to get close."

Wolfe kept at her until after one o'clock, and I could report it all, but it wouldn't get you any farther than it did him. He couldn't trip her or back her into a corner. She hadn't been to Arbor Street for two months. She hadn't seen Chaffee or Aland or Talento for weeks, and of course not Meegan, since she had never heard of him before. She couldn't even try to guess who had killed Kampf.

The only thing remotely to be regarded as a return on Wolfe's investment of a full hour was her statement that, as far as she knew, there was no one who had both an attachment and a claim to Bootsy. If there were heirs, she had no idea who they were. When she left the chair to go, the dog got up, too. She patted him, and he went with us to the door. I took her to Tenth Avenue and put her in a taxi, and returned.

"Where's Bootsy?" I inquired.

"No," Wolfe said emphatically.

"Okay." I surrendered. "Where's Jet?"

"Down in Fritz's room. He'll sleep there. You don't like him."

"That's not true, but you can have it. It means you can't blame him on me. Anyhow, that will no longer be an issue after Homicide comes in the morning with a document and takes him away."

"They won't come."

"I offer twenty to one. Before noon."

He nodded. "That was, roughly, my own estimate of the probability, so while you were out I phoned Mr. Cramer. I suggested an arrangement, and I suppose he inferred that if he declined the arrangement the dog might be beyond his jurisdiction before tomorrow. I didn't say so, but I may have given him that impression."

"Yeah. You should be more careful."

"So the arrangement has been made. You are to be at Twenty-nine Arbor Street, with the dog, at nine o'clock in the morning. You are to be present throughout the fatuous performance the police have in mind, and keep the dog in view. The dog is to leave the premises with you, before noon, and you are to bring him back here. The police are to make no further effort to constrain the dog for twenty-four hours. While in that house you may find an opportunity to flush something or someone more contributive than Jewel Jones. . . ."

It was a fine, bright morning. I didn't take Meegan's raincoat, because I didn't need any pretext, and I doubted if the program would offer a likely occasion for the exchange.

The law was there in front waiting for me. The plain-clothesman who knew dogs was a stocky, middle-aged guy who wore rimless glasses. Before he touched the dog he asked me its name, and I told him Bootsy.

"A heck of a name," he observed. "Also, that's some leash you've got."

"I agree. His was on the corpse, so I suppose it's in the lab." I handed him my end of the heavy cord. "If he bites you it's not on me."

"He won't bite me. Would you, Bootsy?" He squatted before the dog and started to get acquainted.

Sergeant Purley Stebbins growled a foot from my ear, "He should have bit you when you kidnapped him."

I turned. Purley was half an inch taller than I am and two inches broader. "You've got it twisted," I told him. "It's women that bite me. I've often wondered what would bite you."

We continued exchanging pleasantries, while the dog man, whose name was Larkin, made friends with Bootsy. It wasn't long before he announced that he was ready to proceed. He was frowning. "In a way," he said, "it would be better to keep him on leash after I go in, because

Kampf probably did. . . . Or did he? How much do we actually know?"

"To swear to," Purley told him, "very little. But putting it all together from what we've collected, this is how it looks: When Kampf and the dog entered, it was raining and the dog was wet. Kampf removed the leash, either in the ground-floor hall or one of the halls above. He had the leash in his hand when he went to the door of one of the apartments. The tenant of the apartment let him in and they talked. The tenant socked him, probably from behind without warning, and used the leash to finish him. The murderer stuffed the leash in the pocket of the raincoat.

"It took nerve and muscle to carry the body out and down the stairs to the lower hall, but he had to get it out of his place and away from his door, and any of those four could have done it in a pinch. Of course, the dog was already outside, out on the sidewalk. While Kampf was in one of the apartments getting killed, Talento had come into the lower hall and seen the dog and chased it out."

"Then," Larkin objected, "Talento's clean."

"No. Nobody's clean. If it was Talento, after he killed Kampf he went out to the hall and put the dog in the vestibule, went back in his apartment and carried the body out and dumped it at the foot of the stairs, and then left the house, chasing the dog on out to the sidewalk. You're the dog expert. Is there anything wrong with that?"

"Not necessarily. It depends on the dog and how close he was to Kampf. There wasn't any blood."

"Then that's how I'm buying it. If you want it filled in you can spend the rest of the day with the reports of the other experts and the statements made by the tenants."

"Some other day. That'll do for now. You're going in first?"

"Yeah. Come on, Goodwin." Purley started for the door, but I objected: "I'm staying with the dog."

Purley looked disgusted. "Then keep behind Larkin."

I changed my mind. From behind Larkin the view wouldn't be good. So I went into the vestibule with Purley. The inner door was opened by a homicide colleague, and we crossed to the far side of the small lobby. The colleague closed the door. In a minute he pulled it open again, and Larkin and the dog entered.

Two steps in, Larkin stopped, and so did the dog. No one spoke. The leash hung limp. Bootsy looked around at Larkin. Larkin bent over and untied the cord from the collar, and held it up to show Bootsy he was free. Bootsy came over to me and stood, his head up, wagging his tail.

"Nuts," Purley said, disgusted.

"You know what I really expected," Larkin said. "I never thought he'd show us where Kampf went when they entered yesterday, but I did think he'd go to the foot of the stairs, where the body was found, and I thought he might go on to where the body came from—Talento's door, or upstairs. Take him by the collar, Goodwin, and ease him over to the foot of the stairs."

I obliged. He came without urging, but gave no sign that the spot held any special interest for him. We all stood and watched him. He opened his mouth wide to yawn.

"Fine," Purley rumbled. "Just fine. You might as well go on with it."

Larkin came and fastened the leash to the collar, led Bootsy across the lobby to a door, and knocked. In a moment the door opened, and there was Victor Talento, in a fancy rainbow dressing gown.

"Hello, Bootsy," he said, and reached down to pat.

Purley snapped, "I told you not to speak!"

Talento straightened up. "So you did." He was apologetic. "I'm sorry; I forgot. Do you want to try it again?"

"No. That's all."

Talento backed in and closed the door.

"You must realize," Larkin told Purley, "that a Labrador can't be expected to go for a man's throat. They're not that kind of dog. The most you could expect would be an attitude, or possibly a growl."

"You can have 'em," Purley said. "Is it worth going on?"

"By all means. You'd better go first."

Purley started up the stairs, and I followed him. The upper hall was narrow and not very light, with a door at the rear end and another toward the front. We backed up against the wall opposite the front door to leave enough space for Larkin and Bootsy. They came, Bootsy tagging, and Larkin knocked. Ten seconds passed before footsteps sounded, and then the door was opened by the specimen who had dashed out of Wolfe's place the day before and taken my coat with him. He was in his shirt sleeves and he hadn't combed his blond hair.

"This is Sergeant Larkin, Mr. Meegan," Purley said. "Take a look at the dog. Have you ever seen it before? Pat it."

Meegan snorted. "Pat it yourself."

"Have you ever seen it before?"

"No."

"Okay; thanks. Come on, Larkin."

As we started up the next flight the door slammed behind us, good and loud. Purley asked over his shoulder, "Well?"

"He didn't like him," Larkin replied from the rear, "but there are lots of people lots of dogs don't like."

The third-floor hall was a duplicate of the one below. Again Purley and I posted ourselves opposite the door, and Larkin came with Bootsy and knocked. Nothing happened. He knocked again, louder, and pretty soon the door opened to a two-inch crack and a squeaky voice came through:

"You've got the dog."

"Right here," Larkin told him.

"Are you there, Sergeant?"

"Right here," Purley answered.

"I told you that dog didn't like me. Once at a party at Phil Kampf's—I told you. I didn't mean to hurt it, but it thought I did. What are you trying to do—frame me?"

"Open the door. The dog's on a leash."

"I won't! I told you I wouldn't!"

Purley moved. His arm, out stiff, went over Larkin's shoulder, and his palm met the door and shoved hard. The door hesitated an instant, then swung open. Standing there, holding to its edge, was a skinny individual in red-and-green striped pajamas. The dog let out a low growl and backed up a little.

"We're making the rounds, Mr. Aland," Purley said, "and we couldn't leave you out. Now you can go back to sleep. As for trying to frame you—" He stopped because the door shut.

"You didn't tell me," Larkin complained, "that Aland had already fixed it for a reaction."

"No, I thought I'd wait and see. One to go." He headed for the stairs.

The top-floor hall had had someone's personal attention. It was no bigger than the others, but it had a nice, clean tan-colored runner, and the walls were painted the same shade and sported a few small pictures. Purley went to the rear door instead of the front, and we made room for Larkin and Bootsy. When Larkin knocked, footsteps responded at once, and the door swung wide open. This was the painter, Ross Chaffee, and he was dressed for it, in an old brown smock. He was by far the handsomest of the tenants—tall, erect, with features he must have enjoyed looking at in the mirror.

I had ample time to enjoy them, too, as he stood smiling at us, completely at ease, obeying Purley's prior instructions not to speak. Bootsy was also at ease. When it became quite clear that no blood was going to be shed, Purley asked, "You know the dog, don't you, Mr. Chaffee?"

"Certainly. He's a beautiful animal."

"Pat him."

"With pleasure." He bent gracefully. "Bootsy, do you know your master's gone?" He scratched behind the black ears. "Gone forever, Bootsy, and that's too bad." He straightened. "Anything else? I'm working. I like morning light."

"That's all, thanks." Purley turned to go, and I let Larkin and Bootsy by before following. On the way down the three flights no one had any remarks. As we hit the lower hall Victor Talento's door opened, and he emerged.

"The District Attorney's office telephoned," he said. "Are you through with me? They want me down there."

"We're through," Purley said. "We can run you down."

Talento said that would be fine and he would be ready in a minute. Purley told Larkin to give me Bootsy, and he handed me the leash.

I departed. Outside, the morning was still fine. The presence of two PD cars in front of the scene of a murder had attracted a small gathering, and Bootsy and I were objects of interest as we appeared and started off. We both ignored the stares. We moseyed along, in no hurry, stopping now and then to give Bootsy a chance to inspect something if he felt inclined. At the fourth or fifth stop, more than a block away, I saw the quartet leaving Number 29. Stebbins and Talento took one car, Larkin and the colleague the other, and they rolled off.

I shortened up on Bootsy a little, walked him west until an empty taxi appeared, stopped it, and got in. I took a five-dollar bill from my wallet and handed it to the hackie.

"Thanks," he said with feeling. "For what—down payment on the cab?"

"You'll earn it, brother," I assured him. "Is there somewhere within a block or so of Arbor and Court where you can park for anywhere from thirty minutes to three hours?"

"Not three hours for a finif."

"Of course not." I took out another five and gave it to him. "I doubt if it will be that long."

"There's a parking lot not too far. On the street without a passenger I'll be hailed."

"You'll have a passenger: the dog. I prefer the street. Let's see what we can find."

There are darned few legal parking spaces in all Manhattan at that time of day, and we cruised around several corners before we found one, on Court Street two blocks from Arbor. He backed into it and I got out, leaving the windows down three inches. I told him I'd be back when he saw me, and headed south, turning right at the second corner.

There was no police car at 29 Arbor, and no gathering. That was satisfactory. Entering the vestibule, I pushed the button under "Meegan" and put my hand on the knob. No click. Pushing twice more and still getting no response, I tried Aland's button, and that worked. After a short wait the click came, and I entered, mounted two flights, and knocked with authority on Aland's door.

The squeaky voice came through: "Who is it?"

"Goodwin. I was just here with the others. I haven't got the dog."

The door swung slowly to a crack, and then wider. Jerome Aland was still in his gaudy pajamas. "What do you want now?" he asked. "I need some sleep!"

I didn't apologize. "I was going to ask you some questions when I was here before," I told him, "but the dog complicated it. It won't take long." Since he wasn't polite enough to move aside, I had to brush him, skinny as he was, as I went in.

He slid past me, and I followed him across the room to chairs. They were the kind of chairs that made Jewel Jones hate furnished apartments. He sat on the edge of one and demanded, "All right; what is it?"

It was a little tricky. Since he was assuming I was one of the homicide personnel, it wouldn't do for me to know either too much or too little. It would be risky to mention Jewel Jones, because the cops might not have got around to her at all.

"I'm checking some points," I told him. "How long has Richard Meegan occupied the apartment below you?"

"I've told you that a dozen times."

"Not me. I said I'm checking. How long?"

"Nine days. He took it a week ago Tuesday."

"Who was the previous tenant? Just before him."

"There wasn't any. It was empty."

"Empty since you've been here?"

"No, I've told you, a girl had it, but she moved out about three months ago. Her name is Jewel Jones, and she's a fine artist, and she got me my job at the night club where I work now." His mouth worked. "I know what you're doing. You're trying to make it nasty, and you're trying to catch me getting my facts twisted. Bringing that dog here to growl at me— Can I help it if I don't like dogs?"

He ran his fingers, both hands, through his hair. When the hair was messed good he gestured like the night-club comedian he was. "Die like a dog," he said. "That's what Phil did—died like a dog."

"You said," I ventured, "that you and he were good friends."

His head jerked up. "I did not!"

"Maybe not in those words.... Why? Weren't you?"

"We were not. I haven't got any good friends."

"You just said that the girl who used to live here got you a job. That sounds like a good friend. Or did she owe you something?"

"Of course not. Why do you keep bringing her up?"

"I didn't bring her up—you did. I only asked who was the former tenant in the apartment below you. Why? Would you rather keep her out of it?"

"I don't have to keep her out. She's not in it."

"Perhaps not. Did she know Philip Kampf?"

"I guess so. Sure, she did."

"How well did she know him?"

He shook his head. "If Phil was alive you could ask him, and he might tell you. Me, I don't know."

I smiled at him. "All that does, Mr. Aland, is make me curious. Somebody in this house murdered Kampf. So we ask you questions, and when we come to one you shy at, naturally we wonder why. If you don't like talking about Kampf and that girl, think what it could mean. For instance, it could mean that the girl was yours, and Kampf took her away from you, and that was why you killed him when he came here yesterday."

"She wasn't my girl!"

"Uh-huh. Or it could mean that although she wasn't yours, you were under a deep obligation to her, and Kampf had given her a dirty deal; or he was threatening her with something, and she wanted him disposed of, and you obliged. Or of course it could be merely that Kampf had something on you."

"You're in the wrong racket," he sneered. "You ought to be writing TV scripts."

I stuck with him only a few more minutes, having got all I could hope for under the circumstances. Since I was letting him assume that I was a city employee, I couldn't very well try to pry him loose for a trip to Wolfe's place. Also, I had two more calls to make, and there was no telling when I might be interrupted by a phone call or a courier to one of them from downtown. So I left.

I went down a flight to Meegan's door, and knocked, and waited. Just as I was raising a fist to make it louder and better, there were footsteps inside, and the door opened. Meegan was still in his shirt sleeves and still uncombed.

"Well?" he demanded.

"Back again," I said, firmly but not offensively. "With a few questions. If you don't mind?"

"I certainly do mind."

"Naturally. Mr. Talento has been called down to the District Attorney's office. This might possibly save you another trip there."

He side-stepped and I went in. The room was the same size and shape as Aland's, above, and the furniture, though different, was no more desirable. The table against a wall was lopsided, probably the one that Jewel Jones hoped they had fixed for him. I took a chair beside it, and he took another and sat frowning at me.

"Haven't I seen you before?" he wanted to know.

"Sure, we were here with the dog."

"I mean before that. Wasn't it you in Nero Wolfe's office yesterday?"

"That's right."

"How come?"

I raised my brows. "Haven't you got the lines crossed, Mr. Meegan? I'm here to ask questions, not to answer them. I was in Wolfe's office on business. I often am. Now—"

"He's a fat, arrogant half-wit!"

"You may be right. He's certainly arrogant. Now I'm here on business." I got out my notebook and pencil. "You moved into this place nine days ago. Please tell me exactly how you came to take this apartment."

He glared. "I've told it at least three times."

"I know. This is the way it's done. I'm not trying to catch you in some little discrepancy, but you could have omitted something important. Just assume I haven't heard it before. Go ahead."

He groaned and dropped his head on his hands. Normally, he might not have been a bad-looking guy, with his blond hair and gray eyes and long, bony face; but now, having spent most of the night with Homicide and the D.A., he looked it, especially his eyes, which were red and puffy.

He lifted his head. "I'm a commercial photographer. In Pittsburgh. Two years ago I married a girl named Margaret Ryan. Seven months later she left me. I didn't know whether she went alone or with somebody. She just left. She left Pittsburgh, too—at least I couldn't find her there—and her family never saw her or heard from her. About five months later, about a year ago, a client of mine came back from a trip to New York and said he saw her in a theater here with a man. He spoke to her, but she claimed he was mistaken. He was sure it was her. I came to New York and spent a week looking around, but didn't find her. I didn't go to the police, because I didn't want to. You want a better reason, but that's mine."

"I'll skip that." I was writing in the notebook. "Go ahead."

"Two weeks ago I went to look at a show of pictures at the Fillmore Gallery in Pittsburgh. There was a painting there—an oil—a big one. It was called *Three Young Mares at Pasture*, and it was an interior, a room, with three women in it. One of them was on the couch, and two of them were on a rug on the floor. They were eating apples. The one on the couch was my wife. I was sure of it the minute I saw her, and after I stood and studied it I was surer than ever. There was absolutely no doubt of it."

"We're not challenging that," I assured him. "What did you do?"

"The artist's signature was Ross Chaffee. I went to the gallery office and asked about him. They thought he lived in New York. I had some work on hand I had to finish, and then I came to New York.

"I had no trouble finding Ross Chaffee; he was in the phone book. I went to see him at his studio, here in this house. First, I told him I was interested in that figure in his painting, that I thought she would be just right to model for some photographs I wanted to do, but he said his opinion of photography as an art medium was such that he wouldn't care to supply models for it. He was bowing me out, so I told him how it was. I told him the whole thing. Then he was different. He sympathized with me and said he would be glad to help me if he could, but he had painted that picture more than a year ago, and he used so many different models for his pictures that it was impossible to remember which was which."

Meegan stopped, and I looked up from the notebook. He said aggressively, "I'm repeating that that sounded phony to me."

"Go right ahead. You're telling it."

"I say it was phony. A photographer might use hundreds of models in a year, and he might forget, but not a painter. Not a picture like that. I got a little tactless with him, and then I apologized. He said he might be able to refresh his memory and asked me to phone him the next day. Instead of phoning him I went back the next day to see him, but he said he simply couldn't remember and doubted if he ever could. I didn't get tactless again. Coming in the house, I had noticed a sign that there was a furnished apartment to let, and when I left Chaffee I found the janitor and rented it, and moved in. I knew my wife had modeled for that picture, and I knew I could find her. I wanted to be as close as I could to Chaffee and the people who came to see him."

I wanted something, too. I wanted to say that he must have had a photograph of his wife along and I would like to see it, but of course I didn't dare; it was a cinch that he had already either given it to the cops, or refused to, or claimed he didn't have one. So I merely asked, "What progress did you make?"

"Not much. I tried to get friendly with Chaffee, but I didn't get very far. I met the other two tenants, Talento and Aland, but that didn't get me anywhere. Finally I decided I would have to get some expert help, and that was why I went to see Nero Wolfe. You were there, so you know how that came out—that big blob!"

I nodded. "He has dropsy of the ego. What did you want him to do?"

"I've told you."

"Tell it again."

"I was going to have him tap Chaffee's phone."

"That's illegal," I said severely.

"All right; I didn't do it."

I flipped a page of the notebook. "Go back a little. During that week, besides the tenants here, how many of Chaffee's friends and acquaintances did you meet?"

"Just two, as I've told you. A young woman, a model, in his studio one day—I don't remember her name—and a man Chaffee said buys his pictures. His name was Braunstein."

"You're leaving out Philip Kampf."

Meegan leaned forward and put a fist on the table. "Yes, and I'm going on leaving him out. I never saw him or heard of him."

"What would you say if I said you were seen with him?"

"I'd say you were a dirty liar!" The red eyes looked redder. "As if I wasn't already having enough trouble, now you set on me about the murder of a man I never heard of! You bring a dog here and tell me to pat it!"

I nodded. "That's your hard luck, Mr. Meegan. You're not the first man who's had a murder for company without inviting it." I closed the notebook and put it in my pocket.

I rose. "Stick around, please. You may be wanted downtown again."

I would have liked to get more details of his progress, or lack of progress, with Ross Chaffee, and his contacts with the other two tenants, but it seemed more important to have some words with Chaffee before I got interrupted. As I mounted the two flights to the top floor my wrist watch said twenty-eight minutes past ten.

"I know there's no use complaining," Ross Chaffee said, "about these interruptions to my work. Under the circumstances." He was being very gracious about it.

The top floor was quite different from the others. I don't know what his living quarters in front were like, but the studio, in the rear, was big and high and anything but crummy. There were pieces of sculpture around, big and little, and canvases of all sizes were stacked and propped against racks. The walls were covered with drapes, solid gray, with nothing on them. Each of two easels, one much larger than the other, held a canvas that had been worked on. There were several plain chairs and two upholstered ones, and an oversized divan.

I had been steered to one of the upholstered numbers, and Chaffee, still in his smock, had moved a plain one to sit facing me.

"Only don't prolong it unnecessarily," he requested.

I said I wouldn't. "There are a couple of points," I told him, "that we wonder about a little. Of course, it could be merely a coincidence that Richard Meegan came to town looking for his wife, and came to see you, and rented an apartment here, just nine days before Kampf was murdered, but a coincidence like that will have to stand some going over. Frankly, Mr. Chaffee, there are those—and I happen to be one of them—who find it hard to believe that you couldn't remember who modeled for an important figure in a picture you painted."

Chaffee was smiling. "Then you must think I'm lying."

"I didn't say so."

"But you do, of course." He shrugged. "To what end? What deep design am I cherishing?"

"I wouldn't know. You say you wanted to help Meegan find his wife."

"No, not that I wanted to. I was willing to. He is a horrible nuisance."

"It should be worth some effort to get rid of him. Have you made any?"

"I have explained what I did. In a statement, and signed it. I have nothing to add. I tried to refresh my memory. One of your colleagues suggested that I might have gone to Pittsburgh to look at the picture. I suppose he was being funny."

A flicker of annoyance in his fine dark eyes warned me that I was supposed to have read his statement.

I gave him an earnest eye. "Look, Mr. Chaffee. This thing is bad for all concerned. It will get worse instead of better until we find out who killed Kampf. You men in this house must know things about one another, and maybe some things connected with Kampf, that you're not telling. I don't expect a man like you to pass out dirt just for the fun of it, but any dirt that's connected with this murder is going to come out, and if you are keeping any to yourself you're a bigger fool than you look."

"Quite a speech." He was smiling again.

"Thanks. Now you make one."

"I'm not as eloquent as you are." He shook his head. "No, I don't believe I can help you any. I can't say I'm a total stranger to dirt—that would be smug; but what you're after—no. You have my opinion of Kampf, whom I knew quite well; he was in some respects admirable, but he had his full share of faults. I would say approximately the same of Talento. I have known Aland only casually. I know no more of Meegan than you do. I haven't the slightest notion why any of them might have wanted to kill Philip Kampf. If you expect—"

A phone rang. Chaffee crossed to a table at the end of the divan and answered it. He told it "Yes" a couple of times, and then: "But one of your men is here now. . . . I don't know his name; I didn't ask him. . . . He may be; I don't know. . . . Very well. The District Attorney's office. . . . Yes, I can leave in a few minutes."

He hung up and turned to me. I spoke first, on my feet: "So they want you at the D.A.'s office. Don't tell them I said so, but they'd rather keep a murder in the file till the cows come home than have the squad crack it. If they want my name they know where to ask."

I marched to the door, opened it, and was gone.

I was relieved to find the cab still waiting with its passenger perched on the seat looking out on the scenery. Jet seemed pleased to see me, and during the drive to 35th Street he sat with his rump braced against me for a buttress. The meter said only six dollars and something, but I didn't request any change from the ten I had given the driver. If Wolfe wanted to put me to work on a murder merely because he was infatuated with a dog, let it cost him something.

I noticed that when we entered the office Jet went over to Wolfe, behind his desk, without any sign of bashfulness or uncertainty, proving that the evening before, during my absence, Wolfe had made approaches; probably had fed him something, possibly had even patted him. Remarks occurred to me, but I saved them. I might be called on before long to spend some valuable time demonstrating that I had not been guilty of impersonating an officer, and that it wasn't my fault if the murder suspects mistook me for one.

Wolfe inquired, "Well?"

I reported. The situation called for a full and detailed account, and I supplied it, while Wolfe leaned back with his eyes closed. When I came to the end he asked no questions. Instead, he opened his eyes, and began, "Call the—"

I cut him off: "Wait a minute. After a hard morning's work I claim the satisfaction of suggesting it myself. I thought of it long ago. I'll call the gallery in Pittsburgh where Caffee's picture was shown."

"Indeed. It's a shot at random."

"I know it is but I'm calling anyway."

I reached for the phone on my desk and got through to the Fillmore Gallery in no time, but it took a quarter of an hour, with relays to three different people, to get what I was after. I hung up and turned to Wolfe:

"The show ended a week ago yesterday. And I won't have to go to Pittsburgh. The picture was lent by Mr. Herman Braunstein of New York, who owns it. It was shipped back to him by express four days ago. They wouldn't give me Braunstein's address."

"The phone book."

I had it and was flipping the pages. "Here we are. Business on Broad Street, residence on Park Avenue. There's only one Herman."

"Get him."

"I don't think so. It might take all day. Why don't I go to the residence without phoning? The picture's probably there, and if I can't get in you can fire me. I'm thinking of resigning anyhow."

He had his doubts, since it was my idea, but he bought it. After considering the problem a little, I went to the cabinet beneath the bookshelves, got out the Veblex camera, with accessories, and slung the strap of the case over my shoulder. Before going I dialed Talento's number, to tell him not to bother to keep his appointment, but there was no answer. Either he was still engaged at the D.A.'s office or he was on his way to 35th Street, and if he came during my absence that was all right, since Jet was there to protect Wolfe.

A taxi took me to the end of a sidewalk canopy in front of one of the palace hives on Park Avenue in the Seventies, and I undertook to walk past the doorman without giving him a glance, but he stopped me. I said professionally, "Braunstein, taking pictures, I'm late," and kept going, and got away with it. I crossed the luxurious lobby to the elevator, which luckily was there with the door open, said, "Braunstein, please," and the operator shut the door and pulled the lever. We stopped at the twelfth floor, and I stepped out. There was a door to the right and another to the left. I turned right without asking, on a fifty-fifty chance, listening for a possible correction from the elevator man, who was standing by with his door open.

It was one of the simplest chores I have ever performed. In answer to my ring, the door was opened by a middle-aged female husky, in uniform with apron, and when I told her I had come to take a picture she let me in, asked me to wait, and disappeared. In a couple of minutes a tall and dignified dame with white hair came through an arch and asked what I wanted. I apologized for disturbing her and said I would deeply appreciate it if she would let me take a picture of a painting which had recently been shown at a Pittsburgh gallery, on loan by Mr. Braunstein. It was called *Three Young Mares at Pasture*. A Pittsburgh client of mine had admired it, and had intended to go back and photograph it for his collection, but the picture was gone before he had got around to it.

She wanted some information, such as my name and address and the name of my Pittsburgh client, which I supplied gladly without a script, and then she led me through the arch into a room not quite as big as Madison Square Garden. It would have been a pleasure, and also instructive, to do a little glomming at the rugs and furniture and especially the dozen or more pictures on the walls, but that would have to wait.

She went across to a picture near the far end, said, "That's it," and lowered herself onto a chair.

It was a nice picture. I had half expected the mares to be without clothes, but they were fully dressed. Remarking that I didn't wonder that my client wanted a photograph of it, I got busy with my equipment, including flash bulbs. She sat and watched. I took four shots from slightly different angles, acting and looking professional, I hoped. Then I thanked her warmly on behalf of my client, promised to send her some prints, and left.

That was all there was to it.

Out on the sidewalk again, I walked west to Madison, turned downtown, and found a drug store. I went into the phone booth, and dialed a number.

Wolfe's voice came: "Yes? Whom do you want?"

I've told him a hundred times that's no way to answer the phone, but he's too pigheaded.

I spoke: "I want you. I've seen the picture, and it glows with color and life; the blood seems to pulsate under the warm skin. The shadows are transparent, with a harmonious blending—"

"Shut up! Yes or no?"

"Yes. You have met Mrs. Meegan. Would you like to meet her again?"

"I would. Get her."

I didn't have to look in the phone book for her address, having already done so.

I left the drug store and flagged a taxi. . . .

There was no doorman problem at the number on East Forty-ninth Street. It was an old brick house that had been painted a bright yellow and modernized, but getting in was a little complicated. Pressing the button marked *Jewel Jones* in the vestibule was easy enough, but then it got more difficult.

A voice crackled from the grille: "Yes?"

"Miss Jones?"

"Yes. Who is it?"

"Archie Goodwin. I want to see you."

"What do you want?"

"Let me in and I'll tell you."

"No. What is it?"

"It's very personal. If you don't want to hear it from me I'll go and bring Richard Meegan, and maybe you'll tell him."

I heard the startled exclamation. After a pause: "Why do you say that? I told you I don't know any Meegan."

"You're 'way behind. I just saw a picture called *Three Young Mares at Pasture*. Let me in."

I turned and put my hand on the knob. There was a click, and I pushed the door and entered. I crossed the little lobby to the self-service elevator, pushed the button marked 5, and ascended. When it stopped, I opened the foyer and emerged into a tiny foyer. A door was standing open, and on the sill was Miss Jones in a giddy négligée. She started to say something, but I rudely ignored it.

"Listen," I said, "there's no sense in prolonging this. Last night I gave you your pick between Mr. Wolfe and Sergeant Stebbins; now it's either Mr. Wolfe or Meegan. I should think you'd prefer Mr. Wolfe, because he's the kind of man who understands; you said so yourself. I'll wait here while you change, but don't try phoning anybody, because you won't know where you are until you've talked with Mr. Wolfe—and also because their wires are probably tapped."

She stepped to me and put a hand on my arm. "Archie, where did you see the picture?"

"I'll tell you on the way down. Let's go."

She gave the arm a gentle tug. "You don't have to wait out here. Come in and sit down."

I patted her fingers, not wishing to be boorish. "Sorry," I told her, "but I'm afraid of young mares. One kicked me once."

She turned and disappeared into the apartment, leaving the door open.

"Don't call me Mrs. Meegan!" Jewel Jones cried.

Wolfe was in as bad a humor as she was. True, she had been hopelessly cornered, with no weapons within reach, but he had been compelled to tell Fritz to postpone lunch until further notice.

"I was only," he said crustily, "stressing the fact that your identity is not a matter for discussion. Legally, you are Mrs. Richard Meegan. That understood, I'll call you anything you say. Miss Jones?"

"Yes." She was on the red-leather chair, but not in it. Perched on its edge, she looked as if she were set to spring up and scoot any second.

"Very well," Wolfe regarded her. "You realize, madam, that everything you say will be received skeptically. You are a competent liar. Your offhand denial of acquaintance with Mr. Meegan last night was better than competent.

Now. When did Mr. Chaffee tell you that your husband
was in town looking for you?"

"I didn't say Mr. Chaffee told me."

"Someone did. Who and when?"

She was hanging on. "How do you know someone
did?"

He waggled a finger at her. "I beg you, Miss Jones, to
realize the pickle you're in. It is not credible that Mr.
Chaffee couldn't remember the name of the model for that
figure in his picture. The police don't believe it, and they
haven't the advantage of knowing, as I do, that it was you
and that you lived in that house for a year, and that you
still see Mr. Chaffee occasionally. When your husband
came and asked Mr. Chaffee for the name of the model,
and Mr. Chaffee pleaded a faulty memory, and your husband rented an apartment there and made it plain that he
intended to persevere, it is preposterous to suppose that
Mr. Chaffee didn't tell you. I don't envy you your tussles
with the police after they learn about you."

"They don't have to learn about me, do they?"

"Pfui. I'm surprised they haven't got to you already,
though it's been only eighteen hours. They soon will, even
if not through me. I know this is no frolic for you, here
with me, but they will almost make it seem so."

She was thinking. Her brow was wrinkled and her eyes
stared straight at Wolfe. "Do you know," she asked, "what
I think would be the best thing? I don't know why I didn't
think of it before. You're a detective, you're an expert at
helping people in trouble, and I'm certainly in trouble. I'll
pay you to help me. I could pay you a little now."

"Not now or ever, Miss Jones." Wolfe was blunt.
"When did Mr. Chaffee tell you that your husband was
here looking for you?"

"You won't even listen to me," she complained.

"Talk sense and I will. When?"

She edged back on the chair an inch. "You don't know
my husband. He was jealous about me even before we
married, and then he was worse. It got so bad I couldn't
stand it, and that was why I left him. I knew if I stayed in

Pittsburgh he would find me and kill me, so I came to New York. A friend of mine had come here—I mean just a friend. I got a job at a modeling agency and made enough to live on, and I met a lot of people. Ross Chaffee was one of them, and he wanted to use me in a picture and I let him. Of course, he paid me, but that wasn't so important, because soon after that I met Phil Kampf, and he got me a tryout at a night club and I made it. About then I had a scare, though. A man from Pittsburgh saw me at a theater and spoke to me, but I told him he was wrong, that I had never been in Pittsburgh."

"That was a year ago," Wolfe muttered.

"Yes. I was a little leery about the night club, appearing in public like that, but months went by and nothing happened. And then all of a sudden Ross Chaffee phoned me that my husband had come and asked about the picture. I begged him not to tell him who it was, and he promised he wouldn't. You see, you don't know my husband. I knew he was trying to find me so he could kill me."

"You've said that twice. Has he ever killed anybody?"

"I didn't say anybody—I said me. I seem to have an effect on men." She gestured for understanding. "They just go for me. And Dick—well, I know him, that's all. I left him a year and a half ago, and he's still looking for me, and that's what he's like. When Ross told me he was here, I was scared stiff. I quit working at the club because he might happen to go there and see me, and I hardly left my apartment till last night."

Wolfe nodded. "To meet Mr. Talento. What for?"

"I told you."

"Yes, but then you were merely Miss Jones. Now you are also Mrs. Meegan. What for?"

"That doesn't change it any. I had heard on the radio about Phil being killed and I wanted to know about it. I rang Ross Chaffee and I rang Jerry Aland, but neither of them answered; so I rang Vic Talento. He wouldn't tell me anything on the phone, but he said he would meet me."

"Did Mr. Aland and Mr. Talento know you had sat for that picture?"

"Sure they did."

"And that Mr. Meegan had seen it and recognized you, and was here looking for you?"

"Yes, they knew all about it. Ross had to tell them, because he thought Dick might ask them if they knew who had modeled for the picture, and he had to warn them not to tell. They said they wouldn't, and they didn't. They're all good friends of mine."

She stopped to open her black leather bag, took out a purse, and fingered its contents. She raised her eyes to Wolfe. "I can pay you forty dollars now, to start. I'm not just in trouble; I'm in danger of my life, really I am. I don't see how you can refuse— You're not listening!"

Apparently he wasn't. With his lips pursed, he was watching the tip of his forefinger make little circles on his desk blotter. Her reproach didn't stop him, but after a moment he moved his eyes to me and said abruptly, "Get Mr. Chaffee."

"No!" she cried. "I don't want him to know—"

"Nonsense," he snapped at her. "Everybody will have to know everything, so why drag it out? . . . Get him, Archie. I'll speak to him."

I dialed Chaffee's number. I doubted if he would be back from his session with the D.A., but he was. I pitched my voice low so he wouldn't recognize it, and merely told him that Nero Wolfe wished to speak to him. Wolfe took it at his desk.

"Mr. Chaffee? This is Nero Wolfe. I've assumed an interest in the murder of Philip Kampf and have just done some investigating. . . . Just one moment, please; don't ring off. Sitting here in my office is Mrs. Richard Meegan, alias Miss Jewel Jones. . . . Please let me finish. I shall, of course, have to detain her and communicate with the police, since they will want her as a material witness in a murder case, but before I do that I would like to discuss the matter with you and the others who live in that house. Will you undertake to bring them here as soon as possible? . . . No, I'll say nothing further on the phone. I want you here, all of you. If Mr. Meegan is balky, you might as well tell him his wife is here—"

She was across to him in a leap that any young mare might have envied, grabbing for the phone and shrieking at it, "Don't tell him, Ross! Don't bring him! Don't—"

My own leap and dash around the end of the desk was fairly good, too. I yanked her back with enough enthusiasm so that I landed in the red-leather chair with her on my lap, and since she was by no means through, I wrapped my arms around her, pinning her arms to her sides, whereupon she started kicking my shins with her heels. She kept on kicking until Wolfe had finished with Chaffee. When he hung up she suddenly went limp against me.

Wolfe scowled at us. "An affecting sight," he snorted.

There were various aspects of the situation. One was lunch. For Wolfe it was unthinkable to have company in the house at mealtime, without feeding him or her, but he certainly wasn't going to sit at table with a female who had just pounced on him and clawed at him. The solution was simple: She and I were served in the dining room and Wolfe ate in the kitchen with Fritz. We were served, but she didn't eat much. She kept listening and looking toward the hall, though I assured her that care would be taken to see that her husband didn't kill her on these premises.

A second aspect was the reaction of three of the Arbor Street tenants to their discovery of my identity. I handled that myself. When the doorbell rang and I admitted them, at a quarter past two, I told them I would be glad to discuss my split personality with any or all of them later, if they still wanted to, but they would have to file it until Wolfe was through. Victor Talento had another beef that he wouldn't file—that I had double-crossed him on the message he had asked me to take to Jewel Jones. He wanted to get nasty about it and demanded a private talk with Wolfe, but I also told him to go climb a rope.

I also had to handle the third aspect, which had two angles. There was Miss Jones's theory that her husband would kill her on sight, which might or might not be well-founded; and there was the fact that one of them had killed Kampf and might go to extremes if pushed. On that I took three precautions: I showed them the Carley .38 I had put in my pocket and told them it was loaded; I insisted on patting them from shoulders to ankles; and I kept Miss Jones in the dining room until I had them seated in the office, on a row of chairs facing Wolfe's desk. When he was in his chair behind his desk I went across the hall for her and brought her in.

Meegan jumped up and started for us. I stiff-armed him, and made it good. His wife got behind me. Talento and Aland left their chairs, presumably to help protect her. Meegan was shouting, and so were they. I detoured with her around back of them and got her to a chair at the end of my desk, and when I sat down I was in an ideal spot to trip anyone headed for her. Talento and Aland had pulled Meegan down onto a chair between them and he sat staring at her.

"With that hubbub over," Wolfe said, "I want to be sure I have the names right." His eyes went from left to right. "Talento, Meegan, Aland, Chaffee. Is that correct?"

I told him yes.

"Then I'll proceed." He glanced up at the wall clock. "Twenty hours ago Philip Kampf was killed in the house where you gentlemen live. The circumstances indicate that one of you killed him. But I won't rehash the multifarious details which you have already discussed at length with the police; you are familiar with them. I have not been hired to work on this case; the only client I have is a dog, and he came to my office by chance. However—"

The doorbell rang. I asked myself if I had put the chain bolt on, and decided I had. Through the open door to the hall I saw Fritz passing to answer it. Wolfe started to go on, but was annoyed by the sound of voices, and stopped. He shut his eyes and compressed his lips, while the audience sat and looked at him.

Then Fritz appeared in the doorway and announced: "Inspector Cramer, sir."

Wolfe's eyes opened. "What does he want?"

"I told him you were engaged. He says he knows you are—that the four men were followed to your house and he was notified. He says he expected you to be trying some trick with the dog, and he knows that's what you are doing, and he intends to come in and see what it is. Sergeant Stebbins is with him."

Wolfe grunted. "Archie, tell— No. You'd better stay where you are. Fritz, tell him he may see and hear what I'm doing, provided he gives me thirty minutes without interruptions or demands. If he agrees to that, bring them in."

"Wait!" Ross Chaffee was on his feet. "You said you would discuss it with us before you communicated with the police."

"I haven't communicated with them. They're here."

"You told them to come!"

"No, I would have preferred to deal with you men first, and then call them, but here they are, and they might as well join us. Bring them, Fritz, on that condition."

"Yes, sir."

Fritz went. Chaffee thought he had something more to say, decided he hadn't, and sat down. Talento said something to him, and he shook his head. Jerry Aland, much more presentable now that he was combed and dressed, kept his eyes fastened on Wolfe. For Meegan, apparently, there was no one in the room but him and his wife.

Cramer and Stebbins marched in, halted three paces from the door, and took a survey.

"Be seated," Wolfe invited them. "Luckily, Mr. Cramer, your usual chair is unoccupied."

"Where's the dog?" Cramer demanded.

"In the kitchen. It's understood that you will be merely a spectator for thirty minutes?"

"That's what I said."

"Then sit down. But you should have one piece of information. You know the gentlemen, of course, but not the lady. Her current name is Miss Jewel Jones. Her legal name is Mrs. Richard Meegan."

"Meegan?" Cramer stared. "The one in the picture Chaffee painted?"

"That's right. Please be seated."

"Where did you get her?"

"That can wait. No interruptions and no demands. Confound it, sit down!"

Cramer went and lowered himself onto the red-leather chair. Purley Stebbins got one of the yellow ones and planted it behind Chaffee and Aland.

Wolfe regarded the quartet. "I was about to say, gentlemen, that it was something the dog did that pointed to the murderer for me. But before—"

"What did it do?" Cramer cut in.

"You know all about it," Wolfe told him coldly. "Mr. Goodwin related the events to you exactly as they happened. If you interrupt again, by heaven, you can take them all down to headquarters—not including the dog— and stew it out yourself!"

He went back to the four: "But before I come to the dog, another thing or two. I offer no comment on your guile with Mr. Meegan. You were all friends of Miss Jones's, and you refused to disclose her to a husband whom she had abandoned and professed to fear. I will even concede that there was a flavor of gallantry in your conduct. But when Mr. Kampf was murdered and the police swarmed in, it was idiotic to try to keep her out of it. They were sure to get to her. I got to her first, only because of Mr. Goodwin's admirable enterprise and characteristic luck."

He shook his head at them. "It was also idiotic of you to assume that Mr. Goodwin was a police officer, and admit him and answer his questions, merely because he had been present during the abortive experiment with the dog. You should have asked to see his credentials. None of you had any idea who he was. Even Mr. Meegan, who had seen him in this office in the morning, was bamboozled. I mention this to anticipate any possible official complaint that Mr. Goodwin impersonated an officer. You know he didn't. He merely took advantage of your unwarranted assumption."

He shifted in his chair. "Another thing: Yesterday morning Mr. Meegan called here by appointment to ask me to do a job for him. With his first words I gathered that it was something about his wife. I don't take that kind of work, and I was blunt with him. He was offended. He rushed out in a temper, grabbing a hat and raincoat from the rack in the hall, and he took Mr. Goodwin's coat instead of his own. Late in the afternoon Mr. Goodwin went to Arbor Street with the coat that had been left in error, to exchange it. He saw that in front of Number 29 there were collected two police cars, a policeman on duty, some people, and a dog. He decided to postpone his errand and went on by, after a brief halt during which he patted the dog. He walked home, and had gone nearly two miles when he discovered that the dog was following him. He brought the dog in a cab the rest of the way, to his house and this room."

He flattened a palm on his desk. "Now. Why did the dog follow Mr. Goodwin through the turmoil of the city? Mr. Cramer's notion that the dog was enticed is poppycock. Mr. Goodwin is willing to believe, as many men are, that he is irresistible both to dogs and to women, and doubtless his vanity impeded his intellect, or he would have reached the same conclusion I did. The dog didn't follow him; it followed the coat. You ask, as I did, how to account for Mr. Kampf's dog following Mr. Meegan's coat. I couldn't. I can't. Then, since it was unquestionably Mr. Kampf's dog, it couldn't have been Mr. Meegan's coat. It is better than a conjecture—it is next thing to a certainty—*that it was Mr. Kampf's coat!*"

His gaze leveled at the deserted husband. "Mr. Meegan. Some two hours ago I learned from Mr. Goodwin that you maintain that you had never seen or heard of Mr. Kampf. That was fairly conclusive, but before sending for you I had to verify my conjecture that the model who had sat for Mr. Chaffee's picture was your wife. I would like to hear it straight from you. Did you ever meet Philip Kampf alive?"

Meegan was meeting the gaze. "No."

"Don't you want to qualify that?"

"No."

"Then where did you get his raincoat?"

Meegan's jaw worked. He said, "I didn't have his raincoat, or if I did I didn't know it."

"That won't do. I warn you, you are in deadly peril. The raincoat that you brought into this house and left here is in the hall now, there on the rack. It can easily be established that it belonged to Mr. Kampf and was worn by him. Where did you get it?"

Meegan's jaw worked some more. "I never had it, if it belonged to Kampf. This is a dirty frame. You can't prove that's the coat I left here."

Wolfe's voice sharpened: "One more chance. Have you any explanation of how Kampf's coat came into your possession?"

"No, and I don't need any."

He may not have been pure boob. If he hadn't noticed that he wore the wrong coat home—and he probably hadn't, in his state of mind—this had hit him from a clear sky and he had no time to study it.

"Then you're done for," Wolfe told him. "For your own coat must be somewhere, and I think I know where. In the police laboratory. Mr. Kampf was wearing one when you killed him and pushed his body down the stairs—and that explains why, when they were making that experiment this morning, the dog showed no interest in the spot where the body had lain. It had been enveloped, not in his coat but in yours. If you won't explain how you got Mr. Kampf's coat, then explain how he got yours. Is that also a frame?"

Wolfe pointed a finger at him. "I note that flash of hope in your eye, and I think I know what it means. But your brain is lagging. If, after killing Kampf, you took your raincoat off of him and put on him the one that you thought was his, that won't help you any. For in that case the coat that was on the body is Mr. Goodwin's, and certainly that can be established, and how would you explain that? It looks hopeless, and—"

Meegan was springing up, but before he even got well started Purley's big hands were on his shoulders, pulling him back and down.

And Jewel Jones was babbling, "I told you he would kill me! I knew he would! He killed Phil!"

Wolfe snapped at her, "How do you know he did?"

Judging by her eyes and the way she was shaking, she would be hysterical in another two minutes. Meanwhile, she poured it out:

"Because Phil told me—he told me he knew Dick was here looking for me, and he knew how afraid I was of him, and he said if I wouldn't come back to him he would tell Dick where I was. I didn't think he really would—I didn't think Phil could be as mean as that—and I wouldn't promise.

"But yesterday morning he phoned me and told me he had seen Dick and told him he thought he knew who had posed for that picture. He said he was going to see him again in the afternoon and tell him about me if I didn't promise, and so I promised. I thought if I promised, it would give me time to decide what to do. But Phil must have gone to see Dick again, anyway."

"Where had they met in the morning?"

"At Phil's apartment, he said. And he said—that's why I know Dick killed him—he said Dick had gone off with his raincoat, and he laughed about it and said he was will-ing for Dick to have his raincoat if he could have Dick's wife." She was shaking harder now. "And I'll bet that's what he told Dick! I'll bet he said I was coming back and he thought that was a good trade—a raincoat for a wife! That was like Phil!"

She giggled. It started with a giggle, and then the valves burst open and here it came. When something happens in that office to smash a woman's nerves—as it has more than once—it usually falls to me to deal with it. But that time three other guys, led by Ross Chaffee, were on hand, and I was glad to leave Jewel Jones to them. As for Wolfe, he skedaddled. If there is one thing on earth he absolutely will not be in a room with, it's a woman in eruption. He got up and marched out. As for Meegan, Purley and Cramer had him.

When they left with him, they didn't take the dog. To relieve the minds of any of you who have the notion, which I understand is widespread, that it makes a dog neurotic to change its name, I might add that he responds to "Jet" now as if his mother had started calling him that before he had his eyes open.

As for the raincoat, Wolfe had been right about the flash in Meegan's eye. Kampf had been wearing Meegan's raincoat when he was killed, and of course that wouldn't do, so after strangling him Meegan had taken it off and put on the one he thought was Kampf's. Only, it was mine. As a part of the D.A.'s case I went down to headquarters and identified it. At the trial it helped the jury to decide that Meegan deserved the big one. After that was over I suppose I could have claimed it, but the idea didn't appeal to me. My new coat is a different color.

<< Puzzle for Poppy >>

by

Patrick Quentin

"YES, MISS CRUMP," snapped Iris into the phone. "No, Miss Crump. Oh, nuts, Miss Crump."

My wife flung down the receiver.

"Well?" I asked.

"She won't let us use the patio. It's that dog, that great fat St. Bernard. It mustn't be disturbed."

"Why?"

"It has to be alone with its beautiful thoughts. It's going to become a mother. Peter, it's revolting. There must be something in the lease."

"There isn't," I said.

When I'd rented our half of this La Jolla hacienda for my shore leave, the lease specified that all rights to the enclosed patio belonged to our eccentric co-tenant. It oughtn't to have mattered, but it did because Iris had recently skyrocketed to fame as a movie star and it was impossible for us to appear on the streets without being mobbed. For the last couple of days we had been virtually beleaguered in our apartment. We were crazy about being beleaguered together, but even Héloise and Abelard needed a little fresh air once in a while.

That's why the patio was so important.

Iris was staring through the locked French windows at the forbidden delights of the patio. Suddenly she turned.

"Peter, I'll die if I don't get things into my lungs—ozone and things. We'll just have to go to the beach."

"And be torn limb from limb by your public again?"

"I'm sorry, darling. I'm terribly sorry." Iris unzippered herself from her housecoat and scrambled into slacks and a shirt-waist. She tossed me my naval hat. "Come Lieutenant—to the slaughter."

When we emerged on the street, we collided head-on with a man carrying groceries into the house. As we disentangled ourselves from celery stalks, there was a click and a squeal of delight followed by a powerful whistle. I turned to see a small girl who had been lying in wait with a camera. She was an unsightly little girl with sandy pigtails and a brace on her teeth.

"Geeth," she announced. "I can get two buckth for thith thnap from Barney Thtone. He'th thappy about you, Mith Duluth."

Other children, materializing in response to her whistle, were galloping toward us. The grocery man came out of the house. Passers-by stopped, stared and closed in—a woman in scarlet slacks, two sailors, a flurry of bobby-soxers, a policeman.

"This," said Iris grimly, "is the end."

She escaped from her fans and marched back to the two front doors of our hacienda. She rang the buzzer on the door that wasn't ours. She rang persistently. At length there was the clatter of a chain sliding into place and the door opened wide enough to reveal the face of Miss Crump. It was a small, faded face with a most uncordial expression.

"Yes?" asked Miss Crump.

"We're the Duluths," said Iris. "I just called you. I know about your dog, but . . ."

"Not *my* dog," corrected Miss Crump. "Mrs. Wilberframe's dog. The late Mrs. Wilberframe of Glendale who has a nephew and a niece-in-law of whom I know a great deal in Ogden Bluffs, Utah. At least, they *ought* to be in Ogden Bluffs."

This unnecessary information was flung at us like a

challenge. Then Miss Crump's face flushed into sudden, dimpled pleasure.

"Duluth! Iris Duluth. You're *the* Iris Duluth of the movies?"

"Yes," said Iris.

"Oh, why didn't you tell me over the phone? My favorite actress! How exciting! Poor thing—mobbed by your fans. Of course you may use the patio. I will give you the key to open your French windows. Any time."

Miraculously the chain was off the door. It opened halfway and then stopped. Miss Crump was staring at me with a return of suspicion.

"You *are* Miss Duluth's husband?"

"Mrs. Duluth's husband," I corrected her. "Lieutenant Duluth."

She still peered. "I mean, you have proof?"

I was beyond being surprised by Miss Crump. I fumbled from my wallet a dog-eared snapshot of Iris and me in full wedding regalia outside the church. Miss Crump studied it carefully and then returned it.

"You must please excuse me. What a sweet bride! It's just that I can't be too careful—for Poppy."

"Poppy?" queried Iris. "The St. Bernard?"

Miss Crump nodded. "It is Poppy's house, you see. Poppy pays the rent."

"The dog," said Iris faintly, "pays the rent?"

"Yes, my dear. Poppy is very well-to-do. She is hardly more than a puppy, but she is one of the richest dogs, I suppose, in the whole world."

Although we entertained grave doubts as to Miss Crump's sanity, we were soon in swimming suits and stepping through our open French windows into the sunshine of the patio. Miss Crump introduced us to Poppy.

In spite of our former prejudices, Poppy disarmed us immediately. She was just a big, bouncing, natural girl unspoiled by wealth. She greeted us with great thumps of her tail. She leaped up at Iris, dabbing at her cheek with a long, pink tongue. Later, when we had settled on striped mattresses under orange trees, she curled into a big clumsy ball at my side and laid her vast muzzle on my stomach.

"Look, she likes you." Miss Crump was glowing. "Oh, I knew she would!"

Iris, luxuriating in the sunshine, asked the polite question. "Tell us about Poppy. How did she make her money?"

"Oh, she did not make it. She inherited it." Miss Crump sat down on a white iron chair. "Mrs. Wilberframe was a very wealthy woman. She was devoted to Poppy."

"And left her all her money?" I asked.

"Not quite all. There was a little nest egg for me. I was her companion, you see, for many years. But I am to look after Poppy. That is why I received the nest egg. Poppy pays me a generous salary too." She fingered nondescript beads at her throat. "Mrs. Wilberframe was anxious for Poppy to have only the best and I am sure I try to do the right thing. Poppy has the master bedroom, of course. I take the little one in front. And then, if Poppy has steak for dinner, I have hamburger." She stared intensely. "I would not have an easy moment if I felt that Poppy did not get the best."

Poppy, her head on my stomach, coughed. She banged her tail against the flagstones apologetically.

Iris reached across me to pat her. "Has she been rich for long?"

"Oh, no, Mrs. Wilberframe passed on only a few weeks ago." Miss Crump paused. "And it has been a great responsibility for me." She paused again and then blurted: "You're my friends, aren't you? Oh, I am sure you are. Please, please, won't you help me? I am all alone and I am so frightened."

"Frightened?" I looked up and, sure enough, her little bird face was peaked with fear.

"For Poppy." Miss Crump leaned forward. "Oh, Lieutenant, it is like a nightmare. Because I know. I just know they are trying to murder her!"

"They?" Iris sat up straight.

"Mrs. Wilberframe's nephew and his wife. From Ogden Bluffs, Utah."

"You mentioned them when you opened the door."

"I mention them to everyone who comes to the house. You see, I do not know what they look like and I do not want them to think I am not on my guard."

I watched her. She might have looked like a silly spinster with a bee in her bonnet. She didn't. She looked nice and quite sane, only scared.

"Oh, they are not good people. Not at all. There is nothing they would not stoop to. Back in Glendale, I found pieces of meat in the front yard. Poisoned meat, I know. And on a lonely road, they shot at Poppy. Oh, the police laughed at me. A car backfiring, they said. But I know differently. I know they won't stop till Poppy is dead." She threw her little hands up to her face. "I ran away from them in Glendale. That is why I came to La Jolla. But they have caught up with us. I know. Oh, dear, poor Poppy who is so sweet without a nasty thought in her head."

Poppy, hearing her name mentioned, smiled and panted.

"But this nephew and his wife from Ogden Bluffs, why should they want to murder her?" My wife's eyes were gleaming with a detective enthusiasm I knew of old. "Are they after her money?"

"Of course," said Miss Crump passionately. "It's the will. The nephew is Mrs. Wilberframe's only living relative, but she deliberately cut him off and I am sure I do not blame her. All the money goes to Poppy and—er—Poppy's little ones."

"Isn't the nephew contesting a screwy will like that?" I asked.

"Not yet. To contest a will takes a great deal of money—lawyer fees and things. It would be much, much cheaper for him to kill Poppy. You see, one thing is not covered by the will. If Poppy were to die before she became a mother, the nephew would inherit the whole estate. Oh, I have done everything in my power. The moment the—er—suitable season arrived, I found a husband for

Poppy. In a few weeks now, the—the little ones are expected. But these next few weeks . . ."

Miss Crump dabbed at her eyes with a small handkerchief. "Oh, the Glendale police were most unsympathetic. They even mentioned the fact that the sentence for shooting or killing a dog in this state is shockingly light—a small fine at most. I called the police here and asked for protection. They said they'd send a man around some time but they were hardly civil. So you see, there is no protection from the law and no redress. There is no one to help me."

"You've got us," said Iris in a burst of sympathy.

"Oh . . . oh . . ." The handkerchief fluttered from Miss Crump's face. "I knew you were my friends. You dear, dear things. Oh, Poppy, they are going to help us."

Poppy, busy licking my stomach, did not reply. Somewhat appalled by Iris' hasty promise but ready to stand by her, I said:

"Sure, we'll help, Miss Crump. First, what's the nephew's name?"

"Henry. Henry Blodgett. But he won't use that name. Oh, no, he will be too clever for that."

"And you don't know what he looks like?"

"Mrs. Wilberframe destroyed his photograph many years ago when he bit her as a small boy. With yellow curls, I understand. That is when the trouble between them started."

"At least you know what age he is?"

"He should be about thirty."

"And the wife?" asked Iris.

"I know nothing about her," said Miss Crump coldly, "except that she is supposed to be a red-headed person, a former actress."

"And what makes you so sure one or both of them have come to La Jolla?"

Miss Crump folded her arms in her lap. "Last night. A telephone call."

"A telephone call?"

"A voice asking if I was Miss Crump, and then—

silence." Miss Crump leaned toward me. "Oh, now they know I am here. They know I never let Poppy out. They know every morning I search the patio for meat, traps. They must realize that the only possible way to reach her is to enter the house."

"Break in?"

Miss Crump shook her tight curls. "It is possible. But I believe they will rely on guile rather than violence. It is against that we must be on our guard. You are the only people who have come to the door since that telephone call. Now anyone else that comes to your apartment or mine, whatever their excuse . . ." She lowered her voice. "Anyone may be Henry Blodgett or his wife and we will have to outwit them."

A fly settled on one of Poppy's valuable ears. She did not seem to notice it. Miss Crump watched us earnestly and then gave a self-scolding cluck.

"Dear me, here I have been burdening you with Poppy's problems and you must be hungry. How about a little salad for luncheon? I always feel guilty about eating in the middle of the day when Poppy has her one meal at night. But with guests—yes, and allies—I am sure Mrs. Wilberframe would not have grudged the expense."

With a smile that was half-shy, half-conspiratorial, she fluttered away.

I looked at Iris. "Well," I said, "is she a nut or do we believe her?"

"I rather think," said my wife, "that we believe her."

"Why?"

"Just because." Iris' face wore the entranced expression which had won her so many fans in her last picture. "Oh, Peter, don't you see what fun it will be? A beautiful St. Bernard in peril. A wicked villain with golden curls who bit his aunt."

"He won't have golden curls any more," I said. "He's a big boy now."

Iris, her body warm from the sun, leaned over me and put both arms around Poppy's massive neck.

"Poor Poppy," she said. "Really, this shouldn't happen to a dog!"

The first thing happened some hours after Miss Crump's little salad luncheon while Iris and I were still sunning ourselves. Miss Crump, who had been preparing Poppy's dinner and her own in her apartment, came running to announce:

"There is a man at the door! He claims he is from the electric light company to read the meter. Oh, dear, if he is legitimate and we do not let him in, there will be trouble with the electric light company and if . . ." She wrung her hands. "Oh, what shall we do?"

I reached for a bathrobe. "You and Iris stay here. And for Mrs. Wilberframe's sake, hang on to Poppy."

I found the man outside the locked front door. He was about thirty with thinning hair and wore an army discharge button. He showed me his credentials. They seemed in perfect order. There was nothing for it but to let him in. I took him into the kitchen where Poppy's luscious steak and Miss Crump's modest hamburger were lying where Miss Crump had left them on the table. I hovered over the man while he located the meter. I never let him out of my sight until he had departed. In answer to Miss Crump's anxious questioning, I could only say that if the man had been Henry Blodgett he knew how much electricity she'd used in the past month—but that was all.

The next caller showed up a few minutes later. Leaving Iris, indignant at being out of things, to stand by Poppy, Miss Crump and I handled the visitor. This time it was a slim, brash girl with bright auburn hair and a navy-blue slack suit. She was, she said, the sister of the woman who owned the hacienda. She wanted a photograph for the newspapers—a photograph of her Uncle William who had just been promoted to Rear Admiral in the Pacific. The photograph was in a trunk in the attic.

Miss Crump, reacting to the unlikeliness of the request, refused entry. The red-head wasn't the type that wilted. When she started talking darkly of eviction, I overrode

Miss Crump and offered to conduct her to the attic. The girl gave me one quick, experienced look and flounced into the hall.

The attic was reached by the back stairs through the kitchen. I conducted the red-head directly to her claimed destination. There were trunks. She searched through them. At length she produced a photograph of a limp young man in a raccoon coat.

"My Uncle William," she snapped, "as a youth."

"Pretty," I said.

I took her back to the front door. On the threshold she gave me another of her bold, appraising stares.

"You know something?" she said. "I was hoping you'd make a pass at me in the attic."

"Why?" I asked.

"So's I could tear your ears off."

She left. If she had been Mrs. Blodgett, she knew how to take care of herself, she knew how many trunks there were in the attic—and that was all.

Iris and I had dressed and were drinking Daiquiris under a green and white striped umbrella when Miss Crump appeared followed by a young policeman. She was very pleased about the policeman. He had come, she said, in answer to her complaint. She showed him Poppy; she babbled out her story of the Blodgetts. He obviously thought she was a harmless lunatic, but she didn't seem to realize it. After she had let him out, she settled beamingly down with us.

"I suppose," said Iris, "you asked him for his credentials?"

"I . . ." Miss Crump's face clouded. "My dear, you don't think that perhaps he wasn't a real police . . . ?"

"To me," said Iris, "everyone's a Blodgett until proved to the contrary."

"Oh, dear," said Miss Crump.

Nothing else happened. By evening Iris and I were back in our part of the house. Poppy had hated to see us go. We had hated to leave her. A mutual crush had developed between us.

But now we were alone again, the sinister Blodgetts did not seem very substantial. Iris made a creditable *Boeuf Stroganov* from yesterday's leftovers and changed into a lime green négligée which would have inflamed the whole Pacific Fleet. I was busy being a sailor on leave with his girl when the phone rang. I reached over Iris for the receiver, said "Hello," and then sat rigid listening.

It was Miss Crump's voice. But something was horribly wrong with it. It came across hoarse and gasping.

"Come," it said. "Oh, come. The French windows. Oh, please . . ."

The voice faded. I heard the clatter of a dropped receiver.

"It must be Poppy," I said to Iris. "Quick."

We ran out into the dark patio. Across it I could see the light French windows to Miss Crump's apartment. They were half open, and as I looked Poppy squirmed through to the patio. She bounded toward us, whining.

"Poppy's all right," said Iris. "Quick!"

We ran to Miss Crump's windows. Poppy barged past us into the living room. We followed. All the lights were on. Poppy had galloped around a high-backed davenport. We went to it and looked over it.

Poppy was crouching on the carpet, her huge muzzle dropped on her paws. She was howling and staring straight at Miss Crump.

Poppy's paid companion was on the floor too. She lay motionless on her back, her legs twisted under her, her small, grey face distorted, her lips stretched in a dreadful smile.

I knelt down by Poppy. I picked up Miss Crump's thin wrist and felt for the pulse. Poppy was still howling. Iris stood, straight and white.

"Peter, tell me. Is she dead?"

"Not quite. But only just not quite. Poison. It looks like strychnine. . . ."

We called a doctor. We called the police. The doctor came, muttered a shocked diagnosis of strychnine poisoning and rushed Miss Crump to the hospital. I asked if she had a chance. He didn't answer. I knew what that meant. Soon the police came and there was so much to say and do and think that I hadn't time to brood about poor Miss Crump.

We told Inspector Green the Blodgett story. It was obvious to us that somehow Miss Crump had been poisoned by them in mistake for Poppy. Since no one had entered the house that day except the three callers, one of them, we said, must have been a Blodgett. All the Inspector had to do, we said, was to locate those three people and find out which was a Blodgett.

Inspector Green watched us pokerfaced and made no comment. After he'd left, we took the companionless Poppy back to our part of the house. She climbed on the bed and stretched out between us, her tail thumping, her head flopped on the pillows. We didn't have the heart to evict her. It was not one of our better nights.

Early next morning, a policeman took us to Miss Crump's apartment. Inspector Green was waiting in the living room. I didn't like his stare.

"We've analyzed the hamburger she was eating last night," he said. "There was enough strychnine in it to kill an elephant."

"Hamburger!" exclaimed Iris. "Then that proves she was poisoned by the Blodgetts!"

"Why?" asked Inspector Green.

"They didn't know how conscientious Miss Crump was. They didn't know she always bought steak for Poppy and hamburger for herself. They saw the steak and the hamburger and they naturally assumed the hamburger was for Poppy, so they poisoned that."

"That's right," I cut in. "The steak and the hamburger were lying right on the kitchen table when all three of those people came in yesterday."

"I see," said the Inspector.

He nodded to a policeman who left the room and returned with three people—the balding young man from the electric light company, the red-headed vixen, and the young policeman. None of them looked happy.

"You're willing to swear," the Inspector asked us, "that these were the only three people who entered this house yesterday."

"Yes," said Iris.

"And you think one of them is either Blodgett or his wife?"

"They've got to be."

Inspector Green smiled faintly. "Mr. Burns here has been with the electric light company for five years except for a year when he was in the army. The electric light company is willing to vouch for that. Miss Curtis has been identified as the sister of the lady who owns this house and the niece of Rear Admiral Moss. She has no connection with any Blodgetts and has never been in Utah." He paused. "As for Officer Patterson, he has been a member of the police force here for eight years. I personally sent him around yesterday to follow up Miss Crump's complaint."

The Inspector produced an envelope from his pocket and tossed it to me. "I've had these photographs of Mr. and Mrs. Henry Blodgett flown from the files of the Ogden Bluffs *Tribune*."

I pulled the photographs out of the envelope. We stared at them. Neither Mr. or Mrs. Blodgett looked at all the sort of person you would like to know. But neither of them bore the slightest resemblance to any of the three suspects in front of us.

"It might also interest you," said the Inspector quietly, "that I've checked with the Ogden Bluffs police. Mr. Blodgett has been sick in bed for over a week and his wife has been nursing him. There is a doctor's certificate to that effect."

Inspector Green gazed down at his hands. They were competent hands. "It looks to me that the whole Blodgett story was built up in Miss Crump's mind—or yours." His grey eyes stared right through us. "If we have to eliminate the Blodgetts and these three people from suspicion, that leaves only two others who had the slightest chance of poisoning the hamburger."

Iris blinked. "Us?"

"You," said Inspector Green almost sadly.

They didn't arrest us, of course. We had no conceivable motive. But Inspector Green questioned us minutely and when he left there was a policeman lounging outside our door.

We spent a harried afternoon racking our brains and getting nowhere. Iris was the one who had the inspiration. Suddenly, just after she had fed Poppy the remains of the *Stroganov*, she exclaimed:

"Good heavens above, of course!"

"Of course, what?"

She spun to me, her eyes shining. "Barney Thtone," she lisped. "Why didn't we realize? Come on!"

She ran out of the house into the street. She grabbed the lounging policeman by the arm.

"You live here," she said. "Who's Barney Stone?"

"Barney Stone?" The policeman stared. "He's the son of the druggist on the corner."

Iris raced me to the drugstore. She was attracting quite a crowd. The policeman followed, too.

In the drugstore, a thin young man with spectacles stood behind the prescription counter.

"Mr. Stone?" asked Iris.

His mouth dropped open. "Gee, Miss Duluth. I never dreamed ... Gee, Miss Duluth, what can I do for you? Cigarettes? An alarm clock?"

"A little girl," said Iris. "A little girl with sandy pigtails and a brace on her teeth. What's her name? Where does she live?"

Barney Stone said promptly: "You mean Daisy Kornfeld. Kind of homely. Just down the block. 712. Miss Duluth, I certainly ..."

"Thanks," cut in Iris and we were off again with our ever growing escort.

Daisy was sitting in the Kornfeld parlor, glumly thumping the piano. Ushered in by an excited, cooing Mrs.

Kornfeld, Iris interrupted Daisy's rendition of *The Jolly Farmer.*

"Daisy, that picture you took of me yesterday to sell to Mr. Stone, is it developed yet?"

"Geeth no, Mith Duluth. I ain't got the developing money yet. Theventy-five thenth. Ma don't give me but a nickel an hour for practithing thith gothdarn piano."

"Here." Iris thrust a ten-dollar bill into her hand. "I'll buy the whole roll. Run get the camera. We'll have it developed right away."

"Geeth." The mercenary Daisy stared with blank incredulity at the ten-dollar bill.

I stared just as blankly myself. I wasn't being bright at all.

I wasn't much brighter an hour later. We were back in our apartment, waiting for Inspector Green. Poppy, all for love, was trying to climb into my lap. Iris, who had charmed Barney Stone into developing Daisy's films, clutched the yellow envelope of snaps in her hand. She had sent our policeman away on a secret mission, but an infuriating passion for the dramatic had kept her from telling or showing me anything. I had to wait for Inspector Green.

Eventually Iris' policeman returned and whispered with her in the hall. Then Inspector Green came. He looked cold and hostile. Poppy didn't like him. She growled. Sometimes Poppy was smart.

Inspector Green said: "You've been running all over town. I told you to stay here."

"I know." Iris' voice was meek. "It's just that I wanted to solve poor Miss Crump's poisoning."

"Solve it?" Inspector Green's query was skeptical.

"Yes. It's awfully simple really. I can't imagine why we didn't think of it from the start."

"You mean you know who poisoned her?"

"Of course." Iris smiled, a maddening smile. "Henry Blodgett."

"But . . ."

"Check with the airlines. I think you'll find that Blodgett flew in from Ogden Bluffs a few days ago and flew back today. As for his being sick in bed under his wife's care, I guess that'll make Mrs. Blodgett an accessory before the fact, won't it?"

Inspector Green was pop-eyed.

"Oh, it's my fault really," continued Iris. "I said no one came to the house yesterday except those three people. There was someone else, but he was so ordinary, so run-of-the-mill, that I forgot him completely."

I was beginning to see then. Inspector Green snapped: "And this run-of-the-mill character?"

"The man," said Iris sweetly, "who had the best chance of all to poison the hamburger, *the man who delivered it*— the man from the Supermarket.

"We don't have to guess. We have proof." Iris fumbled in the yellow envelope. "Yesterday morning as we were going out, we bumped into the man delivering Miss Crump's groceries. Just at that moment, a sweet little girl took a snap of us. This snap."

She selected a print and handed it to Inspector Green. I moved to look at it over his shoulder.

"I'm afraid Daisy is an impressionistic photographer," murmured Iris. "That hip on the right is me. The buttocks are my husband. But the figure in the middle—quite a masterly likeness of Henry Blodgett, isn't it? Of course, there's the grocery apron, the unshaven chin . . ."

She was right. Daisy had only winged Iris and me but with the grocery man she had scored a direct hit. And the grocery man was unquestionably Henry Blodgett.

Iris nodded to her policeman. "Sergeant Blair took a copy of the snap around the neighborhood groceries. They recognized Blodgett at the Supermarket. They hired him day before yesterday. He made a few deliveries this morning, including Miss Crump's, and took a powder without his pay."

"Well . . ." stammered Inspector Green. "Well . . ."

"Just how many charges can you get him on?" asked my wife hopefully. "Attempted homicide, conspiracy to defraud, illegal possession of poisonous drugs. . . . The rat, I hope you give him the works when you get him."

"We'll get him all right," said Inspector Green.

Iris leaned over and patted Poppy's head affectionately.

"Don't worry, darling. I'm sure Miss Crump will get well and we'll throw a lovely christening party for your little strangers. . . ."

Iris was right about the Blodgetts. Henry got the works. And his wife was held as an accessory. Iris was right about Miss Crump too. She is still in the hospital but improving steadily and will almost certainly be well enough to attend the christening party.

Meanwhile, at her request, Poppy is staying with us, awaiting maternity with rollicking unconcern.

It's nice having a dog who pays the rent.

The Case of the
Canine Accomplice

<< >>

by

John Lutz

SAM GROWLED BESIDE me, as if he didn't like the looks of the rambling mansion beyond the car's windshield. The place didn't seem particularly forbidding to me, maybe because there was a fee involved in our coming here.

I pulled my Beetle into the circular drive and stopped in the shadow of one of the house's many gables. Parked on the other side of the driveway was a plain gray sedan I recognized and wasn't at all surprised to see. As I held the door open for Sam, I glanced at the miles of wooded hills surrounding the house and wondered how much of them the Creel family owned.

I rang the bell. A butler opened the door six inches and peered down an aristocratic nose at me. "Milo Morgan to see Vincent Creel," I said.

The nose dipped a few degrees as the butler took in Sam's low, squat frame. "Come in, sir. But the, er . . ."

"Mr. Creel hired both of us," I said.

Lieutenant Jack Redaway, whose unmarked police car was parked outside, was in a large Victorian room talking to the Creel family. Vincent Creel shook my hand and introduced me to the other family members. There was tall and elegant Robert, short and muscular James, short and almost as muscular Millicent. Like Vincent Creel, who was silver-haired, urbane, and very rich, they were all the brothers and sister of homicide victim Carl Creel.

It had been Carl Creel who had replenished the family coffers with his bestselling book on how to survive the ravages of inflation. The Creel family, struggling along on dwindling wealth from the oil dealings of their forebears, had no further financial problems after a big movie studio bought the rights to Carl Creel's book and made it into a successful comedy.

"Mr. Morgan and I have met all too often," Lieutenant Redaway said. He glanced at Sam. "I heard you had a new partner."

"This is Sam," I said. "He doesn't bite or make a mess."

"The gentleman of the firm. As a private detective, Morgan, I would think you'd have noticed that 'Sam' doesn't suit that animal's gender."

"It's short for Samantha," I explained. "Since Sam's been neutered, we use the male pronoun for the sake of convenience. But we have impressive, and accurate, business cards."

"Don't tell me. I already heard. Sam Spayed."

"Correct. And he's got a bloodhound nose." Which was true. Sam is a drab brown animal who looks like a mixture of a hundred breeds, the last generation of which might have been bulldog, but his nose is one hundred percent pedigreed bloodhound. "We'd like to examine the death scene," I said, to both Vincent Creel and Redaway, "before the scent grows any colder or is obliterated by official bungling."

Vincent led me, Sam, and Redaway to a ground floor study. "I've heard you employ unusual methodology," he said to me. "I've also heard you get results. I want this stigma removed from our family at any cost. As we agreed at your office, I will give you carte blanche in every respect to solve my brother's murder."

I nodded. Sam shoved his pushed-in bloodhound nose against Creel's pants leg, snuffled, and gave Creel his weird kind of canine grin that might mean anything.

When Vincent had left us in the study, Redaway rolled out the hostility. "I hate to see you here," he said. "You can muddle a case more thoroughly than any shamus I know."

"If the case weren't muddled to begin with," I replied, "Sam and I wouldn't have been hired by Vincent Creel." I looked down at the large ova bloodstain that Sam already was sniffing. "That's where Carl Creel's body was discovered, I suppose."

"Your deductive powers are at full strength," Redaway said. He was as mean as his hatchet face and tiny glittering black eyes suggested.

"Fill us in," I told him, knowing he couldn't refuse. Vincent Creel had hired me, and like any smart cop, Redaway respected the Creel family's political clout.

"Carl was working here in his study the night before last," Redaway said around a smelly cigar he was lighting, "when the other family members heard a shot. They all rushed in from their various places in the house. Carl was lying on the carpet, having died from a single .22 bullet to the brain. Those french windows were wide open, and the family dog, Caster, a big Irish setter, was seen running up that hill as if chasing someone into the woods. It was obvious to all that Carl was dead, so Vincent phoned the police first, then a doctor." Redaway crossed his arms and pretended to be a smokestack.

"That's it?" I asked.

"That's a quick overview," Redaway said. He looked down and grinned as Sam coughed at the cigar smoke and glared at him.

I looked around the study. Not a large room, it was furnished expensively with a desk, small sofa, velvet chair, bookshelves, oak filing cabinets. Besides the french windows there were two other windows. The door to the hall was spring-loaded and had no latch.

"Not your locked-room type of crime," I said. "What about motive?"

"Carl had announced his intention of donating all his movie and book sale profits to the Insomniacs Society, a research group in New York. Creel himself was a chronic insomniac. The rest of the family were losing sleep because they might lose the money."

"What you're saying is—"

"That everyone in the house at the time of Carl Creel's death had a motive. Furthermore, everyone had opportunity."

Sam sighed and stretched out where a sunbeam cast a bar of light across the floor. He gets discouraged easily. I have to do the heavy thinking.

"One of the Creels in that other room did the killing," Redaway said, "but there's no way we can get an indictment as long as they can claim it was the work of an intruder whom Carl Creel surprised."

"A jury won't buy that old intruder line," I told him.

"They will if we can't produce a weapon. And no gun was found. The Creels were all here together less than a minute after the shot was fired, so there was little or no time to hide the weapon. We've searched this house and the surrounding grounds thoroughly. No gun. The defense attorney can say, quite logically, that the intruder took it with him."

"So maybe it was an intruder after all. A burglar surprised by an unlucky Creel."

Redaway sneered around his cigar. "Maybe the butler did it?"

Sam and I exchanged glances. "What *about* the butler?"

"Bart—that's the butler—was off that night and has a concrete alibi. He was at the racetrack with Jenny, the Creels' cook. Witnesses confirm."

"What about footprints outside? And you said the dog chased someone."

"We're in the middle of a drought; the ground was too hard for footprints. And Caster wandered home after an hour or so, empty pawed."

Sam seemed to smile, baring his teeth for an instant in that quick, good-natured snarl of his.

"If there was no intruder," I asked, "what do you suppose the dog was chasing into the woods?"

Redaway shrugged. "A squirrel, a rabbit—who knows? Dogs are always running after something."

Still grinning, Sam got up and sat by the door. He had an uncanny sense of timing in a case.

"It's time for me to talk to each of the suspects," I said.

"Sure," Redaway said. "Especially the butler."

The family members told Sam and me what they'd already told the police. Not one of them didn't complain about having to tell the story again.

Millicent Creel had been in the sewing room, talking on the phone to a friend, when she'd heard the shot. The friend had verified Millicent's story, and had even heard the shot herself over the phone. Millicent had excused herself and rushed to investigate. She'd reached Carl's study at almost the same time as her brothers. They knocked several times in quick succession, then threw open the door to find Carl dead on the floor. The french windows were standing open, and in the distance they saw Caster running into the woods as if in pursuit of something or someone.

Robert Creel had been in his upstairs bedroom taking a late afternoon nap. James, having just returned from hunting with Caster, had been showering in the bath adjoining his own bedroom. Wearing only a towel, he had rushed from his room and seen Robert already running down the stairs. They had reached the study door in time to see Vincent Creel burst onto the scene from the basement, where he had been engaged in his hobby of woodworking, and they'd seen Millicent scurrying along the hall from the direction of the sewing room.

"Calculate the distances," Redaway said when we were again alone. "Any one of them could have shot Carl Creel, then made it back to where he or she could pretend to be rushing to the study with the rest of the Creels."

"After stashing the gun," I added.

"Now if you'll just tell me where," Redaway said, "we'll simply pick up the gun, make an arrest, and wind this thing up." He was the only man I knew who could gnash his teeth and smoke a cigar simultaneously.

Sam stretched out near the sofa and made a sound somewhere between a growl and a chortle.

"Is that dog laughing at me?" Redaway demanded, seriously.

"The smoke bothers him, is all," I said. "I'd like to speak to the butler and the cook."

Redaway rolled his eyes, but he sent for Bart and Jenny.

Bart the butler told me he'd been at the racetrack at the time of the murder. At the moment the trigger was pulled, he was losing ten dollars on the daily double and he had the witnesses and worthless stubs to prove it. He said Jenny had been with him, using her complicated system of astrology in conjunction with the names of exotic spices to place her bets. She had won twenty-seven dollars; Bart had lost fifty. They often went to the track together, usually with similar results.

Jenny was busy preparing lunch so I went to the kitchen to question her, and to see what sort of exotic spices she used. The Creel kitchen was as large and efficient looking as the kitchen of a good-sized restaurant. There were food grinders, heavy-duty processors, a commercial-size freezer, and a gas double oven that covered half of one wall. Something smelled good.

Jenny was a middle-aged, round-shouldered woman with her blond hair pinned in a bun above a wary frown. Sam whiffed the aroma of cooking and sidled right up to her as I introduced us. Also in the kitchen was a tall, gangly Irish setter I took to be Caster. Sam and Caster ignored each other, which didn't strike me as odd. That was Sam's way, and apparently Caster's.

"I'm told you were at the track at the time Carl Creel was murdered."

Jenny nodded. She was adjusting the temperature on the eye-level oven.

"What did you think of Carl Creel?"

"Did you ask the others that?" She fixed her shrewd, gambler's eyes on me.

"No. Their alibis aren't as good as yours and Bart's. They'd be less likely to give an honest answer."

She smiled faintly. "I didn't like him," she said. "Carl Creel was a vicious and miserly man. No one liked him."

"Do you think anyone here disliked him enough—"

"I wouldn't know. I'm a cook, not a psychologist." She reached into the sink and picked up a steak bone. "You have a nice dog." She offered the bone to Sam, who turned his head away in refusal. He was poisoned on the Hatfield case and has since been leery of food from strangers.

"The hell with you," Jenny said, and gave the bone to Caster, who promptly took it out the back door.

"Sam's independent," I said.

"Bad mannered is what he is." She began chopping onions.

"Is this the daily menu?" I asked. A list was attached to the refrigerator with a magnet.

"It is."

"The same every week?"

"Every other week," Jenny said, "for variety."

"Roast beef on Mondays? Ham on Thursdays? Steak on Fridays?"

"On odd weeks," Jenny told me acidly.

"Who does the shopping?"

"Either me or Bart."

"What do you do with the garbage?"

"We put it outside in a can with a plastic liner. It's picked up once a week and taken to the dump." *Chunk!* went the knife through the onion.

Sam and I got out of there. Sam's eyes were watering.

I talked to James again, next. He told me he hadn't really been hunting on the day of his brother's death, merely walking in the woods and shooting at various objects for target practice. I went down to see Vincent, in the basement. He had his power tools out; he was making a handsome walnut plaque featuring the Creel family crest of two crossed oil derricks on a field of green. Nothing illuminating in that conversation. When I left Vincent, I hunted up Lieutenant Redaway.

"Making any progress?" he asked sarcastically.

Sam glared at him.

"I think I have this one about wrapped up," I said. "Will you arrange for everyone to meet in Carl Creel's study after lunch?"

Redaway stood staring at me with an expression of hostile incredulity. "Okay," he said, "but if you ask me, it's all a ruse so you can stay for lunch."

"Steak and salad today," I said.

"Now how would you know that?"

I smiled. "A little detective work, lieutenant." Sam gave his chortling little growl and we moved on. I had a few things to do before lunch.

After lunch, the household, including Bart and Jenny, gathered in Carl Creel's study as I'd suggested. We were joined by a tall, stoic police sergeant named Evans, sent for by Redaway at my request. Everyone stood about uneasily, trying to avoid stepping on the bloodstain. Caster sat near Robert Creel, enjoying an ear rub.

"It's time for the Milo Morgan show," Redaway said with a sneer. All eyes in the room rotated in my direction, even Sam's.

Since I already had everyone's attention, I figured I'd keep it. "I know who the killer is," I said, "and I will set about proving it."

Sam ambled over and say by the door, wearing his stern expression.

"The key to the case is Caster," I said. "When he was seen dashing into the woods, everyone assumed he might be chasing someone. But perhaps he was running *from* someone, or, more accurately, *to* someplace. When I saw him leave the kitchen with a bone this morning, it occurred to me that many dogs have special areas where they bury their bones or go to chew on them, and usually the instant they're given a bone they dash for that place. It's an instinctive thing involving protection of food, and dogs are such slaves to instinct that their behavior seldom varies." Sam seemed to be frowning at me. "Most dogs," I added.

"Murderers are not as predictable as dogs," Redaway said. "Unless you think Caster shot Carl Creel, get to the point."

"Your story, James," I said to the youngest Creel, "is that you were out shooting the day of the murder, and that Caster was with you."

James nodded, his gray eyes cool and unblinking.

"That indicated to me that Caster, who was in the room when Carl Creel was shot, was not gunshy."

An expression of disbelief suddenly transformed Redaway's narrow face. "You're not saying that Caster was trained to get rid of the gun!"

"A dog couldn't be reliably trained to do that—not to the point where anyone would stake a murder charge on it. Not to mention that the gun still might be found."

"This seems to be leading us nowhere, then," Millicent Creel said impatiently, her pudgy features arranged in a frown. When she subsided, I turned to Vincent.

"I've been down to the basement to examine your woodworking tools," I said calmly. "I found what I was looking for."

"Which was?"

"Bone," I said. "Minute fragments of bone." Vincent's feet edged him a little toward the door. Sam growled and Redaway moved over to stand by Vincent. Redaway, though still disbelieving, was catching on.

"You used your skill with tools to fashion a simple gun out of bone," I said. "Something like the homemade zip guns street gangs carry. Only instead of using a metal barrel, you drilled a hole in the bone the exact diameter of the bore of a .22 pistol, then created a functional hammer and firing pin. Oh, the weapon was crude, and you probably had to use both hands to aim and fire it, but it only had to fire one shot, and at very close range. After you fired that shot, you handed the gun to Caster, knowing he'd run off with it, gnaw on it, and bury it. You hurried to the basement. From there you pretended to be dashing upstairs to investigate the shot that you yourself had fired."

Vincent was obviously flustered. "Morgan, if this is some pathetic attempt of yours to . . ."

"To what, Mr. Creel?" Redaway asked, finally on top of things.

"You have no proof, Morgan!"

That's when I pulled a jar of horseradish from my pocket and rubbed some on Caster's hind paws. I put a leash on Sam and handed the end of it to Sergeant Evans. "Sam is an excellent tracker," I said, "and he loves horseradish. The scent should make it easier." From another pocket I withdrew a steak bone from lunch and handed it to Caster. The big setter clamped his jaws on it, scrambled for traction, and dashed away through the french windows I'd made sure were open.

"If you'll just follow Sam following Caster's scent," I said to Sergeant Evans, "I'm sure you'll come to the spot where a little of your own snooping around will uncover the murder weapon."

Sam had his gnarled nose to the carpet and was already snuffling and snorting like a steam engine straining uphill. Evans was stumbling, holding onto the leash, and leaning backward to keep his balance as Sam yanked him across the room and out the french windows.

"Why don't we go into the den," I suggested.

The atmosphere in that den was cool, I can tell you. Cool and tense. No one said five words until, half an hour later, Sergeant Evans and Sam walked in. I don't know which of those tenacious crimefighters was grinning the widest.

Evans showed us the bone he'd found a few inches beneath freshly turned earth. It was a neat job, all right, a big ham bone tooled into the rough shape of a handgun. A neat round whole had been drilled slightly off center, to avoid the marrow. The empty shell was still stuck inside the drilled hole, which was of larger diameter for about four inches near the butt end, to allow for a tooled cylinder of bone to be propelled, probably by a powerful rubber

strap, up to the cartridge to strike with a firing pin fash-
ioned from a filed-down pointed screw. That screw was
the only metal part of the gun itself; a little more gnawing
by Caster and it would have dropped off, along with the
spent shell, leaving the whole apparatus to look like any
dog-mistreated bone unless someone examined it and noticed the drilled hole. I figured Vincent Creel had shot his
brother, slid the rubber strap up his arm out of sight beneath his sleeve, given Caster the bone-gun, and thought
he was home free. A precision-tooled perfect crime. Almost.

Vincent Creel, his face now nearly Chinese red, snarled
at me and started up from his big leather armchair. But
Redaway and Sam both snarled back at him, and he settled
down.

Redaway got out a little card and read Creel his rights,
then nodded to Evans, who put the cuffs on Creel and led
him away. The rest of the family looked on in a state of
shock, except for Millicent, who was dabbling at her potato
nose with a handkerchief.

"What I don't get," Robert Creel said, "is why Vincent
hired a private detective if he was the murderer."

"To divert suspicion," I explained. "And he thought he
was safe anyway."

"He also hired the most incompetent private detective
he could find." Redaway was his obnoxious self again. He
knew he'd be credited with the arrest.

"He wouldn't be the first to underestimate our firm," I
said pointedly.

Figuring why should we stay around to be insulted,
Sam and I made for the door. Redaway was in our path.
Sam walked right at him and he moved. I turned. "I'm
sorry it couldn't have been an intruder," I said to the still
stunned Creel family. To Redaway I said nothing, not even
goodbye. Sam and I let ourselves out and didn't look back.

It wasn't until we'd got back to the office, Sam gazing
out the window at the city skyline, me at my desk sorting
through the mail, that it occurred to me. Since we'd hung
the crime on our client, there was nobody to pay our fee.

This was some business! I cursed, crumpled the half-written bill into a compact wad and hurled it into the wastebasket.

I couldn't see Sam's face, but his shoulders were shaking as though he might be laughing. It's a dog's life. It really is.

<< Dog Act >>

by

Herbert Resnicow

YOU WANNA HEAR a great joke?

This guy and his dog come into a booking agent's office. "Have I got an act for you," he says.

"I got plenty a acts," the agent says. "Too many."

"This one's different," the guy insists. "A talking dog."

"Ventriloquists I got coming outa my ears."

"No ventriloquism," the guy says. "You can watch my Adam's apple."

"So you do it without moving your Adam's apple, but I still don't need ventriloquists."

"Just listen, willya? As long as I'm here?"

"Okay," the agent says. "You got one minute."

The guy turns to the dog and asks, "What's on top of a house?"

"R-r-r-r-roof," the dog growls.

"And what's the opposite of smooth?"

"R-r-r-r-rough."

"Who's the greatest ballplayer of all time?"

"R-r-r-r-Ruth."

"Out!" yells the agent. "Get out, you phonies, and never come back."

The man and the dog turn around and start walking out, very depressed. At the door, the dog stops, turns to the man, and asks apologetically, "DiMaggio?"

Great joke, right? First time I heard it, it laid me in the

215

aisles. You too, right? But would you've laughed the second time you heard it? A little, maybe? Okay, how about the third time? The sixth time? Believe me, by the tenth time you would stop even a customer from telling it to you.

That's normal. You know why? Because you heard it before? Wrong. Otherwise, tell me why, when Streisand announces she's going to sing a song you heard ninety-nine times before, you applaud before she even opens her mouth. And after you hear it for the hundredth time? You applaud even louder. Why? You love the song? Sure, but you loved the joke too. Okay, I'll give you another for instance. How many times have you heard Abbott and Costello do "Who's on First"? Ten? Fifteen? Twenty? I'm in the profession and I've heard them do it at least fifty times. Hell, I've done it *myself* maybe a *thousand* times—*everybody* steals in this business—and it still kills me. On stage, I can hardly keep from breaking up, and I'm a pro. And Len, my straight man—don't forget, I can't watch myself mug and he can—I don't see how he keeps a straight face. I can make the strain of not laughing look like I'm blowing my top, but Len—if he don't take everything absolutely serious, the whole routine drops dead.

See, that's the answer. It ain't just the words or the music, it's what you do with it. Like taking the Talking Dog gag and making a routine of it. When Len and I do it, he's sitting behind a big desk stage left, lighting a big cigar. I bust in—not just walk in, I *bust* in. I'm so starving for a booking that I can't control myself. As soon as I realize what I did, I'm scared that maybe I blew my last chance to get a gig by the way I showed how desperate I am. The agent fakes looking busy. He don't raise his eyes from the desk for a full minute, while I'm doing a slow burn. I'm wearing schlumpy clothes—not my regular drop pants; just an oversize wrinkled old suit—and a wild grey wig. My mad-scientist costume. Len's wearing a derby. When he looks up, he blows cigar smoke in my face. I'm so anxious to get a gig, I don't even wave it away. I put my hands on his desk and he gives me a *look*. Immediately I take my hands off. Stand at attention. You get the idea? We're not telling a joke; we're acting in a play. *Acting.* A real drama. With a terrific kicker at the end. When Trixie—she's the cutest little sort-of-terrier you ever saw, and the smartest dog I ever worked with—when she looks up at me like she's afraid her wrong answer cost us the job and says, in that sweet, sad voice, "DiMaggio?" and—*BANG!*—blackout—well, I'm telling you, the audience goes wild. Absolutely crazy. We use it for the end of the first act of the show and we get two, three curtain calls, guaranteed. Then, as a kicker, I send Trixie out all by herself, to take the star bow. The audience goes wild again. And, believe me, we could do that routine twice a night and they'd never get tired of it. Because it's a real show, a real piece of life. Sad and funny at the same time. Like how many times have you seen a great movie, or heard a song you loved, or just looked at your grandchildren for the thousandth time? Some things you can't ever get enough of.

Len and me—we're not on any circuit now. We just give shows in the old folks' homes and the veterans' hospitals to keep our hands in. For charity, we keep telling ourselves, but actually, it's to keep from going crazy. And to get the applause; that's another thing you can't get enough of either.

Trixie don't talk, of course. She's a *dog*, for Pete's sake. I do the ventriloquism. You don't have to look hard to see my lips move—I'm not a real ventriloquist—but with me facing upstage, and everybody focused on Trixie, it's good enough. And she plays her part perfect. I touch my left eye, she looks at me. How I move my upstage hand, that's how she opens and closes her mouth. I snap my fingers, she jumps into my baggy pants. Always gets a laugh. And when I drop my pants and Trixie steps out, another boff. Trixie and Len and me, we're old pros. Too old. Dying of boredom. Playing gin all day long. That's when it all came to me. During a game of gin.

"Len," I said, squaring the cards and putting them away, "I got this terrific idea."

"What're you doing, Arnie?" he complains. "You're fifty points down and you're quitting? You stop now and you still owe me fifty cents." With Len it ain't the money, it's the principle. It's his ambition to get me to owe him a dollar. Hah! He should live so long. We *both* should live so long.

"Why are we playing gin?" I asked. You got to be very careful how you talk to a straight man. Straight is the hardest job in comedy and his timing's got to be absolutely perfect, so when you talk to him, it's got to be right on the button. Exact.

"Because me and Jean, and you and Hallie, we got enough put away so we don't have to work anymore, but we don't have enough to join a fancy country club. Besides, I hate golf."

"If you won the lottery, would you join a country club?"

"You kidding?" He gave me a disgusted look. "Who would I talk to there? And what would I say? We're the last of a dying breed, Arnie. Even at the Friars . . . There ain't no real comedians left today; all they got is stand-up comics. With mikes. Can't even project. Telling one-liners they bought off college kids. You ever laugh at one of them?"

"Exactly my point, Len. There's no real comedians left today. We're it. One of a kind." I let him think for a second, that's enough for Len; he's very quick on the uptake. Plenty times when we were working and something went wrong, you think we stopped? Hell, no, a pro never stops; he adjusts. Sometimes it comes out even funnier than before.

"You want to go back to work? Is that it?"

"Don't you?"

"Where? There ain't a burlesque house left in the country."

"We make our own. Ann Corio did it with *This Was Burlesque*. Toured for years."

"That was over twenty years ago. Times are different now. Make our own burlesque house? Forget it." He put out his left hand and began counting fingers. "First, we don't have enough dough to even get started. You know what a union orchestra gets today? What a theater rents for? Eight dancers? A singer? Second, where do we get the girls? Doing a striptease is not the same as just taking off your clothes; it's an art. Today there's nobody who would come even close to Honey Deare and Jasmine Lafleur. Close, did I say? Hell, not fit to even hold their G-strings." He was talking about Hallie and Jean, big headliners in their day. In our day. They could get more applause teasing down to *twice* as much on as some models wear in TV ads today, where little kids could see them. "Third, nobody's going to pay to see girls in pasties and G-strings when you could go to any beach and . . . Hell, there are bars not too far from here where the *waitresses* are almost completely naked."

I waited until he was finished; Len don't like to be interrupted. "Exactly right, Len. But what they don't have is comedians. Real comedians. How many routines you know?"

Len pushed his lower lip out and thought for a second. "Couple of hundred. Maybe three." He saw what I was getting at. "You want to do burlesque without the girls? Impossible. And we need scenery."

"Half the routines can be done in front of a drop. *Fleagle Street. Pickle Persuader. Who's On First.* A lot more can be done with stuff any theater's got in the basement. Like *Here Comes de Judge, Pay the Man the Two Dollars, Dr. Kronkite.* You telling me we can't put a show together?"

"A lot of the routines need a talking woman. Maybe two. Some of the best ones—like *The Gazeeka Box*—need a lot of girls. Where we gonna find girls to fit in? Two months of rehearsals before they even learn the basics. And they'd be *actresses*, wouldn't know what to do unless somebody wrote the lines. Couldn't ad lib. Would you trust an actress to get the feel of the audience, to work in with our timing? Burlesque is different from the legit stage."

"We got two of the best right here on this porch. Hallie and Jean."

He turned to look at our wives, knitting and talking wife stuff. "Yeah, they were the best. But Hallie's put on a little weight and Jean's lost a little."

"They're not going to strip, for Pete's sake; they're going to be in the acts. A little makeup, magenta gels, they'll do fine. All we need is a couple of young girls to fill in where we need them. Walk-ons. Non-talking parts."

"Where's the audience? Who's going to pay? How many of us *alte kockers* are there left who still remember?"

"That's the whole point. *Nobody's* left. We got a whole virgin audience. We'll give them *real* burlesque. I looked it up in the dictionary today. Satire. Parody. Take-offs. Like the old Greeks. Fifteen routines an act. Two acts. Thirty short, funny plays a performance. Play*lets*, if you want to be technical. Look at how big the audience was for *Laugh In*. For *Benny Hill*. We'll knock 'em dead."

"You still didn't answer about renting the theater."

"We don't rent; we sell ourselves as an act. The four of us and the two new girls. Six. and Trixie. Seven. Start in the Borscht Belt. The Catskills. We do good there, we go to Atlantic City, Las Vegas, *Hollywood*, even. We can give two shows a night, each completely different. You know what that means in money? Putting on two complete different shows with only six people?"

"And a dog."

"Trixie don't eat much. And she's a pro."

We didn't get any of the big hotels the first time out; they were all extra careful, wanted to see how we did before they booked us. I don't blame them; they're all run by big corporations now and they can't take chances. They'd rather pay big money for well-established draws. If the big name bombs, no one can criticize the manager. But if we—*The Len and Arnie Show*—bomb at a big holiday weekend, the hotel's booker could be looking for a new job.

The six of us—we'd gotten two nice girls: Elaine Gorton and Isabel Bandera; not much experience, but smart, pretty, and hard-working—had come up to the Restawee Mountain Lodge Hotel in our new van, ready to put on a show that night. It wasn't one of the real big places, and the fee was also not very big, but when you're breaking in you got to pay your dues. The theater manager, Ralph Millry, showed us to our rooms—the worst rooms in the place, naturally—and introduced me to the bandleader. Five-piece band only, but at least I'd have a drum roll and a cymbal clash for the blackouts.

It was Millry I was worried about. I'd met that type before. Soft and slimy looking, with slick black hair and a pale face. Professional, sure, he'd give us a good intro and the backstage work would be okay; no way was he going to screw up his living. It was the girls. Some theater managers think the performers are part of their perks. Well, not with my troupe. What you do outside, I told the two girls, that's your business. Inside the theater, you're working and you act professional. If anybody gives you a hard time, tell me. I'm not big and I'm not tough, but nobody screws around with my act.

The four of us went upstairs to rest after the trip—we're not as young as we used to be—while Elaine and Isabel decided to catch a little sun around the pool. Maybe show off their figures and meet some nice boys too? Why not? They're young. I told everybody to meet in the social hall at four to walk through a couple of the routines, get the feel of the stage, hang up our costumes and wigs, place our props, set the lighting and curtain cues, the usual.

Four o'clock and Isabel wasn't there. This wasn't how she impressed me the two weeks that we'd worked together. Isabel was a serious type; no drink, no dope! Elaine said they'd met a couple of nice young men— Bernie, an accountant, and Harris, a teacher—and arranged to have dinner at their table before the show. I told Elaine to check around and sent Hallie with her. Both the boys were at the pool, and they swore they hadn't seen Isabel since a couple of hours ago.

Now I was really worried. We looked in all the obvious places, but no Isabel. Finally—and I knew in my heart it was too late—I had Elaine bring down the clothes Isabel had worn on the trip here and gave them to Trixie to sniff. She's no bloodhound, but even the worst dog can smell a thousand times better than the best person.

Trixie and I found Isabel in the storage room backstage. Beaten up and choked to death. Ugly. Her dress was ripped and her panties torn off. I told Hallie to call the local sheriff and have him come here fast. Quietly. With Len and Trixie, I stood outside the storage-room door, to make sure nobody changed anything. Whatever evidence there was, I didn't want it messed up, and, at my age, I wasn't about to fight a guy Ralph Millry's age all by myself. I knew he did it; it sure as hell wasn't one of those two nice young fellows. I mean, why would they? Not only is the ratio in places like this about three girls to one boy—so the guys have their pick—they already had dates with Isabel and Elaine, and just letting nature take its course was a lot easier than trying to rape Isabel in a storage room. It had to be that louse, Millry. Prove it? No, I couldn't prove a damn thing, but I've been around long enough so my instincts are right most of the time. Len agreed with me, and when he agrees with me, you can bet your boots I'm right.

Sheriff Dan Kramer was a nice, middle-aged man, average height, a little on the heavy side, glasses. No dope, but no genius either. He went into the storage room to look things over. When he came out, he looked like I felt. "I'll call the coroner," he said.

After he finished the call, I told him who we thought did it. He said—off the record—that he wouldn't be a bit surprised. I was surprised. "If you know it's him, why don't you do something about it?"

"I don't *know*," he said, "I *think*. I need evidence. If there are fingerprints . . . But there wouldn't be. He's too shrewd for that. Not smart, but when it comes to covering himself . . . Just that his reputation . . . I hear things. Rumors, complaints that've never been filed . . . He's not from around here—this is his first season—so the owners of the hotel had no way of knowing."

"You going to let him get away with it? Killing that nice innocent girl?"

He looked sad. "I might have to." I believed him. But if he was ready to let Millry get away with murder, I wasn't. I can take a lot when I have to, but this I wasn't going to stand for. Isabel Bandera was one of my girls, and us professionals got to stick together. If we don't, sure as hell nobody else will stick up for us.

"I didn't want to get involved," I said, acting like an embarrassed civilian, "but what would you say if I told you there was a witness?"

The sheriff's face lighted up. "For real? You should've said so right off."

"Well, the reason was . . . I couldn't just tell you, it's gotta be shown. Look, empty out the social hall and get everybody together."

"Millry too?"

"Especially him. Bring those two young fellows—what's their names?—that Elaine and Isabel had the date with. Bernie and Harris. Elaine will show you who they are. Act like you suspect them too, but believe me, it's gotta be Millry. Put them up on the stage, with lights, so it looks like you're setting up a lineup for identification. A couple of busboys too, so it looks real."

"Not you?"

"I'll be there, but I got other things to do. You just do what I tell you, ask the right questions—I'll write them down so you'll get them exactly right—and the witness will identify the killer."

A half hour later, the suspects, Millry in the middle, were standing on the stage, five feet apart, facing front, about ten feet back of the footlights. Behind them, up against the backdrop, I'd put a chair for me to sit on. The spots were set up so they were shining right in the suspects' faces; if you're not used to it, that can be very upsetting.

Kramer announced that Isabel had been murdered and

he needed everybody's cooperation. They didn't have to cooperate, he said, but he suggested very strongly that they did. The suspects, Millry in particular, looked all shocked and upset, but how else should they have looked?

While the sheriff was talking, holding their attention, I came from behind the backdrop, very quietly, and sat in the chair behind them. Then Len entered from stage right and placed Trixie in front of the lineup, facing the suspects, but in such a way that she could see me clearly, looking just past Millry. With a little luck, Millry would think Trixie was looking right at him. Then Len joined the lineup on the end.

I touched my left eye. Trixie lifted her head and looked at me. I hoped that Millry, that sonofabitch, was sweating. The sheriff stood at the footlights, stage right. "This is Trixie, the famous talking dog," Kramer told the suspects. He then turned and looked right at Trixie. "Are you ready?" he asked.

I made the signs with my hand. "R-r-r-r-ready," Trixie said, opening her mouth in perfect timing. The suspects looked around at each other, sort of uneasy, not yet understanding.

Kramer kept his eyes focused on Trixie. "You were in the storage room when Isabel Bandera was murdered?" he asked.

"R-r-r-right," Trixie said. There was no way Millry could object; if he opened his mouth, that would be like a confession, practically.

"Who murdered Isabel?" Kramer asked Trixie.

"R-R-R-R-Ralph!" Trixie said. Ralph Millry dived at Trixie, hands out, ready to kill her, but I snapped my fingers and she scooted past him to jump into my lap.

"It's a lie!" Ralph screamed, and turned fast. "Don't listen; he's a *dog*." He made for me. Len tried to stop him, but Millry knocked him aside. Just as he got to me, I snapped my foot into his knee, sideways. He screamed, fell down, started crawling toward me, still trying to kill the only witness to the murder. When he came close enough, I smashed my other foot in his ugly face. For Isabel.

Sheriff Kramer had his gun out, covering Ralph Millry. The murderer, hands over his broken, bleeding face, was crying. "I didn't do it. It was self-defense. She attacked me. She started it." Kramer put the cuffs on him.

Hallie came over, took Trixie from my arms, and kissed her. Why not, she deserved it, best animal actress in the Catskills. Elaine came over, kissed me too, crying. Len came over, dusted himself off. "Your timing wasn't too bad for a change, Arnie," he said. "One of these days you'll make a good second banana." He took my arm and lifted me from the chair. "Go upstairs and lay down." He understood how much the strain had drained me, that I wouldn't be up tonight unless I had a chance to relax. "We got two shows to do tonight. Jean and Hallie and I—we'll make sure everything's working right."

"A show tonight?" Elaine couldn't believe it. "*Two* shows?"

"The show must go on," Jean told her. "But tonight, Trixie takes all the bows."